the SPORRAN

G.L. GREGG

To The Scot in You.

All my best,

[signature]

BB

BUTLER BOOKS

Feddinch House

and

The Stone of Destiny

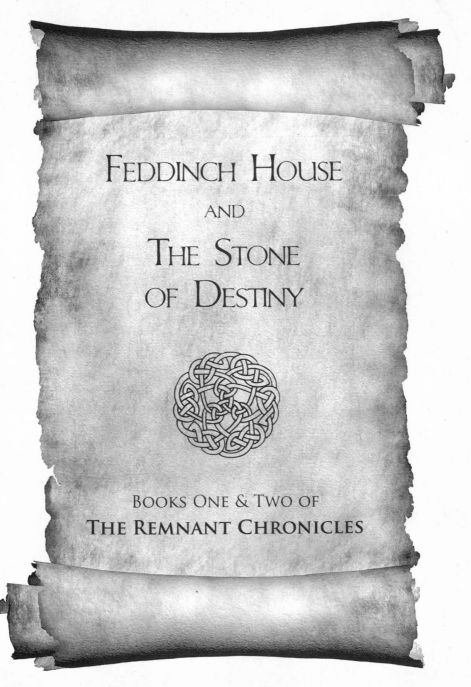

Books One & Two of
The Remnant Chronicles

Copyright © 2007 Gary L. Gregg II
All Rights Reserved
ISBN: 1-884532-88-8
Printed in Canada

Book Designer: Scott Stortz

Published by:

Butler Books
P.O.Box 7311
Louisville, KY 40207
(502) 897-9393
Fax (502) 897-9797
www.butlerbooks.com

www.TheSporran.com

To the wee ones who

keep the magic alive in my life

and for whom

the sporran

entered our world

TABLE OF CONTENTS

Preface – In Catacombs Far Away—A Page is Turned

BOOK ONE
FEDDINCH HOUSE

BOOK TWO
THE STONE OF DESTINY

In Catacombs Far Away—
A Page is Turned

I t was one of *those* mornings. There was no warm sun penetrating his chamber, but Fingus knew it was shining in the world beyond. In his world, he knew it would be one of *those* mornings. His eyes opened slowly to greet the darkness. He had long ago become accustomed to the dark, even in the mornings when it seemed so unnatural and inappropriate.

At first, he did not stir, for it was one of *those* mornings. The air itself demanded contemplation and the dignity of silence. When his legs finally turned off the side of his small bed and he sat up, Fingus had readied himself for his duties. It had been three days since the feeling had come over him and he knew this would be one of *those* mornings. He had been fasting for those three days and was more than ready for the meal he would share later that morning.

He struck a flint and a spark flew onto a cloth that was damp with fuel. The darkness skulked into the corners of his chamber and behind the meager furnishings. Slowly, the small man slipped out of his bed clothes and into his finest white robes. He tied them about his waist with a golden rope. Though no one would be there to see him, it was one of *those* mornings and it demanded respect and the dignity of silence.

Down the corridor he slowly marched until he came to the room. It was one of *those* mornings and this is where he was to be. He paused at the entrance, his waist bending slightly to match the bend in his neck. Entering the room, he bent forward slightly again before placing his torch in an iron sconce to his right.

The small man with a slight paunch bent his body once more before slowly approaching the table near the back wall. His steps were heavy and perfectly placed, as they had been a hundred times before. With care, he reached up to the upper right corner of a large book lying open on the table. Fingus took a deep breath, cleared his mind of the worry and wonder that had been creeping in for the last three days, and pulled the sheet to the left, where he let it fall naturally to its new place of rest. The page had been turned, for it was one of *those* mornings.

FEDDINCH
HOUSE

BOOK ONE OF
THE REMNANT CHRONICLES

THE GIFT

"**C**ome on, Jenny, you will never catch me!" Jacob yelled as he rounded the corner onto Longbranch Drive and headed into the home stretch of the ride from Will's house to his.

As he turned his head back around to face the front of his red mountain bike, he caught sight of Sadie, the neighbor's dog. She was crossing onto the road. Swerving hard to the right to miss hitting the miniature collie, Jacob ended up sprawled face-first in Mr. Wilson's bushes.

"Nice work, Tony Hawk!" Jenny laughed as she sped past her downed friend and headed home.

Picking himself up and trying to hurriedly replace the broken branches of the bush to make it seem like nothing happened, Jacob remembered that he had been expecting a package from his father and quickly sped down the road and up the drive. On the porch he found what he had been waiting for, the latest gift from his father.

Jacob's dad seemed always to be away on business trips. Last summer he missed his son's hitting his first homerun. In the spring he nearly missed being home for his birthday because of a missed flight in Texas. But his dad was always bringing or sending Jacob interesting presents from all over the world.

Jacob ditched his bike on the front lawn, leaped up the three small steps onto his porch and scooped up the small package in one seamless movement. In the house, he took two steps at a time as he ascended the stairs to his room.

Passing his mother as he turned the landing, Jacob flung out a "Hi, Mom," without missing a step. "Nice seeing you as well," said Mrs. Boyd to the closing door where her son stood only seconds before.

Jacob dropped onto his bed and stared at the brown box with the red postage featuring Queen Elizabeth's likeness and the return address as "Feddinch Manor House, St. Andrews, Kingdom of Fife, Scotland, UK."

Jacob Boyd was unlike most other boys in the sixth grade. Rather than new and shiny, he liked things old and dusty and dirty—the dustier and dirtier the better. He liked old, dark rooms and mysterious attics. He liked musty old books with broken-spines and missing pages. He liked old stuff of all kinds better than video games and thinking about ancient battles more than watching television.

His room looked more like a bizarre attraction at a traveling circus than a boy's room. Sure, there was the normal sports stuff that any twelve-year-old would have. But, there was also stuff that made his mother queasy.

There was the ferocious-looking alligator head his dad had brought to him after a trip to New Orleans, its jaws grasping a small toy soldier whose head was long lost to some "accident" around the house. There was the collection of dried tarantulas from Mexico and the door knobs from some old house being torn down up the road. There were the loose bricks scattered here and there from one construction project or another in the neighborhood and the old black and white pictures of mean looking old people from long, long ago that he found at a garage sale on Elm street. He supposed that they must have been someone's relatives and so couldn't be as bad as they looked.

There were large items stacked in the corners and small ones strewn about shelves and his desk. Most of the stuff had been sent by his dad when he was on long business trips and wanted Jacob to know how much he missed him.

His dad was more like him than was his mother. His mother would never buy him dusty old leather books written in Latin (that he couldn't read, of course) or broken powder horns with mildewed leather straps. But, Mr. Boyd knew his son and searched antique shops and back alleys around the world for gifts that he knew would cause his wife to shake her head and roll her eyes but would make Jacob's collection of oddities even more odd, and his son very happy.

Reaching over into his nightstand, Jacob pulled a small dull knife with a turkey-foot handle from his drawer and cut the tape from the box.

Inside he found a small red book with the title "A History of St. Andrews," written by Russell Kirk. He thumbed through the yellowing pages looking at the pictures of old churches and other buildings from the ancient Scottish town then tossed it on the floor and removed the extra paper left in the box, beneath which he found his real prize.

The smell of old leather wafted up from the box as a smile slowly crossed his face. He pulled the small pouch from the box. The dangling ends of its ring belt followed it up and out and back down onto the bed. It was made of tattered brown leather and had three black hair tassels. The flap was held closed by a latch made of an antler tip and a drawstring helped keep it tight.

Jacob's initial excitement turned into confusion as he stared at what he thought looked a bit too much like a girl's purse—though a very, very old one. *How will I explain that being in my room when Will comes over? Maybe I should just give it to Jenny and pretend it was a gift intended for her and not for me.* He wondered what to do.

A note at the bottom of the box said:

> Send me an e-mail when you get this and I will explain.
>
> Love,
> Dad
>
> P.S. It's not a purse!

Jacob went over to his computer and sent a message to his father telling him that he had gotten his package and was looking forward to hearing from him. "Glad it's not a purse," he added, just as mom called him down for dinner.

"So, what did Dad send you?" his Mom asked, as Jacob entered the kitchen.

"Whatever it is, it's NOT A PURSE!" he said, as he sat and took a large gulp from his milk.

THE FIRST DISAPPEARANCE

That night, Jacob did his homework (with his mom waking him out of his daydreams from time to time), watched some TV, and went to bed without thinking much about the gift he had received earlier in the day. He was curious about what it was, but it didn't seem all that important and certainly wasn't as important as thinking about baseball practice. He was really hoping to make the starting line-up for the Pirates this year.

Mrs. Boyd's voice woke Jacob from his sleep (for the third time that morning) at 6:45 A.M.—barely time to dress and rush out of the house before the bus arrived to take him to Buckner Middle School. Bus number 45 was just pulling up when he burst out the door and down the sidewalk. It was the second time in a week that he had barely made it to the bus and the driver raised an eyebrow as Jacob's right foot landed on the second step and he turned down the aisle. He plopped into the seat in front of Jenny.

"What'd your dad send you, Jacob, another dead animal or something?" Jenny asked.

Jacob pretended not to hear her but she repeated her question, this time jabbing him under the arm to assure his attention.

"Well, I am not sure what it is, but I know its NOT A PURSE!" Jacob said assertively but quietly enough so as not to let anyone else hear.

"What does that mean?" said Jenny

"Well, it's just some sort of old leather pouch from England or Scotland or something. I don't know what it is or what it's supposed to be for," he answered.

A few stops later, Will got on the bus and the conversation about Jacob's gift repeated itself with no one very much interested in the leather pouch.

The day went as normally as any other at Buckner Middle School. The bad kids were typically bad. The good kids behaved themselves as usual. The teachers were a typical mix of mean and kind; fun and ruthless. At least the day seemed normal, until science class.

Science was always one of Jacob's favorite subjects, especially, like today, when the topic related to exotic ecosystems and environmental studies. Mrs. Niel was teaching about the lizards of the Galapagos Islands who find food on rocks in the ocean, when something caught Jacob's eye from outside the window.

Jacob's heart jumped as he recognized the form of a man standing outside the window. He wore a tattered jacket and equally well-used cap and had a fuzzy dark beard. He was looking into the classroom but Jacob had the eerie feeling the stranger was actually looking right at him, as if he wanted to communicate with him. Jacob turned his eyes away, feeling uncomfortable. But, Jacob couldn't hold his eyes from the man and turned his eyes back out the window.

The man had turned and was walking away from the school.

"Did you see that creep out the window?" said a note tossed down by Jacob's right shoe. It was from Will Renrut who sat two seats behind Jacob. "Yea, maybe he is the new janitor or something," he scribbled on the note and tossed it behind him when Mrs. Niel turned to look at her slide of two lizards locked in what seemed like mortal combat.

The note banked off the side of Billy Roberts' glasses and landed perfectly on Will's desk, who quickly scooped it up before they were caught. Billy, who was easily the biggest but also the goofiest kid in class, drove a fist into Jacob's back to pay him back for the missile launched off his face. Jacob's grunt caught Mrs. Neil's attention who crossly said, "Problem, Mr. Boyd?" Jacob shook his head and went back to paying attention to the lesson (and occasionally daydreaming about baseball practice.)

That evening, Jacob was sitting having hotdogs and macaroni with his mother when he remembered he probably had a return e-mail message from his dad. "Mom, can I be excused to see if Dad has sent me a message?" he asked as he wolfed down another bite of macaroni and cheese and grabbed the remaining stub of his hotdog. He was ready to sprint to the study where the family computer was kept.

"Sure," she said with a smile. "Go on."

There was a message from his dad waiting on him that said:

Jakester—

I hope you like your gift. I bet you worried it was a purse or something! It's actually called a "sporran" and is worn by Scotsmen around their waist when they wear traditional kilts. Since kilts don't have pockets, they need this pouch to carry things. I figure this one looks like it might have been worn into battle by some old Highland warrior or something.

I wish you could have been here in St. Andrews with me when I found it. I wandered into a little alley off Market Street. The little shop was very dark and full of dusty old junk spread all over the place. I told the owner about you and he really was insistent that this was the proper gift for a young man like you. "Every laddie needs a wee sporran, ya know," he said.

Anyway, I hope you like it. I have another surprise on its way to you and Mom in a few days. Watch the mail!

Love,
Dad

P.S. How is baseball coming?

Heading to bed that night, Jacob picked up the sporran and looked it over again with the kind of appreciation that comes with new knowledge. Made of old brown leather that showed considerable wear, it had three dangling straps hanging from its front, each tipped with a bundle of black horse hair. The top flap was held down by a piece of deer antler. As he pulled back the closing flap, the musty smell of mildewy leather hit his nostrils again and made him wonder how long it had sat hidden in that shop in Scotland and where it had been before that. *Had it really been in battle? Perhaps taken off a soldier's body whose luck had run out?*

Taking the long strap of old leather that hung from the back of the pouch, he tied the sporran around his waist and wondered what it must have been like to have worn it into some great battle against English invaders or against some other Scottish clan.

In the corner by his bookshelf, Jacob kept a small wooden sword his father had made for him many years before. He picked it up and thrust it menacingly at the alligator head on the shelf, then turned with a jerk and slashed at the wooden trout hanging on his wall above his desk. The sword caught one of the many pencils sitting in a can on his desk and sent them and the can flying across the room and crashing to the floor.

"*What* are you doing up there?" came a call from the kitchen.

"Nothing Mom, just dropped my pencils," he replied out the crack of the door.

"Time for bed, anyway, and don't forget to brush your teeth!" Mrs. Boyd announced as she headed up the stairs carrying a basket full of freshly-folded laundry.

Jacob hung the sporran on the coat hanger by the door of his room and then took a baseball from his coat pocket where it had rested since practice that evening and flipped it into the air with his fingertips, wondering when he would be old enough to really try to throw a curveball in a game. "You are too young and will hurt your arm," he kept hearing from his dad, his coach, and nearly everyone else.

The spinning ball landed back onto his right hand with the well-worn "MacGregor Regulation Size and Weight" stamp facing him. Since there was no practice after school the next day, Jacob opened the flap of the sporran and put the ball inside.

Once he laid down, it took Jacob no time at all to fall asleep. Awaking the next morning, he found himself oddly thinking about the man he had seen outside the window in science class the day before.

Walking toward the door, his overlong pajama pants dragging beneath his bare feet as he rubbed the sleep out of his eyes, he reached for the doorknob but stopped. Something seemed out of place to his right. What was it? Looking up and down the coat rack by the door, something just didn't seem right and yet everything seemed there. His Pittsburgh Pirate hat, his coat, the sporran. . . . that was it, the sporran seemed as flat as it did when it arrived two days before but it shouldn't. *I left a bulging baseball in its pouch last night!* he thought.

He lifted the old leather flap. There was nothing inside. The baseball was gone.

MOUSE TRAP

Jacob would blame his little sister for stealing his baseball, but he had none. He would blame an older brother playing tricks on him, but being an only child, he couldn't do that either. *What could have happened to my baseball?* He wondered.

As usual, he was running late for the bus and had just enough time to dress and get out the door as his mother, like a walking alarm clock, would forcefully intone "Let's go, Jacob!" every three minutes until he appeared on the stairs. Finding the ball would have to wait until after school.

He didn't mention the missing ball to anyone at school. After all, there was a good chance he just misplaced it or something. He had lost things before and he was relatively sure regulation size and weight baseballs don't just disappear. *Maybe I didn't really put it in the sporran after all,* he let himself consider.

On the bus that afternoon, Jacob asked Will and Jenny to meet him at his house at 3:30. They agreed and at the appointed time, two bikes approached 10 Longbranch Drive from different directions and raced the last few yards up the driveway. Seeing them coming, Jacob leaned out his bedroom window and yelled down to his two friends, "I am up here, just come on in."

Jenny stepped first into Jacob's room and found him sprawled on the floor pushing the dust around under his bed. He was obviously looking for something.

"What are you searching for?" asked Jenny.

The muffled answer that came from under the bed was unintelligible. Will gave a solid kick to Jacob's foot as he stepped over him and sat down in his chair. Dust-covered and sneezing, Jacob sat up cross-legged.

"I'm hunting for a baseball," Jacob said matter-of-factly.

"Okay, but you have other baseballs in your garage, don't you?" asked Jenny, anxious to get on doing something more interesting than searching for a lost baseball.

"Just help me look. It's a MacGregor Regulation Size and Weight. Jenny, you check down the hallway and in the hall closet while Will and I look in here."

"What is so special about the ball, Jacob?" asked Will.

Jenny paused at the door to listen.

"Probably nothing, but somehow it seems to have disappeared and unless you . . ."

Jenny cut him short and added "Unless we want to get into more trouble by following you on another crazy adventure like last month, when you had us believing Mrs. James was somehow keeping man-eating piranhas in her koi pond . . ."

"Blah. Blah. Blah . . . . Anyway, just help me look for it, please," Jacob replied.

The team searched for more than an hour before Jacob finally gave up and called Jenny and Will together on his bed.

Laying the sporran in the middle of the bed between them, he looked each of them in the eye with a seriousness that they had seen before.

"Oh, no. . . not again. . . " Jenny and Will said simultaneously.

The musty smell of old leather made them both curl their nose as they braced themselves for what tall tale was to come next from their friend who seemed always to be thinking of tall tales to tell.

"Last night," Jacob began, "I took my baseball from my jacket pocket, since I didn't want to take it to school . . . ." He recounted how the baseball had somehow disappeared during the night while no one was in the house except him and his mother.

"Now, let's think reasonably about this," said Jenny who was always trying to be reasonable about everything. "What could have happened to the ball? You either didn't put it in your little purse last night at all or your mother is playing a trick on you. . ."

"Its NOT A PURSE!" Jacob scolded her.

"Or," Will interjected, "maybe you were sleepwalking last night, thought you were on the ball field, opened the window, and fired it out into the night."

Realizing the ball would still be on the lawn if that were the case, all three rushed to the window to look. No speck of white on the green lawn. Nothing.

"Maybe it landed in the back of a pick-up truck that was passing by and now it is somewhere like Montana or Utah or somewhere else," Will hypothesized, attempting to salvage his theory.

Raising his eyebrows, Jacob offered, "Or maybe this is some magical sporran that sends all things in its pouch to some other dimension where someone may be wondering right now what a "MacGregor Regulation Size and Weight" might be.

"Let's come back to reality now, Batman," Jenny said as she walked across the floor and picked up the lump of leather and hair lying on the bed. "What we need is a plan to come up with a *reasonable* solution to this mysterious disappearance!" she offered.

The three would-be detectives sat and thought and puzzled until Will finally came up with the greatest possible plan any of them could imagine.

"Okay, now," he started, "the way I see it, either you are sleepwalking, or your mom is playing a trick on you, right?" he asked.

"Go on," said Jacob wondering where he was going with this line of unmagical reasoning.

"What we need, then, is a trap," Will continued. "A trap that will either catch you when you are sleepwalking or will catch your mother when she sneaks into your room tonight to continue her dastardly plan."

"Okay, so what kind of trap could we set?" asked Jenny. With a tinge of sarcasm she continued, "Tin cans around the door, maybe? How about a bucket of water balanced on top of the coat rack? How about putting a slimy dead fish in the pouch and then just listening for the scream? Or maybe some worms and dirt?"

"A mousetrap," Will interrupted, very proud of his developing plan. "Whoever reaches into the pouch will get their fingers caught in the trap and will give out a loud yell. If it's your mother, she will wake you up with her yelp and you will have her! If it's you, the snap of the trap will wake you up and the mystery will be solved."

"Easy for you to say," said Jacob. Holding up his fingers he added, "Remember these are my fingers, not yours, that are going to get smashed!"

But none of them could think of another plan that was remotely as good, so they headed to the basement to search for a mousetrap.

"Where are you guys going," Mrs. Boyd asked the gang as they headed toward the door that led from the kitchen to the basement.

"Uhhhh. . . just down stairs to look for some stuff, Mom," Jacob answered as he turned the knob and led his friends down into the basement.

The three searched for half an hour until finally they came across what they were looking for in the drawer of an old dresser. It had been holding junk rather than clothes for years and Mr. Boyd always said that anyone who looked long enough would find whatever they were looking for in all the junk it contained.

That night, after math homework and a bit of reading in *Mystical Beasts and Magical Feasts,* Jacob worked to set the trap. A few smashed and throbbing fingers later, and he had finally figured out how to make it work and slipped the set trap into the sporran which was hanging on the coat rack in the exact place it had been the night before.

He went to sleep that night hoping he hadn't been the one to take the ball. The thought of sleepwalking in the dead of night really freaked him out.

He didn't awaken at all that night and heard not a thing until precisely 6:15 AM the next morning when the door creaked open and his mom said, "Time to get up, bud." He sprang up immediately and was disappointed to realize nothing seemed to have happened in the night.

Oh well, he thought to himself, *maybe I didn't put the ball in the sporran the other night after all.*

Just the same, he looked his mother's fingers over a bit as they exchanged places in the bathroom down the hall but saw no sign that they might have been snapped in the night.

He dressed and picked up his coat off the top rung on his coat rack and fingered the hairy tassels on the sporran hanging next to it. *Better un-set that trap before I forget it's in there and get my fingers ripped off when I get home tonight,* he thought. Taking a pencil from his desk, he slowly lifted the flap and stuck in the yellow No. 2 and swished the eraser end around inside.

Nothing happened. No snap. No bang. No jump in the pouch. There was nothing.

Slowly lifting the flap and peeking in, his heart leapt to his throat. The sporran was empty again!

A loud, "Let's go Jacob!" coming from down the stairs snapped him out of the shock that the nothingness in the pouch had caused.

His mind was preoccupied by the latest disappearance in his room as he flew down the stairs and out the door. Not paying attention to what he was doing, his foot caught the bottom step as he came off the porch. His feet held back but his top kept going. His arms flew wildly at his sides trying to regain control until he found himself, fifteen feet later, lying in the dewy grass of his front yard. Jumping quickly to his feet, and looking around to make sure no one had seen, he pulled the backpack down off his head where it ended up from the fall and limped slowly to the end of the drive to await the bus.

THE BLOOD RED BALL

Jenny couldn't wait for an answer when Jacob climbed aboard the bus. She hadn't really believed there was a serious mystery about the baseball's disappearance, but she was hoping to hear a good story about either Jacob or Mrs. Boyd having had their fingers caught in the mousetrap.

"So, who turns out to be the *mouse*?" she asked, as Jacob fell hard into the seat in front of her.

Jacob turned to look her in the eye and whispered, "Wait until Will gets here."

A few stops later, in the subdivision next door to Jacob's and Jenny's, Will climbed aboard. He was followed by his little brother Lenny who never failed to annoy Jacob and Jenny and drove his brother absolutely mad.

Will dropped into the seat next to Jacob and before Jenny could spread her book bag across the seat to keep Lenny away, he was in the seat next to her staring, as always, almost blankly into her face. Lenny, by all accounts, was very creepy.

"What happened?" asked Will with great anticipation.

"Yep, lets have it. . ." added Jenny.

Jacob began to talk but noticed Lenny staring at them. "Do you mind!" he said to Lenny, as the three huddled closer.

With a voice of very serious clarity seldom heard from a boy his age, Jacob told his two friends of the mousetrap missing from the sporran where he had placed it the night before.

Among his friends, Jacob may have had a reputation for having crazy theories and being a real dreamer, but none of them doubted that he always told the truth. There may be a reasonable explanation for the missing ball and mousetrap, but neither Jenny nor Will had any doubt that Jacob genuinely believed they had somehow disappeared.

"Okay. . . its official. . ." Jenny said with resignation, "we have a mystery on our hands. What do we do now?"

"Look," said Jacob, sending a strong look in Jenny's direction. "There are too many ears around here."

"Yep," Will interjected. "Let's meet up at lunch and hatch a plan."

"Deal," said Jacob.

"Fine," confirmed Jenny.

As Jacob turned back to glance out the window, the bus was passing the third hole on Eagle Creek Golf Course. Jacob's curiosity was aroused as he noticed a bearded man look up from his ball on the green and stare at the bus. It was the man from outside the science class window again, he was sure of it. And, just like in science class, Jacob had the eerie feeling the man was looking right at him. It was almost as if the man was recognizing him as someone he knew but hadn't seen in a long time.

When they met up at lunch, Jenny had already been thinking seriously about what needed to happen next. "Okay," she said before Will could even unwrap his sandwich of soggy toast and cheese with ketchup and mustard. It was a sandwich that always weirded the others out.

"Information is what we need. We need research. We need to know everything we can about what a 'sporran' really is," Jenny stated as if she were mustering her troops for battle.

"Yes sir!" said Will, annoyed that she was falling into her "I'm the boss around here" mode again.

"Good idea," said Jacob.

"Now, its Friday night," said Jenny. "I am still not convinced there is not some perfectly reasonable explanation for these disappearances. So, why don't we all spend the night at your house so that we can all be there in case anything strange happens tonight?"

"I'll ask my mom when I get home," replied Jacob. "Ask your parents and wait for my phone call."

All agreed.

The three spent the rest of their lunch dividing up the research jobs each of them would have to do. Jacob's first priority would be to get more information from his father about where he got the sporran and under what circumstances.

Jenny would use her library time that afternoon to find books that might give some insight into traditional Scottish dress and customs.

Will was to check the Internet.

As their lunch period ended, they also agreed with Jacob's assertion that none of them should tell anyone what was going on—at least not yet.

The bus ride home that evening was just like any other. Some students were loud, some were quiet. Some read and others told jokes and stories about their day at school. Jacob was uncharacteristically quiet, as were Jenny and Will.

Daydreaming out the window as trees, houses, and telephone poles rushed by, Jacob was jolted to reality again when he noticed a man walking up the road near Eagle Creek Golf Course which was just around the corner from his home. He snapped his head to the right quickly to watch him disappear behind the bus. It was the bearded man again. *Where did this guy come from? And why does he always seem to be looking at me?*

As soon as Jacob arrived home and had a snack, he e-mailed a message to his father who was still in Scotland on business.

Dad,

Thanks again for the sporran. I am very curious about it and want to know everything you can possibly tell me about it and how you got it. Is there anything else you can tell me about it?

Frankly, it's a little weird, but don't mention that to Mom, please. Sometimes it is better that she not know when out-of-the-ordinary things happen, you know. She is not like us in that way.

I look forward to hearing anything else you know and am looking forward to having you home again.

Love,
Jacob

P.S. Baseball games start in three weeks. Hope you are home for opening day.

He looked around his room again for the baseball and mousetrap until he heard his mom's car pull in the drive.

Jacob was waiting when his mother entered the kitchen from the door that led into the garage.

"Hi Mom, how was your day?" he asked as she crossed the threshold into the kitchen.

"Fine. . ." Mrs. Boyd answered, her voice slow and rising as if to say, "What is going on here, *something* isn't quite right. . . ."

"Oh, excellent," said Jacob. "A fine end to a fine week for a fine mother. That is fine!" he added.

"Okay, what do you want?" said Mrs. Boyd, seeing right through her son's overly dramatic concern for her well-being.

"Can Jenny and Will stay over tonight?"

Mrs. Boyd hesitated with her answer.

"Well, I suppose so, but you will all have to sleep in the family room in sleeping bags. And remember you have baseball practice in the morning and so you'll have to be in bed early enough to be up and gone to the ball field in the morning."

"Done!" agreed Jacob as he turned toward the phone to call Jenny and Will.

That evening Jenny and Will shared the little bit of the information they had been able to gather about sporrans. All in all, it didn't amount to very much.

As it turns out, Will didn't know how to spell it so he spent most of his afternoon typing and retyping various spelling versions such as "Spour-an," "sporn," "sporen," and reading useless items that came up during his search on the Internet.

They quickly decided that in order for this to be a successful experiment, they would have to put something into the pouch. But what could it be?

Will brought what was left of his dinner with him and wanted to put it in the pouch. "Cold beef stroganoff will really weird out anyone who tries to take it out and will make a mess," he argued. "We then could follow the trail of gravy!"

"Disgusting!" said Jenny.

"You aren't putting that in anything of mine!" answered Jacob as he rolled his eyes.

"How about that bizarre little rat skull you have in your room?" suggested Jenny. "That thing always gives me the creeps anyway."

"No way!" Jacob answered as his eyes searched the family room. "I am not putting anything I don't want to lose in that pouch again. Besides, its not a rat's skull, it's the skull of a squirrel that my dad sent me, and please refer to him by his proper name: Merryl!"

"Here," he continued, as he pointed to a small gold-colored metal cup from which he had been drinking milk a short while earlier. "Mom won't miss this old cup, should it disappear."

He placed the cup in the sporran and hung it on the edge of the chair near the fireplace in the family room.

The three lay down in the sleeping bags they had spread all over the room and talked themselves to sleep just as they had so many times before. They had been best friends since they were in Mrs. Boardman's Kindergarten class together. Occasionally, Mrs. Boyd's voice would remind them to be more quiet. "Do I need to separate you three?" she would say. Each call from her room got progressively more loud and serious. Soon sleep came upon the three and none of them stirred until the light rose on the new day.

Jenny awoke first. Through the morning light filtering into the room, she noticed the bulge in the sporran was still there. She laid back down assuming the mystery was about to come to an end and drifted back to sleep.

Will awoke next and shook the other two.

"Don't worry about it," said Jenny. "It's still there!"

Somewhat relieved and somewhat disappointed, Jacob got up and took the sporran from its hanging place. "Hmmm. . . Well, let me put the cup back before mom gets up," he said as he lifted the flap on the pouch.

His hand had barely entered when it shot back out of the sporran as if it had been bitten by a small monster or burned by a flame. He dropped the sporran and backed away.

The sporran hit the floor as Will and Jenny jumped back.

"It's not there!" cried Jacob. "It's not there! Something else! Something else is in there!"

"What is it?" Jenny and Will asked together.

"I don't know, but it's no cup, that's for sure."

"Well, someone has to open it and see and it's not going to be me!" said Will.

Jenny slid her foot closer to the pouch and give it a quick kick.

The flap opened and out of the sporran and across the floor rolled a blood red ball.

THE TICKET

The ball rolled across the floor and came to rest against the stones that made up the base of the Boyd's fireplace. The three partners just sat silently and stared, half frightened and half amazed at the red orb resting on the floor. None of them dared move toward it.

Finally, Will broke the silence. "Looks like your baseball puked itself inside out or something on the way back to you, Jacob."

Will was right. It was about the same size as the baseball that had disappeared into the sporran two nights before. And, if baseballs had blood and guts in them, this one resembled a ball turned inside out.

The three slowly moved closer to the alien orb. They noticed its most distinguishing feature was the one line of bumpy stitches that went straight down the middle of the ball and wrapped all the way around its circumference.

"Should we touch it?" asked Jenny.

"Maybe we should tell your mom," said Will apprehensively.

"No," answered Jacob. "My mom would freak and take it away from me if she knew what was going on. If I need to, I will tell Dad, 'cause he might understand, but not Mom."

"Well, then, someone is going to have to do something with that *thing*," said Jenny.

"I have an idea," Jacob said as he disappeared into the kitchen. He reappeared a minute later with a plastic bag and two forks.

"Plan on making it some lunch?" asked Jenny, sarcastically.

Jacob gave Will the bag and asked Jenny to listen for his mother as he hunched over the ball and began to place the forks on either side of it.

"Wait," said Jenny in an atypical moment of imagination, "What if it's alive or something and you make it angry by stabbing it?"

"It's not alive!" answered Jacob, "Now please . . . let me concentrate!"

Slowly, very slowly, Jacob put the forks solidly against the sides of the ball and began to lift.

Will was so nervous about being touched by the red round visitor that he began swaying and shaking. "Hold still!" insisted Jacob as he swung the ball over toward the bag.

Will closed his eyes, turned his head away from Jacob and the ball and said "I hope this is a zipper seal bag in case it starts to ooze some kind of toxic chemicals or something!"

"Here she comes!" Jenny announced with a forceful whisper, as Mrs. Boyd started down the stairs.

Jacob dropped the ball into the bag and yanked it from Will's shaking hands.

Shoving it behind the stack of wood that rested by the fireplace, he sprang up to meet his mother.

"I will be ready for practice in just a minute, Mom."

"Fine, but wouldn't it be a good idea to have some breakfast first?"

"Great idea, Mrs. Boyd," said Will who was not one to miss a meal, even when mysterious and possibly deadly red balls appear out of nowhere in the family room.

Jacob, Will and Jenny found it impossible to carry on a normal conversation during breakfast. They were dying to talk about the strange red ball and to figure out what to do next. But with Mrs. Boyd hovering around bringing juice and milk and french toast over to them every few minutes, there was really nothing to do but stare and eat. . . fast!

"You three are very quiet this morning," Mrs. Boyd said at one point.

"Just really hungry, I guess," Will responded.

"Can I help you with anything?" offered Jenny, as much to keep her mind off things as to actually be helpful to Jacob's mother.

After breakfast, Jenny and Will headed off on their bikes while Mrs. Boyd drove Jacob to baseball practice.

After telling his mother goodbye and reminding her to please pick him up again in two hours, Jacob retrieved his cleats, glove and bat from the trunk, slammed the lid, and turned toward the field.

Just a few players had arrived before Jacob and they were already out on the field warming up. Jacob sat down on the bottom bench of the bleachers to exchange his sneakers for his cleats. So preoccupied by the appearance of the ball (and disappearance of the gold cup), Jacob didn't even notice there was someone else on the bleachers, too.

"Good morning," said a voice from behind him. Startled, Jacob turned around to find himself looking right into the eyes of the bearded stranger who had shown up in town for the first time a few days before.

"Uh . . . good morning. . ." Jacob stammered.

"What team do you play for, young man?"

"The Pirates, sir,"

"Ah. . . baseball was never my game. I play golf now and used to play a sport like baseball on a team called The Dirks, but that was a long time ago," the man replied.

Jacob turned to head out onto the field but stopped and turned back when the man spoke again.

"Remember, when a mystery has you stuck in a real thicket, the answer may be in the lowly little cricket."

Jacob raised his eyebrows as a way of acknowledging that the man had said something and then turned onto the field and greeted his teammates. Jogging out toward second base to throw with Johnny Jepson, he looked at the bleachers where he and the man had sat just moments before. Nothing. It was empty. The man was gone.

Practice went well, though being understandably distracted, Jacob let a number of balls go through his legs at second base during infield practice and nearly had his head taken off when Jeffrey Mullins smashed a line-drive back at him during batting practice.

"Need a nap, Boyd?" Coach Budd yelled from the dugout more than once that morning.

When Jacob and his mother arrived back at the house that afternoon, the mail had come and a small package was waiting on the doorstep. "Mom, there is a package," he announced to his mother who was coming up the walk behind him.

"Didn't your dad tell you he was sending us something?" she asked, though she knew very well the answer.

"Yep. . . It's from dad," Jacob said as he picked up the package and opened the door.

The package contained a set of small papers and a note. The note read, "I miss you guys so much and want to see you soon. Mom has to work, I know, but here is a ticket for you. See you in Scotland for spring break!"

I am going to Scotland? Spring break is just days away! Jacob missed his dad and wanted to see him, but he wondered how he could leave now. *How can I leave when such strange things are happening at home?* Things were disappearing and appearing in his life and he needed Jenny and Will to help figure out what was going on. *How can I leave my mother alone in the house with that red ball (assuming the ball is still there, that is)?* Then there was the strange bearded man . . . . Well, truthfully, he was glad to be leaving that guy behind.

CRICKET

Jenny and Will were circling their bikes in the cul-de-sac near the Boyd house at 10 Longbranch Drive when Jacob and Mrs. Boyd pulled in from baseball practice. They were talking and wondering and waiting to get back to that blood red ball. They all were concerned about what might have happened since they left it hours before.

Jenny and Will raced their bikes down the hill and into the Boyd drive when they saw Mrs. Boyd's car had returned. Jacob met them at the door with a look of desperation on his face.

"Oh boy, what is wrong?" asked Jenny.

"It's hatched into a baby dragon, hasn't it?" blurted Will with his eyes bulging out like two boiled eggs.

"Worse, maybe," said Jacob, "Dad sent me a ticket to go to Scotland for break."

"Cool," answered Will.

Jenny, however, instantly realized the problem—*What was Jacob supposed to do with that 'thing' of his while he was gone? What if something happened to his mom while he wasn't here?* "We have no time to lose, then," asserted Jenny. "It's time to get to work!"

Taking charge of the situation, Jenny began barking orders to Will and Jacob to gather up the sporran and that ball, if it still was a ball, that is, and to meet her at the library in town in one hour.

"Yes, sir!" both boys said sarcastically and went to their tasks. Will found the sporran and Jacob retrieved the ball or egg or whatever it was which was right where he had left it. Unchanged. Unmoved. Seeming utterly unalive in its little baggie home.

Running out the door a few minutes later, Jacob caught himself in mid-stride on the walkway in front of the Boyd home. "Whoa . . ." he uttered as he held his foot in mid-air and began bouncing on one foot.

"What are you doing?" asked Will.

"It's a cricket on the walk," Jacob answered.

"How exciting, nature lovers!" Will said sarcastically as if he were an announcer on some nature show on TV.

"Well, it just reminded me of what the bearded guy told me today," said Jacob. He went on to explain the story of meeting the bearded man at baseball practice that morning. "He said something about 'When you are in a thicket, look to the cricket.'" Jacob ended his story as he examined the small black bug on the ground.

"He seems even creepier than we thought," added Will.

Jacob just shrugged his shoulders and took a step toward his bike.

The red ball, carefully wrapped in double plastic bags, was in Jacob's backpack with the sporran as they rode northeast toward town.

Arriving, they found Jenny sitting alone in a stack of books about traditional Scottish customs, fairy tales, dress, and history.

"Look at this," Jenny remarked, "a book all about that thing you have, there."

Jacob flipped through the book entitled *Sporrans and Other Pouches through the Ages* which was full of pictures and paintings of sporrans and other purse-like things that people have used to carry things. Some were very fancy and some were very plain.

Meanwhile, Will had wandered off into the stacks. Walking through the fourth aisle behind Mrs. Wiggins' check-out desk, something caught his attention. To his right he noticed a quick movement and then heard a pulsating "hummmmm. . . hummmm. . . hummmm. . ."

Bending over and looking at the third shelf, Will realized that what he had seen and was now hearing was a cricket. . . there was a cricket in the library!

Was it the same cricket that Jacob almost stepped on at his house just moments before? Had it somehow attached itself to us and ridden to the library? Did it somehow have superpowers and made it here on its own? Was it just another stupid little cricket, a coincidence and nothing more? With all that had happened, Will decided to take no chances.

Squatting down, he came face-to-face with the little critter. He jabbed his right hand fast at the humming insect, but not fast enough. The cricket jumped up over the books on the shelf and disappeared behind the stack while Will's hand crashed through the books, causing some to fall hard on the floor and others to fall back into the area between the rows.

A forceful and unquestionably Mrs. Wiggins-like "SHHHHHHHHH-HHH!!!!!!" was hurled his way. Embarrassed, he was attempting to reassemble the shelf of books and had momentarily forgotten about his prey when his eye noticed a book in his hand and on the spine of the book were the letters C-R-I-C-K-E-T. The full title was *An Everyman's Guide to the History and Rules of the Glorious and Royal Game of Cricket.*

Will's heart began to race as fast as the flashes of ideas zinging through his mind. *This could not be a coincidence, could it?*

He turned the book in his hands and then sent it crashing to the floor as he stumbled back into the bookshelf on the opposite side of the aisle. There, staring back at him on the cover of that book, was a basket—a basket of blood red balls!

Recovering his senses, Will grabbed the book and rushed toward the table where Jenny and Jacob sat studying the books Jenny had already found.

"DO NOT RUN!!!" said Mrs. Wiggins, as Will passed her desk holding the book at arms-length as if it were some kind of poisonous snake or something.

Jenny looked up as Will approached the table. Before even seeing Will's face she saw the cover of the book he was carrying. "Uhhhhh, Jacob. . . you better look up. . ." Jenny said, smacking at his arm with her knuckles.

"It's the ball!" Jacob exclaimed, as he stood excitedly. "Where did you find it?" he asked Will but then quickly added, "Never mind, let's see that thing!"

The three huddled close to each other and stared at the picture on the cover. "What on earth is 'cricket'?" said Jenny.

They opened the book and began to look at the pictures of men in white uniforms holding long paddles. There were pictures of men seeming to pitch to the ones with the paddles and others stood behind them. It reminded Jacob of his favorite game and one he played that very morning—baseball.

The three learned that "cricket" is a game something like baseball that is played in England, Australia, and other places where the English have had colonies or where lots of English people live. They learned that the area where the thrower stands is called the "pitch" and that the paddle-thing is called a "wicket." They learned all sorts of things about cricket and about the surprise the sporran had spit out that morning.

"So, the ball that came to me is a cricket ball!" said Jacob. "But why?" he added. "Why would my pouch steal my baseball and return a cricket ball?"

"Jacob, do you suppose that bearded guy has something to do with this?" asked Will anxiously. "After all, you said yourself that he told you to follow the cricket or beware of the cricket or something."

Jacob looked up from the book on the table and glanced at the ceiling in thought. His eyes rose to their destination but then shot back down part way to where they had started. Something had caught his eye. There on the balcony of the second floor was the disheveled bearded man staring back at him. Their eyes caught each other's and Jacob felt a strange sensation—a cross between fear and excitement.

"It's him, come on!" Jacob whispered "but try to act like nothing is going on!"

The two friends followed Jacob, looking around very suspiciously, trying to figure out what was going on without looking like something was going on.

"What, Jacob?" Will asked.

"Who, Jacob?" Jenny whispered.

Jacob ignored the questions as he hurriedly walked to the stairs by the front entrance and climbed to the second floor.

"There!" Jacob announced as he emerged on the top step. His announcement was premature, since he saw nothing.

"What?" his two friends asked simultaneously as they emerged from the stair case behind him.

The man was gone. The second floor was completely empty except for a little girl coloring on the floor near the papier-mâché animal statues in the story corner.

I know I saw him, where could he have gone? Jacob stood confused at the top of the stairs before explaining what he saw to Jenny and Will. As they descended the stairs, the thought slowly started to creep into his imagination that he might well be losing his mind. *But the ball, yes, the red ball, it is real. I know that because I can feel it. Yes, it's real. It's not all in my mind! I must be okay!*

"Well, Jacob, at least we know what that red ball is," Will tried to console his friend.

That part of the mystery was now solved but other things remained just as confusing. Jacob shrugged his shoulders and the three gathered up the books. They checked out the book on sporrans and the one on the game of cricket and headed back toward their homes to think, and for dinner.

That night Jacob lay in his bed studying the book about cricket and spinning the cricket ball in his fingers as he stared at it and wondered where it had come from and why he had it. The ball had become strangely comforting to him. As long as he had it in his hands he knew his mind was not making it all up. When his eyes became heavy, he laid the ball on the table by his bed and dropped the book on the floor.

The next day was Sunday and he awoke to a soft shimmer of light playing through his curtains. As he lay in bed staring at the ceiling, he remembered he had dreamt of being a cricket player and of the bearded man and of a yellow shield with three red lions standing on their hind legs and of a blue flag with white cross.

Sliding his legs out from under his covers, his feet hit the floor and he leaned forward to get up. Jacob fell back onto the bed before he even had completely raised to his feet. *An Everyman's Guide to the History and Rules of the Glorious and Royal Game of Cricket* was sitting upside down on his floor by his bed. He had never bothered to look at the back cover yesterday.

There was the picture of the author . . . a man he had seen before. *It couldn't be!* But it was. Right there on the back of the book in his bedroom was the bearded man who had been around town the last week and who had talked to him at the baseball field. A strange shiver ran across Jacob's shoulder blade and down through his left arm as he read the bio of the author on the back:

A GRADUATE OF OXFORD UNIVERSITY, HAMISH MACGREGOR IS A PROFESSOR OF GEOGRAPHICAL POLITICAL SOCIOLOGY AND ANTIQUITIES AT ST. ANDREWS UNIVERSITY IN SCOTLAND. PREVIOUSLY A PROFESSIONAL CRICKET PLAYER, HE NOW ENJOYS GOLF, WOODWORKING, FALCONRY AND TRAVELS WIDELY WHEN NECESSARY.

TURKISH DELIGHT

This Hamish MacGregor character had to have something to do with all this, Jacob reasoned as he went about his morning. *It all couldn't be just a coincidence, could it? The sporran arriving as he seemed to arrive in town. The cricket ball. The man mentioning to me what I thought at the time to be the insect-type cricket at the baseball field. Will just happening to find a book he wrote and then him appearing and disappearing in the library. It was all weird, too weird.*

Jacob was brushing his teeth when he remembered the sporran—*I haven't checked the sporran this morning!* He quickly went back to his room and opened the flap with great anticipation. There at the bottom of the pouch was a small and shiny purple metallic something. It was square and appeared to be some kind of food in a foil wrapper.

"Turkish Delight," read the foil. *What on earth is 'Turkish Delight?'* He stuck it into his coat pocket and went off to church with his mother. Both Will and Jenny were doing things with their families that afternoon and so they didn't have the chance to meet up. Jacob e-mailed them, though, in hopes that one of them might have a thought:

> Jenny and Will,
>
> As we sort of suspected, that creepy bearded guy is somehow connected to all this. He wrote the book on cricket, in fact! And, do you have any idea what "Turkish Delight" might be? A package of it showed up in the sporran this morning. Let me know if you have any thoughts. It's getting a little too strange around here! See ya tomorrow.

Jacob spent the afternoon with his mother, but was preoccupied by the sporran and worrying about leaving her alone when he left for Scotland. *Who knows what this stranger might do*, he worried.

Checking the computer later that night, there was a message from Will and another from Jenny. Will's message read:

> Jacob,
>
> This is really bizarre. I wish I was getting out of here with you this week. I don't want to be around here with that bearded freak running around. And, on 'Turkish Delight,' well, that is something my Uncle Charlie calls the turkey and biscuits we always have the day after Thanksgiving. So, maybe that package you have is some kind of powdered gravy or something. Hope you make it through the night! See you at school.
>
> > Your friend, alive or not,
> >
> > Will

Jacob then read Jenny's message:

> Jacob and Will,
>
> First, Will, you are the freakiest one around here, not that poor old guy! Second, 'Turkish Delight' is not some kind of leftover poultry food. If I remember correctly, 'Turkish Delight' is that food that the evil witch used to lure Edward into her clutches in Narnia. . . remember the 'Chronicles of Narnia' books? I am looking for my old copy but haven't found it yet. But, if I am right, I WOULD NOT OPEN IT AND CERTAINLY DON'T EAT IT! Hoping to see you both again in the morning,
>
> > Jenny

Of course! He remembered his dad reading *The Lion, the Witch and the*

Wardrobe to him a few years ago. *Yes, "Turkish Delight" was some kind of treat the witch used to get Edward to bring his brothers and sisters back into Narnia to be trapped. But that is just a story. It couldn't really be connected, could it?* he wondered.

Jenny was right, he should take no chances. Barely touching the package with his fingers, he tossed the "Turkish Delight" into the back of his desk drawer and shut it quickly.

That evening he would sit with his mother watching a video and scribbling on a piece of paper. Over and over again he would write down the clues in different orders. "Sporran-Hamish MacGregor-cricket ball-Turkish Delight-Scotland-golf-Dad-Lions-Flags . . . . "

Then "Bearded Man (MacGregor)-Turkish Delight-Sporran-Cricket Ball-Dad-Flags-Lions-Scotland-Dusty Store-St. Andrews . . . . "

"What are you working on, Jakey?" Mrs. Boyd asked him.

"Just puzzling and doodling and stuff," Jacob answered, barely looking up from his paper.

"I know you are nervous about going to Scotland," his mom said, anticipating some of what he was puzzling on. "But, you are going to have a great time with your dad and this is a wonderful opportunity to visit places most kids never get to see in person—castles, ruins, suits of armor, and all that stuff you love."

"I know, it's just that I don't want to leave you here alone and don't want to leave Jenny and Will . . . ." and . . . ." He stopped himself.

"I'll tell you what, if it makes you feel any better, why don't you have Jenny and Will come by and check on me now and again while you are gone?" she said.

"Okay," he answered and went back to puzzling and doodling.

"And, since you are leaving in just two days, why don't I take tomorrow off and we can spend the day together?" Mrs. Boyd offered.

Oh, no, I blew it now, Jacob thought to himself, as he realized spending the day with Mom would not help him get to the bottom of the mysteries now enveloping his life and preoccupying his mind. But there was nothing he could do about that now without hurting his mom's feelings. He wasn't going to do that. And, a full day with his mom would be fun before he left to spend the week in another country. Jacob collected his enthusiasm before answering.

"Great, Mom, let's do it. Is it okay if I go and call Will and Jenny to tell them I won't be able to see them tomorrow?" Jacob's mom smiled and answered, "Sure."

As Jacob left the room, his mom yelled after him, "And have them come over for dinner tomorrow night as a farewell party for you!"

First, Jacob called Will and then Jenny. Because things were getting a bit hairy around there, they decided to take a vote on whether or not they should tell some adults about it all. Will voted "yes," because he had become increasingly nervous since his run-in with the cricket in the library. Jacob's vote was "no," because he was afraid someone would take the sporran away and besides, he would be with his father in a few days and could tell him, if he needed to. He thought his dad may well be the only adult on the planet who was sure to understand and trust in what he would tell him. Surely, if his dad thought this was a dangerous situation, he would call back and alert people. Jenny agreed with Jacob, not wanting her reputation as supreme intellect and overall very reasonable person to be undermined by some crazy accusations about magic purses and disappearing balls, cups, and mousetraps.

The secret of the sporran remained sealed.

LEAVING HOME

The next few days passed without incident. Jacob spent most of his time with his mother shopping and packing for his trip to Scotland. Will and Jenny continued to puzzle on the situation but nothing major happened. There were no more appearances or disappearances and MacGregor, the bearded stranger, seemed to vanish just as he had appeared some days before.

The morning of Jacob's flight arrived sunny and warm, the perfect spring day. Birds were chirping and the spring bulbs that had spent the winter and early spring in hibernation were in full flowery bloom. As it would turn out, it was the last such perfect day he would see in many days.

Jacob's mother was loading his bags into the trunk of their car when up the drive flew Jenny. Out of breath, she dropped her bike and asked Mrs. Boyd where Jacob was.

"He is gathering up his backpack in his room," she answered and then shouted out to Jenny as Jacob's young friend rushed toward the house, "but we have to leave in just a minute!"

"I know," answered Jenny, "I just want to tell him something." Facing the other way as she rushed into the door, Mrs. Boyd could barely make out Jenny's reply.

Jenny found Jacob sitting on his bed putting books and notepads and pencils and snacks in his backpack to occupy his time on the long flight across the Atlantic Ocean.

"Jacob," Jenny said, even more out of breath from the run into the house and up the stairs to his room.

"Jacob," she repeated. "I have it . . . I have the connection!"

"What connection?"

"The connection between the clues. . . it's your trip! Its England and Scotland!"

"What do you mean," Jacob answered, as he stood up from his packing.

"Think about it," said Jenny, excitedly launching into a series of questions that she also answered herself."

"Where do they play cricket? England and Scotland!"

"Where did the *Chronicles of Narnia* take place? Some little English College town, right?"

"Where did the sporran come from? Scotland, which is connected to England in the same nation called the United Kingdom."

"Where did you say that MacGregor guy came from, if that is him? England and Scotland?"

"You see," she concluded her presentation as if she was an excited lawyer trying her first case, "it all connects! It's not very rational of me to believe this, but somehow I think you are *meant* to go on this trip today."

Jacob thought he felt the hair on his toes curl at the realization that things may be soon coming to a head for the mystery and for him. Thoughts, and fears, flooded his mind as he listened to Jenny. *Why me, here on Longbranch Drive? Why on a plane? What will become of me? Will I be next to disappear? What if the sporran makes the pilot or the engines or something disappear in mid-flight? What if a gun shows up in the pouch and sets off a metal detector and gets me arrested or something?*

Just in case something were to happen to him, and with his mom yelling up to his window to hurry him along, Jacob quickly scribbled a note to his mother and slipped it deep into the top drawer of his desk.

"Okay, Jenny old friend, lets go . . ." said Jacob as he slapped his friend gently on the back and jokingly added "its been good knowin' ya."

"Will you have e-mail?" asked Jenny, trying to ignore the sense of doom in Jacob's tone.

"Sure, once I get to St. Andrews with my dad, which should be in about 24 hours, after the plane ride, a taxi or two, and a train. . ."

The thought of all those planes and taxis and trains made him dread his departure even more as he stopped himself and added "maybe it would be better if I just crawled in the sporran and had it take me there, huh?"

"I will e-mail you if I come up with anything else on all this, then," said Jenny. "Good luck!"

Mrs. Boyd had the car running when the two arrived at the car and said goodbye for the last time. "I will check in on you from time to time, just like Jacob asked me to," said Jenny through the open car window on Jacob's side of the car. Mrs. Boyd flashed a "thumbs up" sign to Jenny and started backing the car out of the drive.

Jacob and his mother were both nervous, though they both tried not to show it. Mrs. Boyd was uneasy about her son flying all the way to England by himself and having to then make his way on another plane and trains to meet up with his father in Scotland. Jacob was similarly worried about making all the right decisions that would get him on the right plane and the right trains at the right times to the right places. *That would have been bad enough*, he thought to himself. *But, I also have to carry this "thing."*

The ride to the airport went by in an instant and before he could believe it, Jacob had said goodbye to his mother, made it through security and onto the first leg of his journey across the sea.

The ceiling of the plane's cabin was tall and, passing through first class, he saw what reminded him of a cemetery or factory for blue leather easy chairs. *If all the seats are like this it would be a nice comfy flight*, he thought.

Then a flight attendant asked to see his ticket and walked him back through a curtain where three big rows of much smaller seats were stretched across the width of the jet. *Oh. . . This will not be as comfortable as I first imagined*, a somewhat disappointed Jacob thought.

"Mr. Boyd," the stewardess leaned over him with a big smile, "you need anything at all, you just let me know. My name is Kelly, Okay?" She handed his ticket back to him and walked away.

His was a seat with a window, which Jacob thought he would like. No one sat next to him for awhile as more and more people got on. Then a woman introduced herself as Mrs. Wiley and sat down. She turned out to be a pleasant older lady who made fine company, particularly during the more nerve-wracking moments of the flight like take-off, landing, and when the plane would shake with turbulence. Jacob imagined Mrs. Wiley had the same rumbling in her stomach as he had in his during those moments. Talking about his little league career or Mrs. Wiley's grandchildren seemed to help pass those times for both of them.

Jacob spent the flight reading his tour books that he and his mom had purchased to get him ready for his trip, watching the TV that hung from the ceiling in the aisle in front of his seat, and snoozing. Mrs. Wiley pretty much just snoozed.

Periodically, Jacob would reach down into his backpack, which he stored under the seat in front of him. He wanted to make sure the sporran was still there and in good shape. Since that MacGregor guy was back at home, and since he was somehow connected to this, he wondered what would happen to the sporran as he got farther away.

Will it stop working as it got further from home? Will it disappear altogether? Will it somehow turn on me for taking it away?

Somewhere toward the end of a movie his dad would have called a "chick flick," Jacob's head leaned against the window and he fell asleep.

Sometime later a thud at his feet woke him with a startle. His backpack had slipped off his lap where it was when he fell asleep. Leaning forward to shove it back under the seat in front of him, he felt something was different.

He unzipped it and there, in the dark cave of his backpack he noticed something bulging in the sporran. His heart raced. *Here we go again! Is anyone looking?* Mrs. Wiley was sleeping so it was safe to look again. He opened the flap. Too dark at the bottom of the backpack to see. He would have to lift it out into the light.

Slowly he raised the open sporran up out of the backpack which sat between his feet in front of him. As the illumination from the light above Jacob's head penetrated the darkness that bathed the leather pouch, his eye caught sight of its contents. What he saw caused him to gasp unexpectedly and his heart to race.

With one quick motion, Jacob's hands dropped the sporran back into his backpack, his right foot kicked it under the seat in front of him, and his head flew back into his own seat. His head was swimming in panic.

LADY IN THE LOO

J acob looked all around. No one seemed to be watching. Mrs. Wiley was still asleep. He even unbuckled his seatbelt to stand and look behind him. Almost everyone he could see was sleeping.

No one had seen, he realized with some relief as he sunk back down into his seat. *Now what to do? Was it what I thought it was? Could it be? I must have been mistaken, right? Am I losing my mind?*

He puzzled and wondered and worried.

Mustering his courage, he reached for his backpack again.

Slowly he lifted the sporran to the light and saw it exactly as he thought he had. He slammed it shut again and zipped the backpack up as tight as it would go. Jacob's fear was racing.

A missing baseball; an appearing cricket ball; yes, those are one thing. But now . . . now. . . ah. . . ah. . . What do I do now? He repeated the phrase again and again under his breath while his eyes darted back and forth in his head and his skin grew clammy and cold.

Should I awaken Mrs. Wiley? No. . . she is too old and maybe her heart couldn't take the scare. Should I tell the flight attendant? Yes. She was nice and would understand . . . . No! She wouldn't understand. No one would!

Jacob decided he had better take one more look himself before bringing anyone else into this mess with him. *But, what if it got out and escaped on the plane? What if it ran to the cockpit and scared the pilot causing a crash or something? It is too risky*, he thought. *I will have to come up with a plan to do this right.*

"What would Jenny do? What would Jenny do?" Jacob repeated under his breath.

Of course, it hit him as perfectly reasonable. *Jenny is always in the bathroom, she would go to the bathroom to open it!*

Jacob looked all around and saw the lavatory just to the rear of his section was open. He put the sporran over his left shoulder, holding the flap down tight. *How to get over the sleeping Mrs. Wiley, however?* He was puzzled, and looked around.

Jacob stood on his seat and stretched his left leg far over to the arm of Mrs. Wiley's seat on the aisle. Balancing precariously with one foot on his seat and one on Mrs. Wiley's armrest, he knew it would be all over if he fell flat on the old lady and lost control of the sporran. He couldn't let it happen; not at 30,000 feet with nowhere to run.

The young acrobat prepared to make his move. He shifted his weight from his right foot to his left just as a strong hand grabbed his arm. Jacob gasped and turned.

"Shhhhh. . . its alright, just here to help," said Kelly the stewardess as she steadied his weight and motioned him into the aisle. "Nice of you not to want to wake up the lady," she whispered.

"Thank you," said Jacob as he started back toward the bathroom.

Inside, he quickly locked the door behind him and took a big breath of relief as he leaned against it. *One hurdle down, but, now it could get ugly.*

Still half hoping his tired eyes had played a trick on him, he peeked into the sporran. There, yes, no mistake about it. . . a tiny hand was emerging in the darkness!

He slammed it shut again.

For a few minutes he stood trying to get up the courage to do what he knew he would have to do. . . open the bag and let out whatever it was in there . . . and deal with what might happen then.

The sporran was lying on the stainless steel sink, flap side up. Jacob took a pen from his back pocket. He started to jump back toward the door even before he flipped it open. The pouch opened with the flap and its three dangling tassels lying in the sink.

Nothing. Nothing came out. Nothing stirred.

Jacob gave a quick smack to the old leather bottom of the sporran which then spilled its contents into the sink. He heard himself let out a little squeal as he saw, lying in the sink staring back at him, a tiny little woman. She had black hair and wore a rather normal looking dress but no shoes.

Jacob pressed himself hard against the door and as far away as he could get in that tiny little airplane toilet. Racing a million miles a minute, Jacob's mind prepared him for what would happen next. *Maybe she will say she is a genie here to do my bidding . . . maybe she will just turn me to stone with a look . . . maybe she would say something like "Greetings, master of the sporran . . ."*

Nothing. Nothing. Nothing happened. She just stared back from the sink and Jacob stared back as if transfixed. She held him in her power with an unblinking empty stare.

"Knock . . . knock . . ." the sound of knuckles gently wrapping at the door broke the power of the trance.

"Are you okay?" It was the voice of Kelly the stewardess.

"I . . . .I'm. . . . I'm fine, thanks," he replied.

He slowly approached the sink and the "thing" that was using it as a seat or bed or something.

"H-e-l-l-o?" Jacob said as more of a question than a greeting.

No reply. Nothing.

"Do you speak English?" he asked.

Silence.

"My name is Jacob, what is yours?"

Silence.

"Okay, I really need to get back to my seat now. . . "

Still nothing in reply from the woman. She did not release her cold, empty stare.

He approached and extended his hand as gently as if he were greeting an angry porcupine.

A foot away. . . six inches. . . three inches. . . an inch. . . almost touching, and nothing. Expecting he might lose a finger or worse in the process, he closed his eyes and touched the lady.

"What?" he said aloud as he opened his eyes. *What is going on?*

He put his hands around the lady in a scene that reminded him of an old movie he once saw on a Saturday afternoon with his dad, though he was not a giant ape climbing the Empire State Building.

She was not soft and flesh-like at all. She was hard.

"Dang!" Jacob exclaimed. "It's just a stupid doll!"

He shook the doll as if it were its fault he had been through the biggest panic attack of his life, and then shoved it into his front pocket.

Back at his seat, he was relieved to see Mrs. Wiley was awake. She could let him pass without more gymnastics to get back to his seat.

Angry and exhausted from the tension, he put the doll in his backpack and stared out the window until he again fell asleep.

Into the Kingdom of Fife

The early morning sun shot brightly through the blinds left partly open in the night. The plane was nearly to its destination. As the passengers slowly awoke from their slumber, the bright orange sun began to dim. Having been flying above the clouds, the plane gave a false impression of conditions on the ground. Dipping below the clouds, the sun was replaced by a steady rain pelting the windows.

With the pilot's announcements that they would soon be landing, Mrs. Wiley came to life again and began to nervously chatter with Jacob. This time, however, Jacob was not in the mood to hear about her grandchildren, especially not about precious little Susie, the two-year-old genius from Missouri. Jacob was still angry about what he saw as a "dirty trick" that happened the night before.

Why that doll? Why was it so real? Darn it, I was scared! But he still managed to be pleasant with Mrs. Wiley and they parted, wishing each other the best on their vacations. Mrs. Wiley would be spending a week in London doing typically touristy things like visiting Stonehenge, Big Ben, and Madame Tussauds Wax Museum.

It was 7:30 AM in London, though it was still the middle of the night back home and according to Jacob's tired body. He spotted a McDonald's there in the airport. Aaaahh! *I think people call this "comfort food",* he sighed, as he went over to order some breakfast with the English money he and his mother exchanged at the airport when he left home.

He would now take another plane north from London to Edinburgh, the capital of Scotland and from there a train north and eastward to St. Andrews and his father.

He was pleasantly surprised, when the nice steward on the next plane brought him what would for him be a second breakfast part-way through the flight, complete with a real cup (white ceramic with a handle and everything!) of hot tea—not some paper cup or cheap plastic like the American flights he had been on. His mother had taught him to drink tea on cold afternoons with pancakes back home, and he had read how the English loved to drink tea, so he thoroughly enjoyed his first very English moment.

Before breakfast had arrived, Jacob had fingered the old sporran and gave it another look-over. Before replacing it in his backpack, he put a couple of American coins into the pouch that he found left in his pocket; *of no use to me over here anyway.*

The tea brought back his typically good mood and even if it was still raining, he was looking forward to seeing his father in just a few more hours. When the steward had cleared his tray, he reached down into his backpack to retrieve a book, but decided to check the sporran as well.

Opening the flap, he noticed that nothing was there. He expected those coins to be there. *Why weren't they? Nothing had ever disappeared this quickly before. It's been only about an hour since I put the two quarters and a nickel there.* Previously, things took all night to appear or disappear. He rummaged through the bottom of his backpack to make sure they hadn't just fallen out. They weren't there.

He put a pencil in the pouch and put it away. He checked every twenty minutes or so, and it disappeared about an hour later. In its place was an English pound—a rather small coin, but one worth about five American quarters.

By this time his flight was over and it was time to leave the plane and catch a taxi to the train station. The taxi was the strangest car he had ever been in. Purplish-black in color, its back seat had leg room enough for a giant (if he were younger he might imagine there were giants who lived in those parts and took taxi rides). Two little seats folded down from the backs of the front seats, giving room for at least six people his size, maybe more. The driver, as all drivers in England and Scotland are wont to do, drove on the right side of the car and the left side of the road, which Jacob found very peculiar, even if he was expecting it.

Settling himself into a seat on the train at Rob Roy Station in Edinburgh, he opened the sporran to find a different pencil had replaced the one he put in a couple of hours before. This one seemed made from something like paper, not wood, and had no eraser. He took it and, like he did with everything that appeared from beyond through the sporran, he sealed it in a plastic bag in his backpack...just in case they were somehow contaminated from an alien and noxious world.

Jacob was running out of things he was willing to send to another dimension, likely never to see again. But, it was getting more exciting with the quickness of disappearances and appearances. *It's as if the sporran is gaining strength as it reaches its homeland or something. But if that is the case, what will happen next? What if it is gaining power and I refuse to feed it? What if things get even weirder? What if it gains the power to make ME disappear?*

Well, he couldn't let himself worry about all that now. He settled on just sending the napkin he still had in his pocket from his second breakfast that morning.

It couldn't have been any more than half an hour and the airline napkin was gone. In its place was a small slip of paper with numbers on it. *A dumb receipt*, he thought to himself. *They have receipts in other dimensions, too?*

He sat thinking as he watched the scenery go by, complete with sheep and cattle—though, to his disappointment not the really hairy cows he had seen in the guidebooks for Scotland and postcards from his dad. They were just normal looking cows. A shadow of wings passed quickly across the field to his left and he watched it without thinking to look up. *A plane*, he thought. But the shadow, and the thing making it, turned and followed the train as it moved north.

Jacob now held the sporran in his lap, as if perhaps by holding it he could maintain control of it and keep it from gaining more power. When next he opened the flap, he was shocked at what he found.

Inside the pouch was a ticket, and not just any ordinary or random ticket. Jacob immediately recognized it as a matching ticket of his own. He pulled his from his pocket. *Yes. A match. Same color. Same trip (Edinburgh to Leuchars). Same date. Everything!*

The realization hit him like a bolt of lightning. *This ticket came from somewhere on this very train!* His hands began to sweat and his heart began to race at the possible implications. *Is the sporran now taking over the train? Is its magic growing outward and encompassing the other passengers? Will I ever be allowed off this ride? Or maybe the sporran is just an instrument for a larger and more ominous power that is also on this train with me!* His mind was jumping from one fear to another.

Jacob stood and looked around his train car. There was an Asian family directly behind him. They looked unthreatening. Across the aisle was an elderly couple and behind them was a group of four girls and two boys who looked like college students and their teacher on a trip. They all seemed safe enough.

He sat back down and huddled with his thoughts for a moment more when he heard the door open behind him. It was the sliding electric door connecting his car to the one behind it. A cold chill came over him and a tingling pulse ran down his right arm. He had felt something like that sensation several times in the last few days but never this intense.

Footsteps came up the aisle behind him and suddenly he felt a hard pull on his arms. His body swung down toward the floor. *What?* He was being pulled downward by his backpack with the sporran inside. Jacob struggled with his pack for a moment as he remained stuck down in his seat. Then, just as quickly as it had pulled him down, it released his hands. As he sat back up, the door just ahead of him was closing as a tall man in a wide hat passed into the next car. He couldn't help but wonder if the sporran had just helped him escape some danger he didn't even know he was in.

Jacob was very glad when the train ground to a halt at a very small rural station with the sign "Leuchars" on the wall outside. This was the station that serviced the town of St. Andrews in the area of Scotland known as the Kingdom of Fife.

Jacob quickly gathered his things and hurried off the train with about two dozen other passengers. None of them looked particularly threatening. As he turned to see his father waiting down by the road, he hoped the train would take with it whatever strange power he had come close to in that car.

Reunion

As quickly as he could, being weighed down with a backpack and suitcase, Jacob hurried across the platform and down the reddish metal ramp to where his father, and several taxi drivers, waited.

Mr. Boyd stepped forward and picked up Jacob (backpack, suitcase and all) in a big, air-squashing bear hug. "I have really missed you, Jakester!" he said as he broke the hug. Catching a breath, Jacob returned the sentiment with a very content smile.

"C'mon," his dad said with one arm sweeping down to pick up Jacob's suitcase. "I have reservations for dinner and I want to hear all about your trip and baseball practice and everything back home. Ah. . . , " he stopped himself, "but first we must call your mom and tell her you are here. She will be worried sick."

The call was a lot easier than Jacob thought it would be. He imagined having to call some operator in England who would then call some operator in America, who would then call the Boyd house. Instead, he just punched some extra numbers ahead of his phone number and there his mother was on the line. Jacob could hear the relief in his mother's voice as soon as she recognized his, even if he did try to disguise it with a very poor version of a Scottish brogue.

Seeing his father again for the first time in several weeks, the urgency of the sporran was driven from his mind. He talked a million miles an hour at dinner and his dad listened and asked questions eagerly. They talked of Jenny and Will and of baseball and school. They talked of Mom and the neighbors and Grandma and Grandpa and the cousins. Mr. Boyd was glad for the news of home.

Dinner ended. It was too dark to tour the town, so the Boyd men headed to Feddinch House, a bed and breakfast where his dad had been staying for the last two weeks.

The drive to the bed and breakfast took about five minutes from downtown. Jacob couldn't believe his dad had mastered the art of driving "on the wrong side of the road," as they do in Scotland. He thought it must be terribly hard to do and his dad told him a few funny stories of his first times trying to drive on the opposite side of the road (and the opposite side of the car) than he was used to. Jacob found the one about the rose bushes (that are no longer along the road) the funniest of all.

The dark drive was uneventful except that the car's headlights at one point caught a man walking along the side of the road that looked an awful lot like the bearded stranger Jacob met back home. Jacob craned his neck to watch the man as the car passed him. He had a bushy dark beard and wore shabby clothes and was walking with a golf club slung over one shoulder. *It couldn't be,* he thought, *but it looks like MacGregor alright. Glad he is going the other direction! I hope not to run into him at night before I have time to get some answers in the daylight!*

The road to the Feddinch Manor House turned slowly from side-to-side once they got off the main road from town. They entered onto the grounds of the house as if it were some secluded castle or something, Jacob thought. The branches of the trees hung low over the car as they crossed the last gate to the house, which was the last house on the lane.

Floodlights on the ground illuminated the starkly white walls of the house, and warm golden glows hung in a few of the windows as they approached. "Dad, this is great!" Jacob exclaimed after exiting the car. If there was anything he liked more than dusty old junk, it was exploring old houses that, even if immaculately kept as was the Feddinch Manor House, he could imagine were dusty and creepy and maybe even haunted.

The door opened as they approached. Holding the door was a very tall and balding older man in white pants and a striped dress shirt with reading glasses hung on a chain around his neck. It was Mr. Woods, the innkeeper of the house. "Master Boyd, I presume," the man greeted Jacob as he approached the door. "Your father has talked of nothing but your arrival for days." Jacob smiled but said nothing. "It's a pleasure to make your acquaintance young man," Mr. Woods continued, as he motioned Jacob through the door.

They first entered a small foyer of dark wood and stained glass that sat out from the main house. In the morning he would notice the corner filled with old twisted walking sticks and spare golf clubs and balls, but the inner house had already caught his eye by now, with its deep blue carpet and rather elegant appointments.

Mr. Woods asked if he could have the honor of showing Jacob around the first floor a bit while Mr. Boyd carried Jacob's bags up to his room.

Turning left, they went through a glass door into a room with a warm fire burning, though it was obviously coming to the end of its fuel. This was the parlor. It was exactly what Jacob had imagined. It was wonderfully warm and old and comfortable, as all parlors should be.

Directly across the hall was a dining room, though Mr. Woods just pointed to the door and said that breakfast would be served in there by Mrs. Woods in the morning. The kitchen, he noted, was behind the stair and then Mr. Woods began to tell Jacob of the history of the house.

Jacob learned the house went back as far as 1512. *1512! Just twenty years after Columbus discovered America!* He thought to himself that there was no house anywhere in America remotely as old as the Feddinch House. *How many people had lived there? How many wars had it seen? How many swords had been unsheathed in its defense? How much mystery there must be to this old place.* Jacob looked forward to the coming days when he might explore the place a bit.

"But, you probably are more interested in things you can do during your visit than in history," said Mr. Woods as he changed the subject to the things Jacob and his father could do on the property. There were books in the parlor, a tennis court in back, beautiful places to hike through the fields and woods, and golf. Yes, because St. Andrews is most famous as being the ancient home of golf, Mr. Woods had even put in a small putting area by the house for guests who wanted to claim to have golfed in St. Andrews but who weren't adventurous enough to try one of the real courses.

"I take a constitutional at 7:00 AM sharp every morning, should ya like to join me someday," Mr. Woods said as Jacob's dad started back down the stairs. "Sure, I'd like that," Jacob replied.

Heading up the stairs, Jacob whispered, "Dad, what is a "constitutional" he wants me to join him in?" Mr. Boyd let slip a laugh that was a bit too loud for that time of evening and caught himself with an embarrassed shrug. "It's just a fancy word for taking a walk, son!"

Jacob's room was all the way at the very top of the two twists of the stairs and next to his father's. He had traveled four thousand miles since he left home the day before and he was very much ready for bed!

Mr. Boyd had taken the next day off from all meetings so that he could spend time with Jacob. Their day began early with Mrs. Wood's famous waffles (complete with the fanciest little sliced strawberry Jacob had ever seen), though, to be truthful, the Scottish version of bacon, which seemed more like fatty ham than any bacon he had ever seen, left something to be desired for both Boyd men!

Then it was off. First they played "pitch and putt" golf at a place called the Himalayas which used to be reserved for women when women weren't allowed to play the big courses. Then they took a very wet walk along the beach. Jacob never imagined Scotland would have an actual beach, as he thought such things were for warm climates only. Then it was a tour of the town, lunch, a visit to the ruins of the castle and cathedral, some tennis (rather bad tennis, as Mr. Woods said to them), and through it all they got SOAKED!

It rained on and off all day but Jacob loved playing in the rain and not caring—his mother, and certainly his grandmother, would NEVER have allowed it. But, as Mr. Woods said, "In Scotland, if you don't do things in the rain, they likely won't get done!"

Having such an enjoyable time with his dad, the sporran, which was left in his backpack in his room, passed almost completely out of his mind until that evening.

Jacob spent some time that night exploring around Feddinch House. The parlor, with its toasty fire, was his favorite room by far. His dad settled into a comfortable chair by the fire in the early evening and read a book. Jacob did the same but found it hard to concentrate. His mind kept drifting to the sporran and to related thoughts of things in Scotland. His eyes drifted, too, from the book to the bookshelves and around the room.

Finally, he got up and looked out into the Scottish darkness through the window. Outside by the shed he saw the figure of a man moving back and forth in the shadows cast by the floodlight mounted above the shed door.

"Dad, it's awfully late for Mr. Woods to be working outside, isn't it? Dad?"

Jacob turned to see his father had fallen fast asleep in his chair. His book had slipped down his chest and caught on top of his pants. It was a comforting sight. *How could anything really be wrong in the world when Dad can sleep like that?*

Jacob turned again to the window and watched the shadows move about near the shed and the small woodlot next to it. He backed away from the window slightly, hoping not to be seen. *Is it Mr. Woods? Surely it must be, but what is he doing?*

A voice suddenly startled him from behind. "Watching Mr. Woods practice his putting, are we?" Mrs. Woods was standing in the doorway.

"I'm done for the day and heading to my bed chamber, but you are welcome to go out and putt with him. Mr. Woods always says, 'The day is for puttering—the night is for the putter!'"

"Thank you," Jacob said, and nodded politely. For a moment he thought he might venture out into the night with Mr. Woods but, alas, his courage did not match his curiosity.

He turned to awaken his father and go to bed when something else caught his eye outside. *Did I see something? Is there someone else out there?* Mr. Woods was walking around the small putting greens near the shed, but what was that in the shadow beside the small building? Jacob stared for a moment but could not make anything out. He let his eyes focus in and out. He looked directly at the shadow and then tried looking at it just out of the corner of his eye. He tried every angle he could think of but still he could not make out a distinct figure, only the hint of a presence. Nervously, he backed away from the window for good and shook his father awake and asked to go to bed, ducking slightly and walking quickly, as he passed the window on his way out the parlor door.

STRANGER AT HOME

It was spring break and the school was quiet. Only the secretaries and the administrators were at work when the strange man arrived at the middle school. A man entered the front door but bypassed the office. He did not stop to get his official "Visitors Pass" and somehow slipped beyond the watchful eye of Mrs. Whitefish, which was quite an accomplishment. Almost no one slips passed her. She was known by students and teachers alike as the "Hall Nazi." It was a title she did not shun.

He was seen a few minutes later walking the lower halls.

"May I help you, sir?" said Miss Finnigan, the newest office worker at the school.

"Ahhh, well, yes, yes, you can." The thin man smiled a charming smile of many teeth that stood out white and bright against his dark skin. He extended his hand, which Miss Finnigan shook. Only later that afternoon would she realize that somewhere she had picked up a black ink stain on her hand. "You see, I am looking for Jacob Boyd. He is my grandson and I have come from California to surprise him and his family."

"Well, I'm sorry sir, but this is spring break. The students are all gone and won't be back at school for another week," the secretary recounted with a tone of sadness.

The stranger looked down at the ground sadly and said, "Well, that just blows all my plans. I guess I will have to call his mother and tell them I am coming and ruin the surprise."

"That is a shame! You have come so far and now to be denied the chance to surprise your family, that is really not right," said Mrs. Finnigan.

"Well, what else can I do? I didn't bring their address with me since I thought I would just surprise Jacob here at school first and . . ."

Miss. Finnigan interrupted, "Mr. Boyd, you did say that was your name, didn't you?"

"Uh," the man paused and then caught his own lie. "Yes, that is right, my name is Boyd, miss,"

"Well, I have an idea for you, Mr. Boyd. Why don't I just look up their address and give it to you so you can surprise them?"

"Oh, that would be so kind of you! I have so looked forward to the look on their faces when I show up!"

The two walked back up the stairs to the office where the files were kept on each student. Everyone else was at lunch by now and the office was empty except for Miss Finnigan and the dark stranger claiming to be Jacob's grandfather. At the file, Miss Finnigan hesitated and offered, "If Mrs. Whitefish were here she would not like this! 'Highly irregular, don't you think,' she would say! But I say there is nothing more important than a grandfather's love for his grandson and I can clearly see how much you love Jacob!"

It took Miss Finnigan only minutes to find Jacob's file and copy down the address on a small slip of paper. A few minutes more and the tanned stranger was out the door and on his way to Longbranch Drive.

Jenny and Will had been keeping an eye on Mrs. Boyd as they promised Jacob they would. That morning, though, she left town to visit with Jacob's grandparents while he and his dad were out of town. The two friends were tooling around the neighborhood when a very fancy black sports car drove slowly down the street. They barely noticed it the first time it passed, but then just minutes later it was coming back up the street very slowly. The windows were tinted so dark the driver could not be seen.

As it passed Jenny and Will, it slowed still more and the driver's window slowly came down.

"Excuse me, but I am looking for the Boyd residence, could you tell me if that brick house down the street is theirs?"

"Yes it is," Will blurted out immediately.

"Well, thank you, young man. Very kind of you to help."

"Well, excuse me sir, can I ask why you are interested in the Boyds?" Jenny interjected.

"Of course, I am Jacob's uncle and am here to visit for the first time," the man answered as he started to put his window back up.

"Well, sir, they are. . ." Will was beginning to tell this stranger that the Boyds were out-of-town when Jenny coughed hard and drove her front tire into Will's leg.

"Ouch! Watch it!" Will squealed.

"What was that you were saying?" the stranger asked. He leaned further out of his car and both Jenny and Will noticed his hand was stained with what looked like black ink.

"Oh, he was just saying they are really nice people, the Boyds are, right, Will?"

"Huh? Yes, they are very nice," Will said as he stared at the stains on the man's fingers.

The stranger nodded, closed his window, and slowly drove up the street.

"What were you doing?" Jenny asked Will in a very accusatory tone.

"What? I didn't do anything. I was just going to. . ."

"Exactly! You were going to tell that freaky guy that the Boyd's were out of town so he would feel free to rob them blind or something!"

"Oh, yes, I see what you mean. But, he said he was Jacob's uncle, so he wouldn't steal from them," Will countered.

"Come on, Will, would you think Mrs. Boyd would leave town if Jacob's uncle was coming to visit?" Jenny asked rhetorically. "Uncles just don't show up unannounced the first time they come for a visit, do they? Let's keep an eye out around the neighborhood for this guy and then e-mail Jacob to see if he does have an uncle like this."

The two friends rode their bikes fast down Morris Court to the cul-de-sac behind the Boyd home and stashed their bikes behind the bushes that separated the Boyd home from their neighbors. There they watched the house.

Within a few minutes the black sports car was back slowly driving by the house. Then it passed one more time and the two friends watched. Minutes turned into hours and the stranger did not return to the Boyd home. At dinner time, Will and Jenny split and went to their own homes. But first they had agreed that Jenny, who lived only a few houses up the street from the Boyds, would keep an eye on the Boyd home and would call Will if anything happened.

Immediately after dinner, both Will and Jenny e-mailed Jacob to tell him about this man claiming to be his uncle. As the evening wore on, Jenny walked to the corner of her drive every fifteen minutes but saw nothing out of order. At 9:00 P.M. came the last call of the evening from Will to see if anything was afoot. Then Jenny went to bed, but not to sleep, for too much was on her mind. So much had happened that she couldn't account for and now she was genuinely afraid for the safety of the neighborhood and for Jacob's family in particular.

Will spent a similar early evening, though he was mainly imagining scenarios where he would be able to save the neighborhood from this bad man who meant them harm. He laid traps along the road, ambushed him in the alley, and dropped an old 31-inch Louisville Slugger upside his head when the man tried to get into the Boyd House.

Unable to sleep, Jenny got out of bed and stared out the window at the full moon hanging in the sky. When she looked down, an unfamiliar glow hung in the air down Longbranch Drive. *Is that a fire? It looks like Jacob's house! Holy Cow!*

Jenny grabbed her jeans and pulled them on as she hopped and stumbled across her bedroom. She snuck down the stairs as quietly as she could. In case there was a fire or something else wrong, she grabbed her mother's cell phone off the counter as she went through the kitchen and then she quickly walked out through her garage, surely the quietest way out of the house.

Jenny paused as she passed her bike in the garage, but then decided the road was too dangerous. She would go on foot and through the small wooded lot that separated her house from the Boyd's home. Then, across the tiny creek and up the end of the woodlot by Jacob's house and she could hide among the shadows in the trees and see what was going on.

She had no flashlight but Jenny hurried as best she could through the woodlot. The moon was bright and she knew the woods well from having played in them with Jacob since he moved in when they were five. The sounds of twigs snapping under her feet, a sound she wouldn't even have noticed in the light, sounded like firecrackers in her ears at night. Fearing being found, she slowed her pace as she emerged at the top of the grade near Jacob's house and crouched behind a large maple tree.

Every light in every room of the Boyd house was ablaze. *What is going on? All the Boyds are out of town and no burglar would put all the lights on to rob the place!* Suddenly, a twig cracked behind Jenny and before she could turn, Jenny felt a body crash down next to her and an arm drop around her shoulders. She turned and pushed back, scrambling away in the loose leaves and twigs.

"Shhhhhh. . . It's me!"

Jenny recognized the voice. "What are you doing! You scared me to death!"

"Sorry . . . and, to answer your question, I am doing the same thing you are!"

Will had noticed the strange glow coming from the neighborhood as well and set off to check things out. He had been there about ten minutes and noticed Jenny coming up through the trees. He had made his way around the back of the Boyd's house and into the woodlot where he snuck up on Jenny.

"What have you seen? I can't see anything unusual but all the lights being on," Jenny remarked.

"Its that stranger guy . . . can't you see him?" Will answered.

Jenny looked back up at the house and shook her head from side-to-side, indicating she couldn't.

"Down there, see, in front of the house down by that little tree." Will was pointing to the front of the Boyd home where a small crabapple tree stood in the middle of a rounded stone wall that looked like the remnant of an old well.

Now, Jenny caught sight of him. All in black, he looked more like a shadow than a man. A broadsword was driven into the ground in front of him and he was moving his arms up and down. As he did, the lights in the house also brightened and dimmed. Then he started to speak in a tongue Jenny and Will could not make out. It sounded like a chant, as if he was putting a spell on the house or calling out something from inside.

"Come on, Will, we must get a closer look," Jenny whispered to her friend.

"This is close enough!" Will answered.

"I am going to crawl up by the swing set and then over by the shrubs at the corner of the house."

"I'll stay here and watch to warn you, then." Will was pretending to be brave in his decision to stay put and well hidden in the woodlot.

Jenny ignored his answer and started a slow crawl the few feet between the tree she was hiding behind and the Boyd's swing set. Once safely there, she took a deep breath as if preparing to dive in a pool and started for the shrubs on the corner of the house.

She was going quickly on hands and knees. It was a bit darker on the side of the house as the moonlight was blocked by the house and the tall tree next to it. Moving like a dog, she hurried along until "THUD!" Jenny had forgotten about the Boyd's new lawn swing and had banged her head into one of the metal support poles. She let out a whimper that was louder than was prudent.

Startled, Will looked over at Jenny and then down at the stranger. *Oh no, he's heard her!* The lights in the Boyd house went dark and the stranger lit a lantern. It was an old-fashioned lantern with a candle surrounded by square glass panes. He came out from behind the short stone wall and started toward where Jenny and Will were hiding.

"Jenny! Jenny!" Will was whispering as loudly as he dared. "He has heard you, come on!"

Jenny peeked around the corner to see the light of the lantern approaching. She crawled quickly back into the woodlot and she and Will started to run as quickly as they could down through the trees. They only got a few feet however, when something tripped them both. It could have been any number of roots or downed branches that caused their fall and they both hit hard, catching rotting dry leaves and dirt in their mouths.

The moment they hit, they felt something descend upon them. It felt like a blanket had been placed over them and then a small and high-pitched whisper told them to be still and very quiet!

"Quiet, little ones, and he won't see you."

Jenny and Will were breathing hard and didn't know what to do, but at this time they were less frightened of someone at least claiming to want to help than they were of the footsteps they heard approaching from behind. The boots were now in the woodlot with them cracking twigs as they came. Closer, closer they came and then the two heard the man speak.

"Who is there? Come out and I won't hurt you. What are you doing here at night? Hello? Hello?" The man had now reached where Jenny and Will lay. He came within a few feet of their faces and stood holding his lantern out in front of him and turning around in circles. He was close enough that Jenny and Will could hear him breathe and Will caught sight of the tip of his sword sticking out from under his long black coat.

The kids had somehow been covered by a cloak or cloth that they could see through but it was obviously camouflaging them from the stranger's eyes. Will felt his breaths start to come in quick bursts as he watched the man move within feet of him. Jenny reached over to touch his hand in the hopes of calming her friend.

Then there was another burst of crackling twigs and crunching dry leaves over to their right. The man turned his head quickly in time to see a large deer burst through the woodlot and down the hill toward the stream.

"Darned animal!" the man mumbled and then turned and left the trees. In relief, Jenny exhaled hard and realized she hadn't taken a breath in quite awhile.

"Stay still little ones, stay still," a voice whispered at them. "Danger has not yet passed."

A few moments later and the kids heard the black sports car pull away from the Boyd home. The cloak that covered them began to rise off Jenny and Will and they slowly picked themselves up off the ground.

"Don't turn around, little ones, just listen for a moment." The voice was coming from behind them. The scratchy and high-pitched voice belonged to a very small man, standing no more than a few feet off the ground but fully grown and dressed in flannel clothes cut in a style seldom seen but on Halloween for generations. He had laid down and spread his cloak over the children to help them escape from the dark stranger.

"Your bravery is admirable, but your actions very unwise, little ones! The danger to you has now passed for this night, but your friend is in very great danger. You should warn him, but tell him he must not give up or take the easy way, but should bear the burden of the gift. Do you understand?"

Jenny and Will both nodded affirmatively and waited. The small man said nothing more and even when Will and Jenny finally broke the silence by saying "Hello? Hello? Are you still there?" there was no reply.

Jenny was first to turn and see that they were again alone in the woods. They stood and got out of the woodlot as quickly as they could. They talked for a moment at the road about what happened and who might have saved them. Then both ran home to sneak back into the quiet safety of their beds.

CONTACT

M r. Boyd awoke early the next morning to get to his temporary
office at a small industrial park outside of town. He was
going to put in a few early hours every morning so by mid-
afternoon he could be back with Jacob, spending the day with his son.

A glimmer of sun hit Jacob's eye about 6:40 A.M. "Darn!" he said as his feet
hit the area rug around his bed. He had wanted to be up and have breakfast
and be ready to go with Mr. Woods on his "constitutional," or whatever he
called it.

Jacob threw a flannel shirt over the t-shirt he slept in, put on a pair of jeans
and his ball cap and rushed downstairs to the dinning room. Mrs. Woods was
awaiting his order, which, of course, was for waffles again.

Mr. Woods was lacing his shoes at the head of the dining room table as
Jacob tried to stall him by asking him questions about the house, his past,
how many guests they have each year, and the like. In quick order he learned
of the house originally being just a tower about 500 years ago, of Mr. Woods'
time as a fighter pilot in the Royal Air Force, and that they had been running
the Inn for only a few years.

At 7:00 A.M. sharp, Mr. Woods rose from his seat and started for the door.
"Mr. Woods," Jacob called after him. "What I mean is. . . ," he stammered,
". . . would you mind me joining you this morning?"

"Come along," said Mr. Woods without a pause in his step. Jacob hurried
up from the table and followed the Innkeeper. "But," Mr. Woods added
without even turning toward Jacob, "the stones are a bit rough on the bare
feet."

Embarrassed, Jacob looked down to realize he had forgotten his shoes
in the morning rush. "Be right back!" he said and bolted up the stairs

taking two at a time when he could. Mr. Woods continued out the door and down the drive where Jacob caught up to him, kneeling as he did to tie his second shoe.

"Rubble is good for the mind, it helps smooth your ideas, but it's mighty hard on the soles, I think you would have agreed not long down the road!"

"So, tell me about yourself, laddie," said Mr. Woods as they walked. Jacob told him about baseball and school and Jenny and Will but was stingy with details, not assuming that this man who had traveled the world as a fighter pilot could possibly be interested in the everyday experiences of a middle schooler from Longbranch Drive.

They paused at the stone wall near Feddinch House that overlooked St. Andrews. Golden grasses covered the fields that led down into the ancient town and Jacob imagined a battle that may one day have happened on that very spot hundreds of years ago.

"Did you climb the tower with your father yesterday?" Mr. Woods asked.

"No, we ran out of time," Jacob answered. "Is it a hard climb?"

"The hardest thing you might ever do, if done right," he answered with his right eyebrow raised what looked like at least two inches above the left in a way that made it seem obvious he was trying to communicate more than he was saying.

Mr. Woods was talking about St. Rule's tower, which dates back to the 12th century and was then the tallest building in Scotland. From the description in the guidebook, Jacob was really looking forward to exploring it and with Mr. Woods' remarks, it had just become a priority.

At the end of their walk, Jacob asked how he might be able to get downtown that morning to look around. Mr. Woods offered him a ride down and then the loan of a bicycle that would get him back home again that afternoon.

A half-hour later, the Innkeeper dropped Jacob off at the corner of South and Abbey Streets and gave him a sheet of paper with directions back to Feddinch House and his phone number just in case. "A-goin' to do some shopping, are you, son?" asked Mr. Woods as he unloaded the bike.

Jacob avoided the question as he didn't want to lie, but also knew his host would not understand a twelve-year-old saying "No sir. I have business today at the University." But that is exactly what Jacob had in mind—he would track down Hammish MacGregor, the author of the book on cricket and, Jacob was sure, the same bearded man from the baseball field and school back home. *Surely, he is part of this sporran thing and will have more answers.*

Jacob walked the bike in the light misty morning air down South Street to North Castle Street and then eventually over to The Scores, perhaps the most famous road in all golf history (he knew that from the guidebook). He was surprised how at-ease he felt in the town and how easily he found himself standing outside the office building where the Department of Classics and Antiquities was housed. It was a large gray building that looked hundreds of years old and was surrounded by a tall, black iron fence. Overlooking the ocean, it was very close to the ruins of the ancient castle he had toured with his dad the day before.

He entered the building and was greeted by a pleasant secretary who seemed to have little or nothing to do until he arrived.

"I am looking for Professor MacGregor," he said haltingly.

"Professor MacGregor's office is the third office on the right, just left down the hall. You can see if he is in," answered the secretary as she resumed her career of seeming to do nothing.

Jacob poked his head leftward down the hall and then let his body follow to the third door on the right. A small bronze plaque on the door read "Dr. Hammish MacGregor, Professor of Geographical Political Sociology and Antiquities." He hesitated, and then with a deep breath to muster his courage, Jacob knocked. No answer. He tried again. Nothing. As he waited, Jacob noted a piece of yellowish paper. It was folded three times and taped to the door with "To Whom It May Concern" written on its front.

Jacob hesitated as he stared at the note. *Should I look at it? Surely Professor MacGregor couldn't know I was coming to see him. But, maybe this was just some kind of generic note to anyone who was coming to visit with him and that surely included me, right?* Jacob asked himself, but in a way that was clearly intended to strengthen his ease more than ask himself a question. *It might say "Gone to lunch, be back in one hour," or something,* he reasoned.

Jacob took the paper down and unfolded it. In big, thick, handwritten letters it said nothing but "MAKE CONTACT."

Make contact? What does that mean? I am making contact! I am here, aren't I? Was this some kind of joke? Frustrated, Jacob put the paper back on the door since it probably was meant for someone else and left the building. Turning right down the road, he decided to walk by the beach for awhile and to write a bit in his journal before heading up town and then starting his ride back to Feddinch House. As he walked, Jacob thought about that note. "Make Contact! Make Contact!" he mumbled to himself over and over again.

Near the beach, he noticed a small shelter with a nice view of the sea and the beach where he and his father had walked yesterday. He thought it would be a fine place to write in his journal.

He sat and began to write about the wonderful time he and his father had yesterday and about his walk with Mr. Woods, but the sporran started to weigh heavy on his mind again. The words "MAKE CONTACT" kept coming to his mind and crowding out his other thoughts. He started writing them over and over on his tablet. Make Contact. Make Contact. Make Contact. Make Contact.

Wait a minute . . . wait just a minute! Maybe I'm to make contact with the sporran somehow!

Jacob took the sporran from the bag. He looked around to see if anyone was watching and then began to speak in a low whisper. Then he lifted the pouch to his ear to listen for a reply. He heard nothing. He tried again. No answer. Two attempts at that were enough. He decided to try a less embarrassing tactic. He ripped a piece of paper from his journal and wrote the word "Hello" on it and slipped it into the sporran where there was a small pink and white sea shell sitting at the bottom. It was just like the ones he and his father had picked for his mother on the beach the day before, but he didn't remember putting one there.

He shut the flap and sat thinking and staring out at the sea. He must have sat thinking and admiring the beauty and power of the sea for half an hour. Before he got up to go on his way, Jacob checked the sporran. His note was still there and he thought maybe he should write something a bit more intelligent than just "Hello." He pulled the note from the sporran and opened it.

"Hello" was written in his own handwriting on the paper. But, below it in someone else's hand was written "Hello. Who are you?"

St. Rules Tower

J acob felt like he was melting into the concrete blocks against which he was resting his back, the realization of what had just happened weighed so heavily on his mind. He found it a little hard to breathe as he looked at the paper. *It can communicate,* he realized with shock, and dropped the sporran to the bench and searched it with his eyes.

Do I dare answer the question? Do I dare tell it my name? On the other hand, do I dare not respond? Do I risk angering it?

Well, he thought, *I've come this far, no turning back now.* He took the paper and wrote. "My name is Jacob. What are you?" He slipped it into the sporran and waited anxiously. He peeked at it every few minutes and on the third peek, which couldn't have been more than ten minutes later, the paper was gone. Next check, it was back again.

Swallowing hard, Jacob unfolded the note. Beneath his question was written: "What do you mean WHAT am I? I am not a 'WHAT'!"

Oh no, have I offended it? But how could I offend a sack of leather by asking "What" it was?

Jacob hurriedly scribbled "Sorry. WHO are you?"

A few minutes later an answer appeared. "I am called. . . ," followed by the three letters "I-A-N."

I-A-N? I-A-N? What is an I-A-N? Jacob wondered. Having never seen such a name in America, he hadn't any idea how to pronounce it and went over various possibilities in his head from "I own" to "I'n."

I-A-N? I-A-N? Jacob thought to himself. *What kind of name is "I-A-N" for a pouch of leather?"*

"I-A-N," Jacob wrote, now on the back of the page that was once part of his journal, "I am a human being."

"So am I" was the reply. "So was HE? Or, so was SHE?" Jacob found himself saying under his breath. *What on earth? How could this Sporran be a human being?*

This was too much. He needed help. Jacob gathered up his things and headed back up to town. Not paying attention to things around him, he ran right across the fairway of the famous "Old Course" at St. Andrews, causing golfers to yell at him, "What are you doing, boy?" and, "You are going to get yourself killed!" He just kept running.

When he found a payphone, he pulled the calling card his mother had given him from his backpack and began to dial the number for Jenny's house. Groggily, Jenny answered the phone. "Jacob. . . do you know what time it is here?"

"Yes, well, I had to talk to you, Jenny. . .it's. . . it's speaking to me!"

"Speaking?!" Jenny replied with a higher-pitched voice than he had ever heard from her before.

"Well, not speaking really, but it's communicating to me in writing!"

"It writes, too?"

Jacob explained it all to Jenny and, just as he knew she would, Jenny had a possible solution, though, unlike her, it was far from reasonable.

"Jacob. I don't think that it is the sporran writing to you," she said. "I think that thing is just a portal to some other place where someone else is writing to you and probably has been sending you those things you have gotten."

Jacob felt instantly a bit better as he entertained the thought that the sporran really couldn't hurt him if it was just some kind of door to some other place. After all, it wasn't big enough to suck him in or anything (he hoped.)

"You have come this far," Jacob's best friend from home said. "I think I would write back and see what you can learn about what is going on. If nothing else, we will have a great toy to play around with when you get back."

"Thanks, Jenny," Jacob said and promised to be in contact again in a few days.

"But, Jacob, wait a minute. . . I have to tell you something. First, do you have an uncle that might be popping in for a surprise visit this week?"

Jacob said that he had two uncles but neither of them would be coming without their families and neither looked anything like the way Jenny described the dark, crinkly-skinned stranger. Jenny then recounted the stranger having come to town looking for Jacob and told him of their adventure in the night outside his house. She also gave him the warning she was told to pass along—don't give up or take the easy way, but bear the burden.

"Jenny, what is happening to us? I wish this thing would just go away! Maybe I will toss it into the sea this afternoon and get rid of it!"

"No, Jacob, remember what I was told to tell you. You must bear this burden, which I think means you cannot give up the sporran. Somehow I trust the person (or, thing) that saved Will and me last night. Be careful but don't give it up."

Jacob left the telephone booth and headed down the street to find a bench on which to sit and think. Part way down the street, it began mistily raining again and so Jacob turned into a small little coffee shop connected to a little church bookstore. To his great relief, it was almost empty. He ordered a blueberry scone (though he hadn't a clue what that would be, but with blueberries, it couldn't be all bad) and a cup of tea (which ended up coming in his very own little silver pot.)

He ripped a new page from his notebook and on it wrote "I-A-N, I am from the planet Earth."

Part way done with what turned out to be a very nice sweet biscuit with blueberries in it, the reply came. Strangely, it was on a yellowish piece of paper and was in a different hand than had been responding to his messages. In big block letters it said "ST. RULES TOWER."

Jacob had wanted to go to St. Rules Tower and Mr. Woods had recommended a visit that very morning on their hike. *But, what did this mean? How would a message come through the portal of the sporran that was clearly not referencing some other planet or dimension or somewhere else on Earth, but listed a location right down the road in St. Andrews itself!*

He decided to finish his second breakfast of the morning and while he did he mustered his courage to head directly to St. Rules Tower at the other end of town.

By the time he left the shop, the rain had picked up and he was getting wetter by the minute. He stopped by the place at the University where he had left Mr. Woods' bike and rode it the rest of the way up the street to the ruins of the old cathedral. The last remaining ruined wall of the old Cathedral gave him some shelter from the rain as he walked to the base of the tower. "Darn!" he muttered as he arrived. He needed a special token to get in and the sign told him to go to the Visitor's Center to purchase one.

Even wetter than before, he arrived back at the Tower and dropped the token in the gate which opened as he pushed through.

Jacob found himself alone in a small room with nothing but bare stone walls and a metal staircase reaching up to where the ancient stone stairs began. He took a deep breath and started to climb.

The spiral was tight and the stairs uneven. As he tried to hold onto the cold stone walls as he stepped, he feared the climb itself might prove treacherous. *What if I run into someone coming down the stairs as I go up the stairs?* He soon discovered the answer to that question.

A Japanese mother and father were feeling their way back down the spiraling narrow staircase. Out of breath and obviously nervous, they motioned for Jacob to back up. He took a few slow backward steps until he came to a slightly wider area in the stairs where he could press himself hard against the wall to allow them to pass. When they did, he continued his ascent.

Round and round he went. The stairs seemed to go on forever. He felt his legs tiring and he felt a bit of a burn in his lungs as he ran out of breath the higher he got. Round and round the narrow staircase crept and he found himself half walking upright and half walking on all fours as he began to get a little claustrophobic by the close walls and the height he must have climbed.

Around the final corner, he saw a faint light shining through an old gate that was clanging slightly in the windy rain. The sight brought relief and he scrambled to the top step and then out the gate where he now stood atop the tower looking down on rain-soaked ruins of the Cathedral and tombstones.

The wind was blowing even harder now and he hoped he wouldn't be blown off the very top of the tower to join those who had been resting for centuries beneath the tombstones below. Jacob felt a strange feeling across his shoulder blades and down into his arm. He recognized it as the same feeling he had on the train coming in. Then he heard a louder clang of the gate behind him.

Turning, he saw a small figure heading back down the stairs. It was a boy that looked about his age or thereabouts. He hadn't noticed him when he came out on the roof of the tower, so, Jacob reasoned, he must have been on the other end looking out over the ocean. Otherwise, he was alone and getting wetter by the minute.

Jacob waited a few minutes as he stared over the ancient city of St. Andrews down below and watched the storm that was slowly rolling the sea. Nothing happening, he turned and started down the stairs very slowly as he feared his wet feet might cause him to lose his footing and fall on the hard stone stairs or against the rough-cut stone walls.

Safely at the bottom, he exited the tower and noticed the boy he had seen, now crossing through the cemetery and heading into town. *I could use a friend my age in Scotland,* he thought to himself. But now it was time to get on the bike and head back to Feddinch House to dry off before dad arrived for a late lunch and some time together that afternoon.

Dinner Guests

A lready wet when he got on Mr. Woods' bike and headed up the road to Feddinch House, Jacob looked like he had fallen into the sea by the time he pulled into the drive. Being almost all up hill from St. Andrews, he had a couple of very tired legs to go along with his dripping hair and drenched clothes when Mrs. Woods opened the door for him and handed him a towel.

"Thank you, ma'am."

"It's not a problem. I know you Americans aren't quite as used to the weather as we Scots are. We were expecting you." Mrs. Woods began helping Jacob dry off. "Now, your father will be here soon for lunch, so get out of these wet things and I will have them dried and put back in your room before you two get back tonight."

"Thank you," Jacob said with the feeling that he used to get when his Grandmother Boyd would warm him up after a cold and wet day of sledding at her farm in Pennsylvania. There was always hot chocolate waiting for him and the other kids on those cold days.

"And when you get yourself dressed again, get right down here for a nice hot cup of tea and a cake or two," Mrs. Woods called out, as Jacob climbed the stairs. *Maybe it wouldn't be as good as hot chocolate, but having something warm to drink and something sweet to eat sure would help,* he thought.

Sitting down on his bed to remove his pants, the thought that had kept rolling over in his head again and again came to him as he sat transfixed in his damp underwear and socks. *Why did the sporran send me to St. Rule's Tower? No one was there. All I got was exhausted and wet and saw the back of some boy's head. Was it another cruel joke by this old hunk of leather? Did I miss some clue?*

Did I misunderstand?

A knock on the door woke him from his trance-like state. It was Mrs. Woods asking for his wet clothes so they could be dried. "Okay. Just a second," he replied. Handing Mrs. Woods a pile of dripping laundry, he followed her down to her kitchen where tea and cakes were waiting for him at the little table by the fireplace.

Jacob and Mrs. Woods chatted lightly about his day exploring the town and about the things he might do while he was in town with his dad. *Mrs. Woods is a very kind woman who just has to be someone's grandmother*, Jacob thought as he watched her flit around the kitchen hard at work (though not making it look hard at all).

The kitchen was different from the rest of the house. Where most of the rest of the house (at least the part open to guests) was obviously updated and redecorated recently in a manner that, though antique in style, was obviously new, the kitchen seemed much more ancient and "original" to what must have been there when it was a medieval tower. The floor was made of brick and was rough and uneven. The white ceiling looked like a frosted cake with its waves and dips in the paint and was broken up every few feet by wide and rough beams of wood. The furniture was small, at least by his standards from home, and very old. A fireplace burned behind his seat and warmed his back, as well as a kettle that hung above the small flame on a pivoting black stand. If Mrs. Woods wasn't so wonderfully sweet, he thought to himself, he could easily be scared in a room like this, as it reminded him of old stories of witches' kitchens where they boiled boys with their eggs for lunch.

Among the curiosities Jacob noticed in a room full of curiosities, was a small door on the wall opposite the fireplace. It was made of wood beams with long iron hinges that stretched across its face. As he ate and talked, he tried to take his mind off the door and resolved not to ask anything more about it. It seemed to him that a small door in a strange room of an ancient home was not something you wanted to call attention to. Almost involuntarily, however, he heard himself saying, "Mrs. Woods, that is an awfully small door.

Does it go anywhere?"

Mrs. Woods laughed and answered without turning from her work. "We found that door when we bought the place. It was behind an old stove that sat there. Turns out it goes nowhere, just a stone wall behind it. I have wanted to take it out or at least put some new cabinets in over it, but Mr. Woods will not hear of it. 'How will the Fairy Folk come and go, Momma,' he always says and then promptly leaves the room whenever I bring it up."

"Fairy Folk?" Jacob said, again in a way that seemed involuntary since it didn't strike him as a topic that should be remarked upon further in a house like this in the Kingdom of Fife.

"Well, if you ask me, it's just his way of getting out of work, that's all!" Mrs. Woods said with a wink over her shoulder. "Though," she added as she turned back to her work, "there are some legends, you know, of some spirits about the place, including a green elf, a couple of dead knights, and a witch or two . . . ."

"Jaaakkester!" a voice called down the hall and cut off Mrs. Woods in mid-sentence.

"There is your father," said Mrs. Woods as she came over to hurry him along from the table. "Now off you go. . . ."

"Thanks Mrs. Woods, the cakes and tea really hit the spot!"

Jacob's dad was standing in the hall when he came out of the kitchen. "How ya doing, bud?"

"Fine, Dad."

"Where is Mrs. Woods?" Mr. Boyd asked his son.

"I am right here, Mr. Boyd," said Mrs. Woods as she emerged out of the kitchen behind Jacob.

Jacob's dad asked Mrs. Woods if it would be possible, though he knew it was out of the ordinary, for her to cook dinner that evening for him and Jacob and two friends of his from work. They were up for the week from England and he wanted to introduce Jacob to the man's son, who was about Jacob's age.

"Ahhhh, I would count it my pleasure to serve," was Mrs. Woods' answer.

She was so pleasant Jacob wondered if there would ever be a request that she would not eagerly entertain.

Jacob and his father left Feddinch House nearing 1:00 P.M. and headed downtown for lunch and shopping. Unlike the weather, which continued to be soggy, the day was joyous for the son and his father. Jacob enjoyed spending time with his dad that day very much but the sporran, the new notes, and the stranger from back home weighed heavily on his mind.

That evening, Mr. Boyd explained to Jacob as they dressed for dinner that Mr. Nelson was a colleague of his who lived in England and was, like him, working on a special project in St. Andrews. His son had come up to spend the week with Mr. Nelson and, though he couldn't recall his name, Mr. Boyd thought he was about the same age as Jacob. Jacob wasn't the kind of kid who enjoys the thought of meeting new people or who makes friends easily, but he did not complain at the thought of such a forced friendship being attempted. He hadn't yet met anyone his age since he arrived.

The Boyds were in the parlor talking with Mr. Woods when the Nelsons clanged the door knocker of the Feddinch Manor House. The three clangs sounded much louder than Jacob could have imagined would come from such a primitive device. It seemed just as loud, in its own way, as the doorbell of their home on Longbranch Drive.

Mr. Nelson was tall like Mr. Boyd, though a few years older, Jacob guessed. The Nelson boy was behind his father and out-of-sight as they entered the house. Mr. Woods dismissed himself and the four remaining were in the parlor before formal introductions of the boys were made.

"Jacob, this is Mr. Nelson and his son . . ." Mr. Boyd caught himself, still not remembering the son's name, "Jeff, I am sorry but I think I have forgotten your son's name."

"This is Ian," Mr. Nelson said, pushing his son slightly forward toward the Boyds.

A certain strange feeling came over Jacob at the sight of the boy and upon hearing his name. It was a feeling he had before, something like what he would get when he was in situations that caused him great anxiety, like being in a school play or taking a test he hadn't really studied for. *I must be getting sick or something*, he thought.

His father then presented him with "And this is Jacob, and he is twelve."

Both boys greeted each other with a nod, though in a way that was obviously done more for their fathers' sake than out of genuine interest.

The English boy was about the same height as Jacob, though not as thin. He wore round glasses that seemed a bit too big for his face but not uncomfortably so, and he wore a bowtie. . . something Jacob would never be caught dead in.

Mr. Boyd asked his friend to sit by him in one of the brown leather wingback chairs in the far corner, which left nowhere for the boys to sit but together on the couch. The stage seemed intentionally set by the fathers to get Jacob and Ian to start talking.

No more did they get seated than Mrs. Woods arrived with drinks on a pretty silver tray. "I am afraid dinner will be awhile, gentlemen, but I will have a wee, something to start you here in a moment. Just settle in and enjoy each other's company and give a call if you need anything at all."

"So, you are from America," Ian Nelson asked or observed, Jacob couldn't tell which.

"Yep," Jacob answered, "and you are from England, huh?"

"Yes, Oxford to be precise."

And so the very uninteresting conversation between the two boys went until Jacob said "I climbed St. Rule's Tower today," and Ian replied, "So did I!"

A tingle crept down Jacob's right arm as if a worm had buried itself inside his skin and he felt a flutter in his chest. *Ian? Ian? Could that be the name that was given by the sporran when contact was made this morning?* Jacob moved back slightly.

"How do you spell your name?" Jacob asked.

"Just I-A-N, how else would I spell it?"

Oh boy, Jacob thought to himself, *those were the letters on the paper this morning! Could it just be another bizarre coincidence?*

The boys spent a moment staring at each other until the English boy broke the silence again with a heavily accented ". . . and why were you at the Tower today, might I ask?"

PASS THE SALT

Why did I climb the Tower? I must be careful how I answer that question . . . don't want to give away any secret. Jacob considered his answer carefully.

"Well," he answered, "it was suggested to me that it would be a good day for it."

"A rainy day like today would be a good day for climbing a tower? If you were a fish, maybe," replied Ian with a look of some doubt crossing his face.

"Well, you climbed it today yourself, so why did you do it?" Jacob cocked his head slightly as he was still taking the measure of this boy that had not yet proven either friend or foe or mere acquaintance.

"Oh . . ." Ian paused before answering, "I guess you could say it was suggested to me as well." He quickly added, as if to cover his tracks, "being a visitor, lots of people have suggestions for what you should do while you are here, you know!"

Jacob nodded his head as if to give the impression of agreement while being completely preoccupied with the possibility that somehow this I-A-N might be bound up with the mystery of the sporran. *Must be careful, must be very careful,* he kept telling himself as his mind raced with the possibilities.

Both boys looked over at their fathers and back at each other. Ian's glasses had slipped slightly down his nose and gave the impression that he was almost looking over them as an older man might do when looking up from his book.

"Did you get very wet?" Ian asked, to break the silence.

"I got soaked, it was awesome," Jacob replied, as he momentarily forgot about the gravity of the situation and simply enjoyed the remembrance of having been so very wet without anyone yelling at him or telling him he was going to catch his death of a cold. "How about you?"

"Drenched," answered Ian with a lowered voice that was barely above a whisper and a glance across the room at his father. It was pretty obvious he would rather not have his father know that little fact.

As the boys sat drumming their fingers and trying to continue the small-talk, an idea crept carefully and slowly into Jacob's mind. *What if I show him the sporran? That couldn't hurt, could it? If he was innocent, there would be no harm in letting him see that I had it. If he was bound up with its power, the boy would be outed and perhaps some answers would be found.* He wished Jenny or Will were there with him at that moment. *If this Ian turns out to be a force of evil, it would be better to have them here as backup!*

Swallowing hard, Jacob said, "Would you like a little tour of the house?"

Shrugging his shoulders from lack of real interest in a look-around at old furniture and guest bathrooms, Ian answered, "Sure."

The boys excused themselves from the parlor and headed up the stairs.

Jacob paused at the door to his room. He pawed the rug with his foot as if trying to remember something he desperately wanted to say. He was having second thoughts about being alone with the kid but resolved it was too late now.

He slowly turned the glass door handle and the white wooden door creaked open. Jacob's backpack lay in the corner of the room under the window seat directly opposite the door.

"Have a seat, I want to show you some stuff," Jacob said as he motioned Ian to sit on the bottom of the crisply-made bed.

Jacob pulled out some postcards and small touristy trinkets he had purchased on his trip, trying to make them seem interesting enough to warrant the presentation.

"Oh, " he added as casually as he could fake, "and my dad got me this old thing."

As he lifted the sporran slowly from the bag, his breath stopped and his eyes focused like those of a hawk directly on Ian's eyes. If there would be a reaction, even a slight nervous darting of the boy's eyes, Jacob was not going to miss it!

There was no need for him to concentrate so carefully to discover Ian's reaction. As the old brown leather and hair of the sporran began to emerge, Ian's legs started to raise him up from the bed. When it came free of the book bag, the English boy's legs shot straight and angled back, propelling him up so quickly that he fell backward and landed on his bottom on the far side of the bed.

The commotion caused Jacob to drop the sporran on the floor as his feet peddled him backward hard into the bathroom door. *Where is he? Where is that Ian kid?*

Slowly Ian's hair and then the rest of his head began to re-emerge from behind the bed but the boy rose no further than to his knees. There one boy stood and the other rested nervously on his knees across the room; both staring at the other not knowing what to say. The tension seemed to last a lifetime but could not have been more than a few seconds until, adjusting his glasses, Ian broke the silence.

"Where did you get that?" he asked haltingly, and trying to mask his fright, and then he added, "I mean. . . who are you? What do you want with me? Why have you brought me here? Please don't hurt me . . . ."

"I am not going to hurt you," Jacob said as he found momentary confidence in the uncertainty and nervousness of his companion. "But, what do you know of my little bag?"

"I don't know anything about your sporran, but have one just like it. My dad bought it for me a few days ago just after he came up here for business. It's in the car," he added, "I will be right back."

Ian rushed out the door and down the stairs. Jacob collapsed on the window seat, more confused than ever and almost exhausted by the tension.

Ian arrived a moment later with the backpack he had retrieved from his dad's rental car. From it he produced a sporran that was a near perfect match of the one that had so plagued the last few days of Jacob's life.

Both boys sat holding their sporrans in their laps and looking at each other and at each other's sacks of leather.

"This wouldn't belong to you would it," Ian remarked as he reached into his backpack and from it pulled a MacGregor Regulation Size and Weight baseball. He tossed it to Jacob whose heart leapt and then sunk hard at the thought of yet another confusing twist.

Without thinking or realizing why he was doing it, Jacob reached into his backpack and in one motion tossed the cricket ball to Ian. "You play cricket, I presume?"

"But. . . how?" Ian asked. He asked, even though he realized that Jacob was just as confused and out of answers as he was.

The two boys began trading the stories of the last few weeks of their lives and the tension turned to excited fun as they realized they had been inadvertent pen pals. There was not another dimension or planet collecting their things. It was just another boy like themselves. Ian asked particularly for his sister's doll back, as his parents had become very cross at its disappearance and expressed disappointment that the golden cup he had gotten was nothing more than one of Mrs. Boyd's water glasses.

Ian sent a strong punch into Jacob's left arm and exclaimed "so you are the one that sent that danged mousetrap to crush my fingers! I was hurting for days after that!" Jacob laughed. *Will is going to be glad to hear his trap worked after all.*

They had gone through the items they had collected from their sporrans and exchanged them. Jacob got his things back and Ian explained a bit more about the game of cricket and that the purple package called "Turkish Delight" was actually his favorite kind of candy bar and no lure of an evil witch.

"Laddies. . . dinner!" came the call from Mrs. Woods, who was standing at the bottom of the stairs.

"Just a minute," Jacob said as he poked his head out his door.

"You know what I am thinking?" asked Ian.

"What?"

"Bring your sporran to dinner, come on. . . ."

Both boys put their sporrans into their backpacks and carried them down stairs where their fathers were sitting in the dining room waiting for them. Jacob's seat was directly across from Ian's and the table was set perfectly with candles that cast a subtle but warm light in the otherwise darkened room.

Mrs. Woods had prepared a wonderful dinner . . . well, wonderful for grown-ups anyway. After an appetizer, Mrs. Woods called "cock-a-leekie soup," there was salmon, "forfar bridies," and pease pudding. To Jacob, the tastes were as bad as the names and he would have been very happy for a grilled cheese and french fries (or, "chips" as he had come to learn they called them in England and Scotland.) Not long into the first course, however, the fun began.

"Jacob, you say you wanted me to pass the salt, do you?" Ian said with a devilish look on his face.

"What? No . . ." Jacob stammered, quite confused.

Ian's hand disappeared beneath the table with the salt while silently mouthing the words "Ssssspppoooorrrrraaaaannnnn!" Jacob nodded in recognition of what Ian had in mind.

Jacob snickered as he reached between his feet and picked up the salt which had arrived in his sporran.

He then slipped his fork into his sporran and sent it over to Ian with the announcement "My fork seems to be missing!"

"Oh, here it is by my plate, now how did it get here?" Ian replied.

And so the pranksters sent items magically to one another under the table. Ian got Jacob's peas, Jacob got Ian's jello-like dessert (which made quite a mess in the sporran) and having to spoon it out of his lap and onto his plate nearly cost them their secret. The boys had great fun at the table, even if the food was not what they would have hoped for.

At the end of the evening, Ian and Jacob agreed to meet again in the morning at Feddinch House. Mr. Boyd and Mr. Nelson were pleased that their sons seemed to have gotten along so well.

As the Boyds walked the Nelsons to their car, however, one last question came over Jacob. He pulled Ian aside and asked, "But, why did you ask me to go to St. Rules Tower today?"

"I didn't, I thought you asked me!"

Ian's reply sent a cold chill down Jacob's legs and into his shoes where he felt his toes curl up and down nervously.

St. Andrew's Bones

The Boyd men talked long after dinner in a way that was more mature than Jacob had ever remembered having conversed with his father before. They talked of things to come and hopes and home . . . mostly of home. They both went to bed and closed their eyes, satisfied by a new sense of connection between them that hadn't been there since Mr. Boyd changed jobs a year ago and started traveling more.

Jacob had a hard time falling asleep that night. *Ian could have been just kidding me when he said he had not sent me the note to go to St. Rules Tower.* But, there was something in his voice that made him believe he was telling the truth. *If not sent from Ian, then who? Was there someone else, or* something *else out there?* The thought filled him with dread and gained him a restless night.

In the morning, he remembered having a similar dream to one he'd had back at home. There were three red lions in fighting positions on a shield and a blue and white banner. He recognized the banner, now that he was in Scotland, as the St. Andrews Flag. It has a blue field and a white cross laid out diagonally across it. *But, what of the lions? What could they mean? Why do I keep having this dream?*

The sun rose warm and bright for the first time in days. It was actually the first time it had really been sunny like Jacob was used to back home. Mr. Woods was having breakfast and Mrs. Woods was ready to cook the Boyds theirs when the two arrived. It was 6:30 and Jacob was ready for Mrs. Wood's waffles with the light syrup that he found he enjoyed much more than the maple syrup his mom would buy back home.

"What would you like this morning, Master Boyd," Mrs. Woods asked. Her apron was already sprinkled with flour as if she had already been at work for hours. Whether she had been up for hours or not, she was as pleasant as ever. Jacob wondered if she ever got tired or felt down in the dumps.

"Waffles, if you please," Jacob said with an eager smile.

"I thought you might say that! I've already got 'em on! And for you, Mr. Boyd?"

Jacob's attention was diverted to Mr. Woods who was sitting at the head of the table and looking at him rather peculiarly. Jacob felt his eyes wanting to look away. *Did he know something? Had he heard the boys talking about the sporran last night?* He had never felt at all uncomfortable around Mr. Woods, but this morning was different.

Mr. Woods broke Jacob's tension by saying, "So, up for a constitutional this morning, little master?"

"Yes sir," Jacob replied, already feeling more at ease. "If you don't mind, I have asked Ian, the boy who was here last night, to join us. That is, if you don't mind."

"Well, now, I certainly don't mind, but then again, what would you do if I did? Can't very well un-invite the lad now, can we?"

Jacob smiled not knowing whether to say "No, sir" in a way that would show he got his point that he shouldn't have invited Ian without asking, or if he should have said "No, sir" in a way as to convey that he knew Mr. Woods was just having a bit of fun with him by pointing out that his question, or statement, or whatever it was really didn't make much sense.

Jacob just kept the smile and spread some jam on a piece of toast sitting near him in the little wire toast holder Mrs. Woods always had on the table in the morning. It was one of those little marvels, like the waffle syrup—so simple and yet so fun because he had never before seen them in America and they seemed quite exotic.

Before the Boyd men quite got done with their breakfast, a horn blew outside Feddinch House. It was Ian's father dropping him off and picking up Jacob's father for work. They had agreed to carpool this morning since Mr. Nelson would be bringing Ian by anyway.

Jacob and his father stood simultaneously to thank Mrs. Woods for breakfast and headed toward the door. Jacob turned but was caught by Mr. Woods' voice. "Laddie," it sounded urgent, "you might want to untuck the tablecloth from your belt, lest you're planning to drag along the china with us this morning!"

Jacob looked down to see that instead of tucking the fine cloth napkin into the top of his belt to keep it from sliding onto the floor, he had tucked the end of the tablecloth into his pants. A sense of shame washed over him until his dad punched him gently on the arm and whispered "I've done it too, pal. I've done it too!" *That was a close one*, Jacob realized as he could have made a real mess in Mrs. Woods' dining room.

As soon as Jacob got within arms reach of Ian, he pulled him aside and the two boys began to whisper just outside the entrance way to Feddinch House. They had both spent a rather restless night wondering if the other was pranking them or if something else had sent that message to visit Rule's Tower. Talking at the same time, they barely got a coherent question in before Mr. Woods appeared with three walking sticks.

Pressing a tall twisted stick into each of the boy's hands, he insisted, "let's go boys, light is a burnin' and we have a few miles to cross before we are home again."

Ian and Jacob said goodbye to their fathers and started to follow Mr. Woods down the "wynd," which is what the Mr. and Mrs. Woods called the little lane in front of their home. *The Feddinch Wynd!* Jacob thought it sounded like some kind of great powerful tornado or something.

Eyes straight ahead and not at all looking at the boys following, Mr. Woods called back, "Master Boyd, I note that Master Nelson has brought his backpack for the day, I wonder if you might have forgotten yours?"

Darn! He had. Jacob turned and ran the few steps back into the house and retrieved the bag he had sat in the wooden entryway near the old putters and walking sticks and boots and hats. *How does he do that without even looking*, Jacob marveled as Ian snickered at seeing his new friend scramble back up the road to them.

As they walked down the wynd, both boys tried to hold back and whisper their questions about the note and St. Rules Tower to one another, but it was no use.

"Sharing some secrets about Mr. Woods, are you boys?" said their guide, as he slowly turned his head and raised one eyebrow at them. "Come on now," he added in a more friendly tone than his raised eyebrow would have indicated and without awaiting a reply. "Rule number one is that all members of the party walk together, and rule number two is that no secrets are ever kept from a member of the party taking the constitutional."

It was only about 100 yards down the way where the party would get its first glimpse of the ancient town of St. Andrews. Jacob imagined he could walk that walk a million times and never get tired of looking upon that scene below. The ancient ruins and University buildings were set off by the beauty of St. Andrew's Bay and surrounded by the green and gold grassy hills that seemed to rise right out of the town.

"So, you visited the Tower, did you," Mr. Woods said as a remark more than a question. "Well, was it what you expected?"

"Sort of," Jacob answered as he looked at Ian. "I got soaked and exhausted and nearly killed myself trying to get down with wet shoes, but other than that. . ."

"Same here," Ian interrupted.

"Well, today is a beautiful day and I suppose you will want to try again." Mr. Woods said it without any hint of a question in his voice. He seemed to know the boys would do exactly that, even if they didn't yet know it themselves.

As they turned and continued along the top of the hill with St. Andrews down below on their right, Mr. Woods began a short history lesson of the town.

"You know, this town is both ancient and royal, as the tourist people will tell you, after they sell you on playing golf, anyway. But it is more than that.

Do you know its story?"

Both boys were eager to hear what Mr. Woods was to say but both had part of their minds (and an occasional eye) on St. Rules Tower far below and on the notes that had sent them there the day before.

Before Mr. Woods could begin again, all three heard a crackling behind them. It sounded like twigs breaking off high in the trees. Then bigger branches were breaking and finally a thud as if something had come down through the trees and hit the leaf-covered ground. As best they could, the three looked through the trees but saw nothing.

"Well, probably just a stag testing his new antlers, boys . . . Probably just a stag." Mr. Woods' remark came with a bit of concern on his face, however. They turned to continue their walk when Jacob noticed a small tuft of brown hair dart over the ridge next to them. "A dog, I think I saw a dog," Jacob announced.

"Oh, just a dog. . ." Mr. Woods remarked, "Just a dog, then, yes, all is fine, let's continue our walk, shall we?"

As they walked, Mr. Woods told them of an old Greek monk named Rule who centuries ago brought the bones of St. Andrew from Europe to Scotland's shores for safekeeping. The monk was told to do so in a dream. At the time, Scotland was a wild place almost at the end of the known world. The town that developed was named after St. Andrew, of course, and the tower after St. Rule who courageously brought the relics across the sea. St. Andrew's saltire cross was eventually adopted by Scotland as its flag as the power of what was happening in this town worked its way through the rest of Scotland.

They learned of the Tower being constructed more than 700 years ago and of the workers who tragically lost their lives building what was then the largest man-made thing in Scotland. Somehow, mysteriously, the tower has survived perfectly intact when everything around it has fallen into ruin.

Occasionally, Jacob or Ian would see the little dog scampering along just over the ridge as if it was watching them. When they got a good glimpse of it, they could see its small pug nose and occasionally its curly tail would be seen before it disappeared beneath a log or mound of dirt. It seemed to mean them no harm and Mr. Woods appeared to be oblivious to its following them.

They learned more about the castle, which now lay in ruin near the tower, and of the 400 years of battles it withstood. They learned of the sieges that were laid upon it and the tunnels that enemies dug to try to get into it when they could not breach the walls. And Mr. Woods told a gruesome tale of the infamous "bottle dungeon" where countless enemies of Scotland lost their lives in great pain and agony.

"Now, boys, it seems we are home and have taken many footfalls this day, and many years, too, it seems!" Mr. Woods stopped himself as they emerged from behind some trees. They were standing on the back lawn of Feddinch House by the tennis court. The boys had become so entertained by his stories of ancient St. Andrews that they had lost all track of time or where they had been. It seemed, indeed, that they had only moments before received their walking staffs and now Mr. Woods was collecting them.

"There are two bikes you can borrow in the shed. Enjoy the rest of your day, laddies," said Mr. Woods as he disappeared back into the house.

Ian and Jacob kept walking to the front of the house where they sat next to each other on an iron bench. Finally alone, they began to discuss the note that had taken them to Rule's Tower and where it could have come from. Neither could venture a reasonable guess and both seemed hesitant to verbalize their gravest fears about it and what it meant, as if by saying them they might come true.

"Did you notice anything peculiar about those staffs we carried?" Ian asked.

"No, except that it felt wonderfully old-fashioned and extremely light to carry," Jacob replied. He didn't want to let on his real feelings. He had let his mind wonder if it might have been just the kind of staff carried long ago by some wizard or another going forth to tame dragons or to save a kingdom from horrible men or beasts.

"Yes, but did you notice anything on it?" Ian asked.

"No."

"Mine," Ian said while getting a bit closer and looking Jacob straight in the eye, "said that it was made by a Hammish MacGregor of St. Andrews." "Now," he continued, "that was the name on the baseball that was sent through the sporrans from you to me."

"Well, the ball didn't say 'Hammish' but had the name of the company that produced it: MacGregor," Jacob corrected.

"Still," Ian tried to go on, but Jacob interrupted again.

"But, Hammish MacGregor is the guy who wrote the book about cricket that my friend found in the library *and* who lives in St. Andrews teaching at the University, *and* who may have talked to me back at my home."

"This is too much of a coincidence," Ian muttered, as he sank deep into the bench and turned to look down the wynd toward town.

"And," Jacob added, as if finally putting the last piece of a thousand-piece puzzle together, "it was a note on his door that caused me to contact you with a note of my own. I didn't tell you that."

Ian swallowed hard. "Jacob, we have come this far and I suppose we really can't turn back now. Can we? We know how to play with the sporrans together, but really don't know what power we may be holding or what is meant of us, or what dangers they will put us in. You know we have to go see MacGregor, don't you?"

Jacob nodded and forcefully exhaled a deep breath he had unconsciously been holding. He wondered if he would have to dig up the courage to visit that man many more times on this trip, having done it once already. Still, it all seemed to be a bit easier now that Ian was there with him and now that he knew at least the part of the mystery that had unfolded so far, discovering Ian that is, seemed harmless. It also helped that MacGregor, with his bearded face, didn't meet the description Jenny gave of the guy that may be after him.

The two boys retrieved the bikes out of the shed and headed down the road toward town. "Do you think that old guy's bones really came over here across the ocean and are buried somewhere down there?" Ian asked as they crested the hill and began to descend into town. Running far behind them and out of sight was a little brown dog with a flat face and small curling tail.

THE BLACK WIND

Ian and Jacob didn't exactly race their bikes toward town. Neither seemed particularly anxious to get to their destination. Twelve year-olds on a college campus was bad enough, but here at this University, which was almost six hundred years old, it was even worse. And presuming to have business with a distinguished professor of geographical political sociology and antiquities (*whatever the heck that was*), Jacob thought, seemed positively absurd.

Both boys seemed lost in their own thoughts most of the way as they coasted effortlessly down the hill toward town.

Passing through the old town gate, its stone sides and top still intact, (even though a modern road ran right through the middle), the boys paused for some traffic to pass. A small black car slowly made the turn in front of them and Jacob caught glimpse of the driver as a dull ache started in his shoulder blade and crept down his arm. The feeling was similar to the one he had the night before when he met Ian. As the car passed, Jacob tried to get a look at the driver but the windows were very darkly tinted. He said nothing to Ian, but continued riding silently along-side.

Having ridden through town, they arrived at the University building where Jacob found Professor MacGregor's office the day before. They tied their bikes to a fence out front and went into the old gray building through the large double doors.

They found the same secretary Jacob had talked with the day before and she again seemed to have nothing to do, yet seemed to be very busy at it all the same. "Need directions somewhere, boys?" the youngish woman of middling age said with a look that seemed not to demand an answer.

"MacGregor. . . ah . . . Professor MacGregor, please," Ian answered.

"Third door on the left, if you can find him! Lord knows none of us ever see the man!"

Ian thought he heard the woman mutter under her breath, "not that we would want to," as she turned, seeming anxious to get back to doing nothing in particular.

The boys turned down the hall and Jacob pointed to the door. It was closed once again with a yellowish paper folded into thirds and taped to the door. No reply came to the knock and Ian reached for the note. "No use," Jacob insisted, "it's the same note I read yesterday. All it says is 'MAKE CONTACT,' which, if it was meant for me. . . or us . . . , we already have done."

Ian pulled the note away from the door anyway and unfolded it. It did seem to be the same note from the day before; from the crinkled yellow paper to the handwritten "To Whom it May Concern" on the outside, to the tape with a ripped notch in it that Jacob had caused when removing it from the door yesterday.

When unfolded, however, it was clear this was not the same note. Instead of the words "MAKE CONTACT" the message was in the form of a short poem. The boys stared at each other and then copied it into a notebook Jacob had in his backpack. They scurried out into the courtyard by the sea to discuss it away from the door and the possibility of actually running into MacGregor—both had a degree of appreciation for communicating only indirectly with large hairy men who seemed to have mysterious powers.

Seated in the soft grass beneath a large and shady tree, Jacob opened his notebook so both could see. The poem read:

"A black wind shall fall,
On Rule's Tower and Wall.
Answers will be found,
Tumbling to the ground."

Both boys read it over and over, silently turning the words in their heads. A few drops of rain began to fall but not on the boys who were under the protection of the tree. Jacob watched the few drops splat on the rock wall nearby as Ian stared blankly into the distance. Finally Ian broke the silence. "Well, come on, we are being called back to the Tower!" Ian was on his feet and moving before Jacob's legs would react. Neither wanted to climb that tower again, but, Mr. Woods seemed to suggest it that morning and clearly the note did the same.

As the boys walked up the sidewalk, the tower grew larger and more ominous on the horizon. Jacob was troubled. "You know," he said, "maybe we better think about this. I mean," he hesitated, "I mean, look at that poem!"

"What about it?" Ian asked, but continued his forward progress toward the ruins, the cemetery and the tower at its center.

"Well, look at that line. . . 'tumbling to the ground?' What does that mean? What, or worse yet, WHO will be tumbling to the ground? What if it's us?" Jacob felt himself growing more anxious as he spoke.

"What if we know too much! What if MacGregor wants to kill us and has decided to throw us off the top of the tower and make it look like an accident or something! I can't fly, can you?"

"Look," Ian said, feeling himself growing more sure and not less, that another climb was the right thing to do. "If someone was aiming to throw us from the tower, don't you think he would have done it yesterday when it was really rainy and cold and no one was up there but us? Who is going to believe two healthy boys fell off the tower at the same time on a nice sunny and fairly dry day like today?"

"Well, maybe," Jacob replied, "but *you* are going up first!"

Arriving at the ruins of the old church, the tower was now directly in front of them. The boys first had to turn right through the cemetery and the ruins to purchase the tokens at the gift shop that would give them entrance to the tower.

Both paused at the base and looked up the tower which seemed to sway as the wind moved the clouds above it. "Come on, its something we need to do," Ian said in a way that was meant to reassure himself as much as it was meant for his partner's ears.

The boys climbed the stairs round and round and round, occasionally having to backtrack to allow someone coming back down to pass. The stones seemed so solid as they climbed, Jacob could understand how it had survived all these centuries when the other buildings around it had crumbled. It seemed awesome in its power to withstand the forces that might besiege it.

Ian pushed open the gate at the top with trepidation and Jacob followed closely on his heels as they stepped out onto the roof. Both boys were tired from the climb but their senses were keen as they began looking closely at the other tourists who had made the climb earlier that morning. None seemed to look like MacGregor, in fact, none had facial hair at all.

Together, they walked round and round the roof of the tower, occasionally looking down over the edge or drifting off into thought as they looked out at the sea. After half an hour, the boys began to drift apart and wander around the roof separately searching for clues and looking over the others who would come and go from the stairs as they walked around.

The sounds of a commotion came from the stairwell. Ian and Jacob looked at one another and peered down through the iron gate. Soon, a mother came 'round the corner urging her rather large son to make it up the stairs. His bulk seemed a bit much for his legs to carry up those hundreds of steep stairs and by the time he reached the top, the poor boy was on all fours crawling his way up, with his mother pulling on the hood of his jacket. *Hmmm*, Jacob thought, *she must be trying to help, but that looks positively painful the way she is yanking on him.*

Ian and Jacob moved aside as the mother and boy pushed through the gate. The boy took two staggered steps and came crashing down to the floor of the roof. On his knees, he panted his way to the wall where he rested, as a heaving pile of blue nylon, with his mother waving papers over his face to get him air.

"Mate, let's be sure to get out of here before he starts back down," Ian whispered to Jacob as they walked away from the scene, "I don't want him to come bouncing down those stairs on us!"

It had been over an hour and nothing had happened. It was nearly lunchtime and the magic of Mrs. Woods' waffles was beginning to wear off in Jacob's stomach. "Maybe we should just go," he offered. "Let's come back after lunch."

"Are you crazy? I'm not climbing those stairs again today! I say we stay awhile longer," was Ian's reply just as something far above him caught his attention in the clouds.

"What are you looking at now?" Jacob asked as he watched his friend staring up at the sky.

"Not sure. Do you not see anything? Seems like something small and very faint circling far above us. I noticed it before, but didn't pay much attention."

"Got me. . . I don't see anything, probably just a bird or something," Jacob replied, and walked to the edge of the tower. He flicked a small pebble with his finger, sending it falling down to the grassy tombs below. Lost in thought as he watched it fall, he didn't hear Ian whisper his name.

"Jacob. . . Jacob. . . I do believe our black wind is beginning to fall . . ." Ian whispered, but with an urgency to his voice.

Jacob turned to see a large bird circling down closer and closer to the tower from high above. "It's just a bird, what would that have to do with anything?" Jacob kept his eye on the bird, however, and noticed as it drew closer that it was carrying something in its beak.

Down and down it turned and twisted in the wind until it floated right above the boys and landed on the corner of the tower to the right of the gate at the top of the stairs. The bird was large, black, and powerful in a way that Jacob found quite admirable. In its beak it carried something yellow and flat.

"It's a bird of prey, but do you know what kind?" Jacob whispered.

"No idea."

Without so much as blinking, both boys began to move slowly toward the bird. On one leg they noticed it wore a golden band and, as they got closer, they noticed the yellow object in its beak was a piece of paper. Slowly they crept toward the bird who appeared to be watching them from the corner of its left eye. Ten feet . . . five feet . . . three feet. Their hearts raced as they closed the gap with the feathered beast. Ian's attention was drawn to those large, sharp talons and he feared what they could do to him if he got too close. He stopped.

Jacob took another step forward but fell back quickly into Ian when the bird opened its wings and turned to look him directly in the eye. The eyes were bigger and more serious than Jacob had expected. He felt as if the bird was able to penetrate into his thoughts and understand him. Or, maybe it was a feeling of pity the bird seemed to have for Jacob. Whatever it was, Jacob felt inadequate and alone in the bird's gaze. The bird then turned its head out to sea and opened its beak. Out fell the yellow paper, which seemed to hang suspended in place for a second as the bird leapt from its perch and continued off toward the sea.

Jacob and Ian lunged for the paper but it had already begun its descent. They peered over the edge of the tower as they watched the yellow paper float back and forth on the wind as it fluttered toward the tombstones below.

"Well, there are our answers 'tumbling toward the ground,' " Jacob said, as his fist dropped onto the tower wall in frustration.

"Stay here and watch it blow around. I will run down and you can guide me to where it is," Jacob yelled back at Ian as he hurried to the stairs. He descended the stairs at what was certainly an unsafe speed. Even the few tourists heading up the stairs didn't slow him down. "Excuse me. . . pardon me. . ." he said repeatedly as he pressed himself hard against the wall to get past people, but he kept his momentum headed downward. He emerged from the great stone structure out of breath, but intact.

Jacob ran around the tower to his right until he saw Ian's little head poking out from over the wall high above. They were too far away to hear one another and it was hard to really understand Ian's signals the way his arms were flailing high above. But Jacob did the best he could, walking right and then left; forward and then back; looking up for directions and down for the paper (and to avoid tripping over the tombstones).

After a few moments of frustration and nearly killing himself on the grave markers at his feet, he noticed the yellow paper resting at the base of a tombstone where the wind could blow it no further. He reached down, picked it up, and then waved it triumphantly in the air to call Ian off the tower.

Jacob stood catching his breath. He looked down at the tombstone at his feet. It was a Celtic cross carved out of gray stone sitting on a matching base. The carvings in the cross, which at one time must have been much more ornate, had been worn down by the sea air and rain over many generations. Suddenly, he felt his feet backpedaling fast, almost before he recognized the reason. His left foot caught a tombstone behind him and he fell over flat on his back.

"Uuuugggghhhhhh," the air whooshed out of his lungs as he hit the ground. *Could that be right? Could I have just seen what I thought I saw?* The tombstone that the paper had come to rest against read "MacGregor, 1647-1701." *Holy Man! No, it couldn't be!* He loved old things, but even the possibility of a three-hundred-year-old dead guy sending him messages was not something he thought he enjoyed very much at all. *Was MacGregor dead? Was he a ghost? But he has an office! What kind of ghost has an office?*

After Ian descended the tower, he found Jacob at the opposite end of the cemetery sitting in the grass and leaning against part of the ruined wall of the cathedral. "What are you doing all the way over here?" he asked.

"Let's not talk about that right now," Jacob replied, as he handed Ian the yellow paper. "What do you make of these great answers we got?" Ian's heart sunk as he recognized the sarcasm in his new friend's tone.

ROB ROY

"**D**ang!" Ian exclaimed. "Another darn riddle. Can't we ever be told something just straight away and without all this guessing and puzzling and worrying and such? I wish this MacGregor would just show himself and get on with it."

"Well, maybe he can't show himself," Jacob replied, as he thought of the tombstone he had just seen.

"What do you mean?" Ian asked.

"Oh, never mind, just read the note."

Despite his frustrations, Ian sat next to his friend and studied the paper. On the paper dropped from the tower by the black bird were two lines, written in the same hand of black ink as the previous notes:

> A great warrior was Robert Roy
> Who fought for gold and king

By now the sun had risen directly overhead, causing all shadows to disappear in the graveyard around Rule's Tower. "Shoot!" Jacob said standing up. "Its noon and we are going to be late for lunch! Where were we were supposed to meet our dads today?"

The boys had made plans that morning to meet their fathers for lunch at a restaurant called "The Singing Salmon" near the other end of Market Street. They would have to hurry now or they would be late. The boys sprinted for their bikes and headed down Market Street trying to talk as they rode about the note and what it might mean.

Mr. Boyd and Mr. Nelson had already been seated when they arrived at the Salmon. "Nice of you boys to join us!" Mr. Nelson announced as Ian and Jacob came through the doors catching their breath. Both fathers smiled a welcoming smile that told the boys they were not in trouble but their fathers wanted to have a little fun making them feel like they were.

"So, tell us what you boys have been up to today," Jacob's father requested.

Ian looked at Jacob. Jacob looked at Ian.

Both were as nervous as they could be. What could they tell their fathers? Sure, they would love to know how the boys were lured to St. Rules Tower again, and how they chased a black bird, and how Jacob nearly killed himself when he realized a dead guy might have come back to life, be living in town, have visited him in America, and how they both had magic pouches perfect for sending salt clandestinely from one side of the dinner table to another . . . . Yes, they would love that! They would really believe them!

"Ahhhh. . ." Jacob started.

"We walked around town and climbed Rule's Tower again. . . pretty cool," Ian interrupted, cutting off his friend in mid stall.

"Oh, well, we both have great news," Mr. Boyd said, as if he couldn't contain himself anymore. "Actually, we have both good and bad news," he corrected himself.

"Yes, the bad news is that we are going to have to break our dates with you two this afternoon," Mr. Nelson interjected.

Both boys thought this bad news was not *bad* news at all. They were on a hot trail now for uncovering this whole sporran thing and could use the time to get to the bottom of the latest clue.

"And the good news," Mr. Boyd now spoke up as he leaned into the table and looked at the boys, but particularly at his own son. "The good news is," he repeated, "it looks like Mr. Nelson and I have gotten our jobs here just about completed and if we go back this afternoon we can probably wrap up our work."

Are we going home? Jacob wondered to himself with mixed emotions.

"That means starting tomorrow, we will be free, you and me, to make a real vacation of it, Jacob! I say we head to Edinburgh to explore the great castle there!" Mr. Boyd announced.

Jacob smiled but wasn't completely sure about that. He loved staying at St. Andrews and taking walks with Mr. Woods, and how would he live without Mrs. Woods' waffles and those cute little strawberries she cut up on top of each one? Not to mention this sporran thing. . .

Mr. Nelson took his turn. "And you and I," he said, leaning toward his son and putting one hand on his shoulder, "are going to jump on a train first thing and head to Glasgow to take in the great arms museum they have there and do some shopping for your mother and sister!"

Their fathers were so obviously excited by the prospect of their vacations that the boys knew any protest would be useless and impolite as well, given the circumstances. They both instantly knew what this meant—they would have to work extremely fast now! When morning came, they would separate and all might be lost.

"Dad, Mr. Nelson," Jacob blurted out. "Have either of you ever heard of Rob Roy?"

Ian couldn't believe Jacob had just said that—had given away a clue from the latest note. *Would the fathers realize something was going on?*

"Sure," Mr. Nelson said, "I think he was some Scottish Highlander from a few hundred years ago. Stole cattle or something like that. I remember hearing of a book about him. Actually," Ian's dad paused seeming to be momentarily embarrassed, "I think I was supposed to read it in high school but never did."

"Maybe," Mr. Boyd interjected, "but I thought Rob Roy was some kind of a drink. My granddad used to drink it."

"Why are you interested in Rob Roy, Jacob?" Mr. Nelson asked.

"Ummmm. . . we read the name today and were curious," he answered being very careful not to lie, but without spilling the complete bag of secrets.

A waitress appeared for their drink order and the conversation changed with her appearance and amounted to nothing very memorable or exciting except that Ian ordered a "Rob Roy" to drink, just to try it out. The waitress smiled and said, "I don't believe your father would appreciate me serving you whisky, now would he? Nice try, though!" Ian's father shook his head, Jacob's father snickered, and Ian sunk back in his seat a bit embarrassed.

After their lunch, the boys retired to the yard in front of Holy Trinity Church on South Street where they sat on a bench under a tree and out of what was a very unscottish-like warm sun. They would need a plan if they were to get some answers before morning.

"Well," Jacob offered, "at least we can be reasonably sure the clue doesn't refer to the drink version of Rob Roy since no one would send two boys a clue about a drink they can't have, right?"

"No, I don't think so either," Ian replied and then both grew momentarily silent and thoughtful.

"Okay," Ian began, "It seems to me we would make more progress if we split up for awhile to discover more about this Rob Roy."

"Agreed. I think Mr. Woods might know something, he seems very smart about history and things. I will call him."

"And I will head to the library or a bookstore or something, whatever I come to first, to see if I can't find that book dad mentioned," Ian countered with a slap on Jacob's leg and a "Meet you back here in one hour."

"Deal. . . oh, and. . Ian. . . be careful!"

"You too, Yank!"

Jacob headed to the phone booth from which he had called Jenny and his mother earlier in the week. Finding it, he opened his bag to search for the little card Mr. Woods had given him. There, at the bottom of the bag, just beneath the sporran, was the card, a bit of jello smeared on it from the other night's dinner when Ian had sent his dessert to Jacob through the sporran.

Mrs. Woods answered the phone at Feddinch House. As soon as she was reassured Jacob was not in any trouble, she called Mr. Woods in from the garden where he was turning the still cold spring soil to ready it for the first plantings of the year.

As Jacob suspected, Mr. Woods did know of Rob Roy and shared what he knew. He was a Highlander who wielded a very mean broadsword, killed a number of bad guys, and was an outlaw most of his adult life, yet he was loved by his fellow Highlanders. It was said he had arms which reached all the way down to his knees and made him an accomplished swordsman. According to Mr. Woods, some say Rob Roy was like Robin Hood in England; take from the rich and give to the poor, only he took from the rich by stealing their cattle and then offering to protect what was left for a fee.

Jacob was turning the information over in his head trying to figure out how it all might fit with the riddle. Then Mr. Woods said something that made Jacob drop the phone. "And, I think Rob Roy's full name was Rob Roy MacGregor." The phone swung on its cord and the sound of it smacking the glass walls of the phone booth awakened Jacob from his shock.

"Thank you, Mr. Woods, see you tonight," Jacob said after picking up the phone. He hung up the receiver and turned up the street.

MacGregor! MacGregor again! Everywhere I turn that accursed name comes up! Jacob was thinking about all the information he got from Mr. Woods as he turned down the street and passed the Internet café. He still had half an hour until he was to meet Ian. Just enough time to send an e-mail to Jenny and Will to update them on the developments. He wished his friends could be there with him. They would like Ian a lot. He also sent a note to his mother, telling her of the plan to leave St. Andrews with his father in the morning.

Ian was waiting at the church when Jacob arrived. "Okay, what do you know?" Ian asked. Jacob recounted what he had learned from Mr. Woods, including his frustration at running into that name of MacGregor again.

"Did you have any luck?" Jacob then turned the conversation over to his friend.

"You should know!" was the reply.

"How am I supposed to know?" countered Jacob.

"You should know!"

"How do I know?"

Ian was having fun and couldn't hold his laughter any longer. "Okay, you should know because what I found you've been carrying around! I used the sporran!"

"Jerk!" Jacob tersely replied and gave Ian a forceful but playful kick in the shin.

Encounter in the Bookstore

Jacob slipped his backpack from his shoulders and laid it on the ground in front of him. Opening it, he asked Ian what he had found.

"The book about Rob Roy that my father had mentioned, just what I went after, of course."

The sporran was bursting at the seams at the bottom of Jacob's pack. Inside was a very old book bound in burgundy leather with well-worn and flaking gold letters on its cover. Its title was "Rob Roy" and was written by a Sir Walter Scott.

"Where did you get it, Ian?"

"I was walking toward the University library when I noticed a small sign for an antique book shop down Logies Lane. I walked in and found it after a bit and it was pretty cheap, too. Only cost me a couple of pounds, old boy! I guess because it is in such bad shape."

Jacob nodded in acknowledgment of the story but didn't look up from the book.

"But, Jacob," Ian hesitated, as if rethinking his desire to speak, "I should also tell you that I had a rather odd encounter in the bookstore just now."

Jacob looked up from tattered pages of the old book, "Go on."

"Well, I went into the store, as I said, and began to browse around. I wasn't getting anywhere looking, so I went up and asked the woman at the counter if they had a copy of *Rob Roy*. Her name, I think, was Heather and she was very nice. She had a purple brooch like my Mum wears and . . ."

"Yes, yes, fine, so what was so odd about the woman?" Jacob interrupted.

"Nothing was odd about her, let me finish!" Ian's tone was insistent with a hint of annoyance at being cut off in the middle of his story.

"Anyway, she pointed me to the proper aisle in the back of the store so I went and started to look around on the shelves. Suddenly, I got that feeling, you know what I mean? That feeling that you are being watched?"

Jacob nodded his head slightly as he listened.

"Well, I looked over at the end of the aisle and there stood a man. He had on a long oily trench coat and wore a wide-brimmed hat. He was just there staring at me."

"Did he say anything?" Jacob asked.

"No, it wasn't what he said, it was just that he was there at all. I didn't think anyone was in the store but me and Heather, the clerk, and the bell on the door hadn't rung, I was sure of that. But, there he was, just standing there at the end of the aisle looking at me."

"Well, what did you do?" Jacob's curiosity was piqued.

"Well, I felt very uncomfortable and so walked around the end of the aisle away from him. I diddled around a bit pretending to be browsing, but knowing I had to go back to that aisle again. So, fifteen minutes or so went by and I decided I better get back looking for the book. So, I casually strolled over around the corner, pretending I was looking at a book. When I looked up he was there again walking toward me."

"What did you do?"

"Well, I looked back down at the book and pretended I was reading."

"He didn't attack you did he?" Jacob asked.

"Well no, he didn't, but he did speak to me."

"What did he say?"

"He said, 'Son, books generally work better when they are right side up.' He then reached down, took the book from my hands, turned it around the right way and then walked off."

"Seems to me like you were the creepy one, not him, goofball!" Jacob answered, and then looked down and started thumbing through the book.

"Jacob, wait, I am telling you the guy was very strange. He shouldn't have been there I tell you! And, I no sooner looked up than he was gone again around the end of the stacks and I couldn't find him anywhere in the store. I looked! And the bell didn't go off at the door, either. I know it went off when I came in and I listened when I left and it went off again! He just disappeared."

"Maybe," Jacob answered.

"And, I almost forgot to mention this. . ." Ian started to smile knowing he would get Jacob's attention with the next piece of information he was about to impart, "he had dark browned skin and was very thin. His skin looked like it had shrunk to his cheekbones and he had dark black ink spots on his left fingertips. They left a smudge mark on the end of the page he touched!"

Jacob slammed the book shut and looked Ian hard in the eye. "Dark-skinned? Smudge mark? Ink-stained finger? Do you suppose this is the guy who was at my home in America? Do you suppose he has tracked me down?"

"I'm just reporting the facts, Boyd. I'm not saying what they mean," Ian had the satisfaction of a boy telling a parent interesting information they never knew before. He felt good but also a bit worried."

"Well, if this is the guy who is after me, we know he isn't Hammish MacGregor since MacGregor has a beard and you said this guy was clean shaven."

"No, I never said that," Ian countered, "but, that is right, he didn't have a beard. His face was crinkly and dark, but no hair."

The breeze kicked up and Jacob felt his body shiver with a cold chill as his stomach turned over with nervous fright.

THE KEEP

"**W**ell, let's keep a lookout for that guy, but for now, let's get back to our other mystery," Jacob said to Ian, who was sitting next to him on the wooden bench.

"If we don't see him again, I will be very happy!" Ian said.

"What if the clues are in this book? We can't read it all this afternoon! It's more than 300 pages!" Jacob exclaimed as he thumbed through the antique book.

"Just exactly what I thought!" Ian replied. "That is, until I took a good look at it! Turn to the last pages of the book where the pages are blank."

Jacob carefully turned the book over in his lap and opened the book from the back. The spine was brittle and seemed ready to crack into pieces as he lifted the back cover.

There he saw what Ian was talking about. On the inside of the back cover was written the same two lines that were written on the note dropped by the bird at St. Rule's. "Ah, its only part of a longer poem," Jacob said with a proud sense of satisfaction.

A GREAT WARRIOR WAS ROBERT ROY
WHO FOUGHT FOR GOLD AND KING
THE ANSWER YOU SEEK, IS IN THE
DOOR IN THE KEEP
BEHIND THE MISPLACED RING.

Before he could even wonder what on earth the whole thing now meant, or if it again was just part of a yet longer poem, he noticed a drawing on the opposite page.

It was a diagram drawn by hand and in what obviously was very old and fading ink. The dominant part of the picture was a door. Rounded on top, but flat on the bottom, it looked very ancient. *They don't make doors like that anymore*, Jacob thought as he looked at it. Across from the door was a fire and just above the fire and slightly to the left was what seemed like a box or a square of some sort with a bird or gargoyle or dragon or something in it. A ring encircled its left eye and, though the art was very basic, the beast seemed to be looking at the closed door below.

"Any ideas?" Jacob asked, looking up at Ian.

"Not a one, though I guess we need to find that door, wherever it is."

"There must be a thousand old doors in this town!" Jacob exclaimed.

"And, who says it's even here in St. Andrews? You said that according to Mr. Woods, Rob Roy lived in the Highlands way up north from here. It could be at his house or somewhere that he lived!"

"Could be," Jacob replied with a nod that seemed to show something more was going on in his head than he was saying, "but I think the answers are here. After all, everything so far has led us to this place." He paused and then added, "No . . . I am sure it's here. It only makes sense. The question is, where do we start?"

"Lets start with the words, always start with the words," was Ian's thought.

Both boys looked at the poem and read it over in their heads several times.

A Great Warrior was Robert Roy
Who fought for gold and king
The answer you seek, is in the
door in the keep
Behind the misplaced ring.

"I understand all the words, I think," said Ian, "except the word 'keep' as in 'in the keep'. What does that mean? What is a 'keep'?"

"Hmmm. . ." Jacob shook his head and added, maybe the 'keep' is some place things are 'kept.'"

"Yeah, Einstein! Maybe so."

After mulling the situation over awhile under the tree, the two boys decided to head back to Feddinch House in hopes that Mrs. Woods would make them some afternoon tea and cakes.

"That should help us think," Jacob said.

Nothing like an afternoon cake or sweet biscuit to get you going again when you find yourself stalled. Besides, as Jacob pointed out, the Feddinch parlor had a dictionary and other books that might be useful in figuring out the poem.

When they arrived at Feddinch House, Mrs. Woods was dusting the parlor with a large pink feather duster and, just as predicted, without even being asked, she immediately set off to get the boys some sweets and tea. "A bit-o biscuits and jam will get ya both goin' again till this evening!" she said as she headed to the kitchen.

The boys collapsed onto the couch in the parlor. The morning walk, climbing the tower, and the uphill ride from town made the boys about as tired as they had ever been. They sat silently staring at the opposite wall. Ian even thought he may have dozed off for a minute. When Mrs. Woods came back into the room with a tray of goodies and hot tea, Ian jumped, a bit embarrassed. After all, he was both too old and too young for an afternoon nap.

The sugary cakes and biscuits soon stoked the conversation between the boys once again. In the dictionary Jacob retrieved from the bookshelves around the fireplace, they discovered the word 'keep' had many meanings including to watch out for and to reserve. Two definitions, however, stood out in Jacob's mind.

The two possible definitions for the word 'keep' that together caused Jacob to stand and pace excitedly around the room were: it could mean the innermost part or central tower in a medieval castle or it could mean "to supply with food or lodging for pay."

Food and lodging. A central tower. Keeping things and giving things out. Old castle around here? No, just ruins in town. Food and lodging. A hotel is where you get both of those. Someplace to stay and eat. A tower? Rules Tower? No . . . wait a minute . . . food, lodging, tower! Jacob paced as he thought through the clues and came to a conclusion he was very proud of, but that he should have figured out even sooner.

"Don't you see? Don't you see?" Jacob was pacing back and forth around the parlor. He shut the door and turned back to Ian who sat looking at him as if his friend had finally lost his mind.

"Don't you see? That is it! That is it!"

"What is it? What don't I see?" Ian tried to join the conversation that he imagined was taking place somewhere in Jacob's head, but which Jacob hadn't yet shared.

"This is the answer. This place is the answer! It's why we are here right now!" Jacob spoke, as sure of himself as he had ever been in his life.

"What is this place?" he continued. Without waiting for an answer from Ian, Jacob answered himself. "It is a place where food and lodging are provided for pay! Look around us, beds upstairs, food right here on the table, Dad will pay for both before we leave. . ." Ian moved to the edge of the couch and started really to listen carefully to his new friend.

"And, remember the history of this place? It is a 500-year-old, or something like that anyway, tower!" Jacob said with his eyes growing wide. "It's a central tower! It's the keep! It's the keep!" he exclaimed.

PHOTO SHOOT

I an grabbed the old copy of *Rob Roy* from Jacob's backpack and opened it on the table, picking up another biscuit before turning to the book's final pages. "Okay, maybe this is the place meant in the poem, but then where is this door and the key and the misplaced ring and everything?"

"That is the best part of it," Jacob said, walking back over to his friend and leaning over the book. "I have seen this door before," he said as he pointed at the drawing. "As soon as I saw it this afternoon, I thought there was something familiar about it but I didn't know what. Now I remember. That door is in the kitchen!"

"Are you sure? Where does it go?"

"Well, I am as sure as one can be in a situation like this."

Jacob began to recount a description of Mrs. Wood's kitchen and pointing to things in the drawing that he remembered from his visit with Mrs. Woods the other day. The box with the dragon or gargoyle or whatever it was he certainly didn't remember, but the fire was there across from the little door. He explained what Mrs. Woods said about the door: that there was nothing behind it but the stone wall.

"Okay, it's worth a try. But how do we get back there to check it out?" Ian asked.

"We will need a plan and one not too devious because the Woods are very nice people and I don't want to be sneaking around behind their backs in their own home," Jacob insisted.

Some sneaking around would have to be done, however, no doubt about that, and they both knew it.

Over the remaining biscuits and tea, the boys hatched their plan with an ease that surprised them both. Jacob would ask Mrs. Woods to join him and Mr. Woods in the front of the house so that he could get a picture of them together so he could remember them after he left. Then, when Mr. and Mrs. Woods were both outside with Jacob, Ian would sneak back into the kitchen and open the door.

It all seemed to be coming so simply now! The boys agreed to strike.

Jacob knocked and entered the kitchen. A stroke of great luck had both Mr. and Mrs. Woods in the room together. Mr. Woods was reading a magazine and sipping some tea while Mrs. Woods worked at something in the sink.

"Mr. and Mrs. Woods. . . ah . . ." Jacob momentarily lost his concentration and almost his nerve as the Woods turned to look at him. "Well, I was just wondering," he started again, "would you two mind coming outside the front of the house? I would like to get a picture or two of you two together to help me remember my trip."

"Not at all, laddie," Mr. Woods said without delay. Mrs. Woods wasn't quite as agreeable, mumbling something about her hair not being done and her still being in her work clothes. "Come on, Mother, "Mr. Woods said to his wife, "you look lovely as the day I met ya!" Mrs. Woods rolled her eyes at her husband but took off her apron and followed him out the kitchen door and through the hallway toward the front of Feddinch House. She poked at her hair and pulled to straighten her dress as she walked.

"Might want a camera, mightn' ya?" Mr. Woods said, as he opened the door to lead the party outside. *Darn, a camera! I hadn't even thought of bringing a camera to the photo shoot! How on earth would I pull this off if I couldn't even remember a camera?* Jacob was nearing a nervous panic.

"Just a minute," Jacob said, as he sprinted the stairs to his room. As he climbed the stairs, he marveled again at how Mr. Woods seemed to be able to observe things that no one else could. He seemed to have some special power. On the way back down the stairs and through the hall, he motioned to Ian who was waiting in the parlor. The coast was clear.

Outside, Jacob had the Woods pose together in about every possible configuration. First Mrs. Woods sat on the bench with Mr. Woods standing behind her. Then Mr. Woods sat with Mrs. Woods' hand on his shoulder. Then they sat together. Then they stood together. Jacob felt sure if he wasn't a kid they were trying to humor, they would never have put up with it. In the end, he had taken twenty-two pictures and promised to send the best one back to them when he got home to America. He stopped only when he saw Ian's hand signal emerge from the window of the parlor.

Mission accomplished!

"Thank you, Mr. and Mrs. Woods," Jacob said, and began to tell them how much he had enjoyed himself at Feddinch House and how much he hoped to come back again someday. Mr. Woods said something about hoping there would be no green elves showing up on the pictures and then went off behind the house, leaving Mrs. Woods and Jacob to head back into the house together.

Jacob approached Ian in the parlor with great anticipation. He was searching his English friend's face for a clue to what he found while Mrs. Woods was still within hearing distance and he dare not speak.

"Well," Jacob said, the second he heard the kitchen door close down the hall, "what happened? What did you find?"

"Nothing!" Ian answered.

"Nothing? What do you mean nothing?"

"I mean there was nothing there at all. I mean, the door was there alright, just like you said, and I opened it, but there was nothing behind it! Just a stone wall. Nothing!"

"Did you try the stones for a hidden entrance?" Jacob questioned his friend anxiously.

"Of course I did. I've read books about castles too, you know! I pushed the stones, nothing!"

"Dang," Jacob exclaimed, as both boys resumed their old positions on the couch, staring blankly at the opposite wall and thinking; doing lots of thinking.

Eventually, Jacob broke the silence again by asserting, "I am still sure this is the place. It must be the place! We have to try again."

"No way, I am not sneaking around anymore. We made it once, but I don't want to get caught sneaking around like burglars in the Woods' house. It's too risky," Ian insisted, shifting his eyes back to the ceiling.

A few more moments were passed in silence in the parlor until Jacob had a solution, or sort of a solution.

"It has to be tonight. It has to be tonight, when the Woods and everyone are in bed," Jacob argued.

"Since your sporran seems to have sucked your brain away to another dimension, Einstein," Ian replied, "let me remind you that my father and I don't stay here and I am not going crawling around the Scottish countryside in the middle of the night to get here." Ian glanced at Jacob out of the corner of his eye as he spoke.

"We have become friends, haven't we?' Jacob asked his companion.

"Sure, I guess, but what does that have to do with anything?" Ian asked, turning his head toward Jacob.

"Well, if you promise not to wear that sissy bowtie you wore the other night, I might invite you to stay here tonight!" Jacob jumped out of Ian's reach as he teased his new friend. "After all, we are pals now and surely our dads will allow us to spend our last night in St. Andrews together, don't you think?"

"Worth a try, I guess. You don't snore, do you?" Ian replied.

A few hours later, Mr. Nelson drove up with Mr. Boyd and the boys met them in front of Feddinch House. Both fathers liked the idea of their sons getting along so well, and readily agreed to the plan for Ian to spend the night with Jacob. But only after Ian had dinner and went back to his room to pack, get a change of clothes, and retrieve his toothbrush.

The Door Opens

That evening Jacob and his father discussed their upcoming trip south to Edinburgh. Jacob was eager to spend more time with his father, but was also distracted by the door in the kitchen. *That had to be the door; it only makes sense.* Throughout the evening, he tried to look around for more clues without being conspicuous.

The phone rang as the Boyds sat in the parlor waiting for Ian and his father to arrive. Jacob could hear Mrs. Woods answer it and say "Why yes, he is here, may I tell him who is calling?"

Soon Mrs. Woods entered the parlor and announced, "Mr. Boyd, there is a young lady on the phone for you."

"For me? Not work again!" Mr. Boyd said, as he stood to go to the phone.

"Not for you, Mr. Boyd . . . for the other Mr. Boyd!" Mrs. Woods said with a smile that seemed to say "Isn't it cute that a girl is calling you, Jacob." *Oh brother,* he thought, *you don't understand!*

Jacob picked up the phone to find a panicky Jenny on the line.

"Jacob, I have to be quick. My parents will kill me when they get the bill for calling Scotland, but I had to talk to you!"

"What's up?"

"Well, last night I went back to the woods by your house. I know I shouldn't have after what happened last time, but I just had to. I had to know what was going on. Will, well, you know Will, he met me there but wouldn't go into the trees. He stayed by the road."

Jacob listened intently as Jenny recounted what had happened to her the night before.

She had entered the trees and stood silently while Will watched from the road. After standing around awhile, nothing had happened so she sat down on the hollowed stump at the bottom by the creek. They had played around the hollowed stump for years and called it the "witch's cauldron." It had a birch tree growing out the side of it, which hung over the creek.

As Will sat nervously pulling weeds by the road, a small figure arose from inside the tree cauldron behind Jenny. "I didn't hear a thing, Jacob, it was just like all of a sudden I felt something behind me! Like it came right out of the tree or something!"

Jenny felt frozen as if an invisible force was holding her body and keeping her from running or even turning to see what was behind her. Then it spoke. "Jacob, it spoke to me as if it could do no more than whisper."

"What did it say?"

"Well, it said not to be afraid. And then it told me to give a message to 'the Bearer of the sporran,' which I assume is you."

Great . . .what now? When will the messages stop? He thought. "Okay, go on, I guess. . ."

"It said that you should remember 'Aristotle's maxim' when next amongst the trees. Always choose the mean and you will not go wrong."

"What the heck does that mean?" Jacob asked. The message made Jacob realize how confused he was and he grew frustrated.

"Well, I am not sure, but I spent the day in the library and online to check out Aristotle. Turns out he was an ancient Greek philosopher and he taught that we should take the middle course between extremes. That is what he meant by "the mean," that is, "the middle." Jenny heard the frustration in his voice but ignored it.

"Well that doesn't seem to help. Did he say anything else?"

"No, that was it." Jenny answered, but then went on. "When he was done I felt as if he had put his hand on me, like he was reaching out just for a touch and it felt lonely and sad. Then I felt as if I was released from the force holding me and turned and he was gone again. Will claims not to have seen anything, but I know I couldn't have imagined it!"

"No, I am sure you didn't. We are beyond the world of imagination now, I am afraid, though I wish I were back there right now playing imaginary games with you and Will."

"Jacob, I have to get off this phone now, but why don't you try to get your dad to bring you home? I am worried about you."

"We'll be home soon. Look after my mom when she gets back from my grandparents, and take care of yourself."

After the phone call, Jacob went to his room for a minute to think and compose himself before returning to the parlor to wait with his dad.

It was no longer early, but not quite late when Ian's father dropped him off at Feddinch and they made plans to meet again in the morning where the four would say farewell and head on their separate "holidays," as Mr. Nelson referred to their trips.

The boys spent the early part of the evening playing cards and reading in the parlor with Jacob's father and, occasionally, Mr. Woods who would come and go, seeming to find it difficult to sit still for long.

As the lateness of the night approached, the boys' nerves grew tense. Their work was about to begin and the maximum time of danger was approaching. "Time to hit the sack, boys," Mr. Boyd announced more than once before he actually got up and led the boys upstairs. By then, Mr. Woods had disappeared for the night for good and Feddinch was very quiet. Even the fire had reduced itself to silent embers when the boys and Mr. Boyd climbed the stairs to their rooms.

That night Ian shared Jacob's room on a make-shift bed Mrs. Woods had prepared for him on the floor at the foot of the bed. Both boys went through all the motions of preparing to head to bed. Teeth were brushed, pajamas were put on, the lights went off and the covers went on. Jacob whispered to Ian of the call he had taken from Jenny. Then they lay in their beds in silence for what seemed like an eternity. Only an occasional whisper of "still awake" broke the silence between them until Jacob rose from his bed and slowly opened the door.

The creak of the old door seemed deafeningly loud in the silence of the night. On the tip of his toes, Jacob slowly took the few steps between his door and his father's, where he pressed his ear against the door. Sure enough, he heard what he hoped to hear—the sounds of sleep (or, the sounds of his father sleeping, anyway, which he always thought sounded like a small cow must sound when asleep).

He returned to his room where he and Ian slipped their clothes back on and the two boys started their slow descent down the stairs. They were led by no more light than the soft glow of the nightlights Mr. Woods had placed near the floor on each landing. The stairs were newly carpeted in plush blue, but beneath the new carpet were very old boards. Their weight made every few stairs give a squeak or a crack that would make the boys freeze in their tracks and which sped up their heart rates as they feared being caught.

Rounding the last landing of the stairs, Ian leaned against the rail to avoid a creak in the floor that Jacob had just hit. He didn't know the ball on top of the knoll post was loose and his weight caused it to come off and fall. The heavy wooden ball headed toward the floor, but Ian was able to get one hand under it before it crashed onto the stairs. Ian tried to get a grip on the ball but it just flew off his fingers. Up the ball ascended through the air until it was stopped. What stopped it was the back of Jacob's head! "Ugggggh," Jacob let out without control. Rubbing his head, he turned to see Ian putting the ball back on the post. Ian shrugged his shoulders and silently mouthed the word "Sorry," just as a fake right hook passed his nose in the dark.

Arriving at the bottom of the stairs, the boys paused again to listen for any sign of life in the house. Nothing. If they were going to get caught, it was probably on the stairs near the bedrooms, they both had agreed. Now that they had made it that far, the boys felt some type of relief, but only until they realized the real nature of their situation. They were now stuck. Going back up the stairs might get them caught sneaking around, and going forward into the kitchen might bring unimagined perils. Neither was a great option, but both knew they would forever regret not having had the courage to open the door.

Even though Ian and Jacob had been in that kitchen before, there was something about dark rooms and hallways and kitchens at night that can give a guy the creeps. Being in an old house built around an ancient tower made it seem even more dark and made the nightlights cast shadows that were even more ominous.

Jacob led Ian down the hall under the stairs to the kitchen door. Ian lay down on the ground to see if any light might be shining that would indicate someone was in the room behind the door. He saw nothing. Jacob pushed the door open.

The kitchen seemed even darker than the hallway. There was no nightlight in the room at all and the dark stone of the fireplace and beams on the ceiling made everything seem closer and darker. Ian and Jacob moved to the center of the room. Walking so close to one another that they seemed to be one boy with four legs, they bumped into each other with each step. The only light in the room came from the moonlight filtering through the trees into the windows above the sink and through the glass panes of the door. As their eyes adjusted to the dark, shadows began to brighten into objects in the moonlight.

Jacob turned to the small door and stared. "Come on," Ian whispered, as he knelt and reached for the small brass ring that must have been used for centuries to open the tiny door. Jacob stood back in case something flew out or he needed to run. *At least one of them should survive*, he reasoned to himself.

Ian opened the door with an unexpected quickness that Jacob was not expecting. Jacob jumped back a step.

"See, I told you there was nothing here, just like I said earlier today, or yesterday, now, I guess," Ian whispered. Jacob approached and saw nothing but the old stone wall of the Manor House. He pushed the stones and even kicked the wall in frustration but nothing seemed to give. It seemed to be nothing more than a fake door to nowhere.

Ian closed the ancient door and stood back. Both boys silently looked at one another. *What do we do now?*

Both turned to leave the room when something caught Jacob's eye on the mantel. It was a glint of moonlight bouncing off an object. He walked over to the fireplace with Ian desperately whispering at his back, "What the heck are you doing? Come on, we were wrong. Let's get out of here!"

Jacob reached up to the mantel and pulled down a small piece of stained glass. It was too dark to tell much about it until he held it up to the moonlight in the window. What Jacob saw nearly caused him to falter and drop the piece of glass onto the brick floor. There, in the moonlight, showing as clear as if it were the middle of the day, was a red gargoyle-like bird. Jacob didn't know what kind of a creature it would be called or if such a thing had ever existed.

"Ian, come here, quickly," Jacob said excitedly, almost forgetting the need to whisper. "Remember the poem and the diagram in the book? I've, I mean, *we've* found it!" He held the plate of glass out to his friend and added, "The answer you seek, is in the door in the keep. *Behind the misplaced ring.*" Jacob was quoting from the clue in the book and smiling a proud grin.

Ian said nothing as he looked over the piece of glass in the moonlight.

"You see? You see? The thing that looks like a bird? The gold ring around its eye? It's all there!"

"Okay, maybe," Ian replied, "but what do we do with it now?"

"The diagram showed the bird and ring somewhere over here," Jacob said, as he moved toward the window and the outside door in the far wall. Jacob took the piece of glass and moved it slowly over the wall and around the windows. Nowhere did it really seem to find a home or a resting place proper to it. As he passed back the third time over the window, he heard Ian.

"Jacob. . . right there, stop!"

Jacob turned to see a sharp point of light had been cast down onto a water glass sitting on the counter at the other end of the room and then refracting as a wash of light onto the wall. He looked back at his hands and saw the "bird" on the glass appeared now to be looking back into the room at Ian instead of sideways into the edge of the glass pane it was part of. The golden ring around its head was glowing brightly as the light of the moon passed through it and was focused into the room.

"Quickly, Ian, move that water glass out of the way."

Ian moved uneasily toward the glass and the sharp point of light penetrating into it. As he lifted the glass out of the way, the spray of light on the wall disappeared and the light focused back into a sharp beam hitting the tiny door.

Something seemed to be happening, but what? Both boys could sense it.

Ian turned to Jacob. His eyes focused on the eye of the bird which seemed to be staring right through him. "Jacob. . ." there was a tone of fright in Ian's voice as he continued to look in the direction of his friend and the bird. "Jacob. . . I hear something . . . what is happening . . . Jacob?" Ian couldn't bring himself to turn around and the look on Jacob's face didn't make him any more bold.

"Creeeeeaaaaaakkkkkkk" came the sound getting louder behind him. The door was opening and *they* weren't doing the opening! *This is it, I am a dead man.* Ian's mind started to cloud in a confused panic.

Suddenly the door came flying open all the way and smacked against the wall behind it. Both boys jumped and Jacob let the glass pane slip down to his side as he bounded backwards. The two friends thought they were about to encounter their doom together in the face of some awakened beast of fairy land as they looked into the darkness of the tiny doorway. But nothing stirred. Nothing moved. Silence.

Jacob approached the door, silently passing Ian and kneeling down with a calmness and bravery that surprised them both. The darkness beyond the threshold of the doorway was intense. It was a black like neither of them had remembered experiencing before. Jacob's eyes could barely make out that part of the old stone wall had moved aside and there on the floor inside the door was what looked like a small lump. Jacob's hand reached slowly toward the darkness and then, as fast as it could move, his hand snapped passed the threshold of the door, grabbed the lump and retreated. Both boys stood back from the door and looked at the pouch in Jacob's hand.

Thud! The boys looked up at the sound to see the door had closed again.

Suspended Blade

The bag Jacob had in his hand was of burgundy leather tied with a strap. He handed it to Ian, who took it with hesitation. Jacob turned to replace the piece of stained glass. As he placed it on the mantel, he noticed that the "bird's" eye no longer was looking out, but again was looking straight forward, toward the end of the piece of stained glass and out through the kitchen door.

As Jacob turned to leave the area by the fireplace, the entire room suddenly became filled with intense light, followed closely by a booming crack of thunder. Jacob and Ian both felt the shock of the strike in their bones. A storm had suddenly descended upon St. Andrews with no warning. The moonlight that had streamed through the window just moments before was now hidden deep behind thick black clouds. Tree branches were bending hard from side-to-side in a frightening dance as if they were warning the world of something that was to come.

"Come on, Jacob, let's go upstairs and look in this bag." Ian was heading toward the door into the hallway under the stairs as he spoke.

Another bolt of lightning lit the kitchen and the boys were again shaken with a thunderous crash. This time the light revealed something different outside the window. Both of them saw it and both of them froze with fear. Outside the window in the kitchen door was the silhouette of a man in a large brimmed hat.

Before they could move, another bolt of lightning and then a crash. This time it was the crash of the kitchen door flying open and against the far wall. Dripping wet, the man in a long, dark and oiled raincoat and wide-brimmed hat stepped through the door. More than six feet tall, the man would be an intimidating sight at any time of day. Now, in the middle of the dark night and rain soaked, he was positively awesome.

Their shock kept the boys from even noticing the tightness growing between their neck and shoulder and then running down their right arms.

Neither could make out the stranger's face and neither needed to in order to be scared out of their minds. They stood without moving, as if their legs no longer worked. Jacob felt like he was watching the scene unfold as if in a movie that he was observing from a distance.

"Well, now, boys, I think you have something for me . . . hand it over."

Ian felt a scream escape his body as he turned to run. Two steps and his legs froze again as if being held by an invisible force.

"Scream if you will, but I have put a hold on this manor house. No one will awake until our business is well done," the tall figure moved with long strides into the room and toward the table. As he passed the hearth, he waved his left hand gently at his side and the fire slowly grew to life, casting a dull glow upon his face which was clean-shaven.

He sat and pulled a knife from his side. It was a blade of intricate design that he wielded as if it were part of his own hand. He sliced a piece from the ball of cheese sitting in the middle of the table and thrust it into his mouth on the tip of his silver blade.

"Now, boys, we can do this in a way that will not hurt or we can do this in a way that will hurt very much." The dark figure was now ominously sharpening his knife upon a stone he pulled from his overcoat pocket.

"This is not our house," Jacob interjected, as he hoped this man would turn out to be common thief, despite the trick he pulled with the fire. "What could you possibly want with us?"

"Little Bearer, you are not half so full of wit as you have been told; nor as clever as you like to believe. I am not some common criminal here to take the candle sticks. I am here for you to give me what you owe me."

"Jacob," Ian stammered out a question to his friend who had now backed his way to standing directly next to him, "do you know him?"

"Of course he knows me!" The man's voice was raising and he turned to look them directly in the eye, though his hat still cast a dark shadow over his face. "He knows me as the haunter of his dreams . . . his dreams to come!" The man turned in his chair to face Ian and Jacob and then crossed his legs, revealing that he was wearing two black boots that rose up all the way to his knees and were tied with extremely long laces that ran from his ankle to the top of his boots.

"You have something that once belonged to me and I want it back," he said calmly, and almost quietly, as he played with the blade in his hand.

"Sir," Jacob reacted, "if I have something of yours, I am sure it is a mistake and I would be glad to return it."

"You foolish little boy, you will not be glad to return it, but I assure you that you will do so."

The man's tone turned more angry and agitated.

"You see, like you, I once was innocent and naïve. Then a great power came into my hands and I got what I wanted when I wanted it. Then it was stolen from me before I was old enough and wise enough to use it properly." The man took his blade and slammed it hard into the wooden table where it stuck fast and wobbled ominously.

"Well, sir, if someone stole something from you, maybe you should go to the police," Ian interjected.

A wave of the man's wet finger flicked a droplet of water across the room and a spell to Ian's lips which sealed tightly shut. "I have no use for you, boy. It's Boyd who has what belongs to me."

Ian struggled frantically, his eyes crossing and uncrossing, as he attempted to see his lips and what was clamping them shut. His fingers scratched at the clear gelly-like ooze that covered his mouth.

"Now, Boyd, I suggest you hand over that little sporran of mine." The man crossed his legs and pushed the hat off his face. His face was dark and leathery and his eyes were set deep into his head, as if they were two small pools evaporated from too much time spent in the sun.

"Well . . . ahhhhh. . ." Jacob was stalling as he tried to think of what to do. He started to back up toward the hall door, hoping he and Ian could make a run for it. Two steps back and . . . THUD! Ian's knees had buckled and he hit hard on the floor.

The leathery man let out a wicked laugh that pierced Jacob with added fear and said "Now, Boyd, unless you want your friend hurt even more, I suggest you give up the idea of running away and give me what is mine."

"Okay, okay, it's in my backpack in the parlor," Jacob said, while punctuating his wish for the man not to do anything rash by holding his hands up and turning to show he would get the sporran.

"Well, that is better. Now, go get it quickly." The man sat back confidently in his chair and motioned Jacob to the door. "Oh, Boyd, in case you are thinking of trying anything, remember this . . ." the man pulled his knife from the table, flicked it from handle to blade in his left hand and then threw it hard at Ian. The knife tumbled through the air with Ian in its path, frozen with fear.

"Noooooooooooo!" Jacob yelled as he recoiled from the scene.

The man's right hand went up with an open palm and the knife suddenly stopped. It hung in the air, just inches from Ian's throat, who still was gagged and on his knees where he had been knocked a moment before.

"Now, I suggest you get moving. That knife now belongs to you and his blood will stain your hands. Oh, and if you take too long, be careful when you come back in here. We wouldn't want you to slip and fall in the blood!"

"I am sorry, Ian," Jacob said, as he turned and ran from the room. Down the hall he sprinted and spun into the parlor. Grabbing his backpack, he quickly scribbled a note on the only piece of paper he could immediately see: a birthday card sitting on the coffee table. The note he hurriedly scribbled contained just five words: "FEDDINCH. BIG TROUBLE. PLEASE HELP!" Jacob shoved the card into the sporran and ran back down the hall into the kitchen where the knife still hung in front of a motionless Ian.

"Good boy, now, why don't you see if you can save your little friend, Boyd?

Go on. Take the knife from his throat." The small laugh of a man who has found little amusing lately but himself whimpered from his throat.

Jacob looked into Ian's frightened eyes with pity and slowly approached his friend. Reaching for the knife, he closed his eyes tight at the last second, fearing something would go terribly wrong. His fingers closed on nothing but air and Ian let out a small snort. Jacob's eyes opened cautiously, fearing the knife may have moved and plunged into Ian's body. His eyes opened but did not see the carnage he feared. Instead, he found Ian snorting breaths of air through his nose in great relief. The knife was back in the dark stranger's hand.

"Now, about your little gift for me, Boyd." The man was now standing and walking toward the boys. "I won't take it, but you will give it to me, won't you, Boyd?" His leathery brown hands were caressing the blade of his long knife as he stepped toward Jacob.

Over the stranger's right shoulder, Jacob could see something move in the dark corner beside the fireplace. Jacob could not make out any features, but it appeared to be another person lurking in the shadows.

Suddenly, the fireplace exploded with light and heat. Jacob and Ian ducked as a ball of fire and smoke flew through the room and blinded them with intense light. The sound reverberated through their ears like a gunshot. Then, just as suddenly, they began to fall. Jacob screamed and Ian let out a muffled gasp as they fell.

When the ball of flame returned to the fireplace and the room grew quiet, just two men stood confronting one another. The boys were gone.

SARCOPHAGUS

Jacob and Ian landed hard on a stone floor. They had fallen about ten feet through a trap door and were now alone in the barely-lit basement of Feddinch House.

"Mmmmppphhhhh. . . mmmmpppphhhh," Ian was desperately trying to communicate with Jacob to ask for help in releasing his lips from the oozy jelly that had hardened over them. "Mmmppphhh . . . mmmpphhh,"

"Shhhhhh. . ," Jacob whispered at Ian, "our lives may depend on being quiet. I don't know what happened, but clearly we have been saved somehow and by someone and let's stay saved!"

Ian pointed to his lips and batted his eyes as if begging Jacob to help.

Jacob touched the cloudy gel that held Ian's lips and felt for an edge where it might be loose. Finding just such a corner, Jacob dug a fingernail under its edge and pulled slightly. Ian murmured from a slight pain. Then Jacob yanked with all his strength and the gel ripped from Ian's lips, flew back, and stuck fast to the wall far behind Jacob. Ian yelled in pain and instinctively struck out and slugged Jacob hard in the chest.

"Ugghhh. . . " Jacob grunted as the blow forced air from his chest. "What are you doing?"

"Sorry, old chap, but that hurt like the devil himself!" Ian was licking his lips and patting them with his fingers.

"Well, enough of that, what do you think happened up there?" Jacob whispered his question to Ian.

"I don't know, but I never thought I would be so glad to be in a dungeon before. Any place is better than up there," Ian was pointing to the bottom of the trap door they had fallen through.

"Well, come on, let's see how we can get out of here," Jacob said as he stood and reached to help Ian to his feet.

The only light in the basement was the faint glow that filtered through the small and dirty windows from the light on the tool shed beside the house. It was barely enough for the boys to make their way across the floor without major stumbles. They could hear men talking upstairs and occasional small crashes as they searched the work benches and tables for a light.

After some minutes of feeling around and knocking things over, Ian saw a glint of light and approached it. To their great fortune, it was the glint of light reflecting off the light bulb of a flashlight sitting on a box in the corner. Ian picked it up and tried the button to turn it on. To their relief, it came to life with a dull golden glow.

Ian cast the light from side-to-side around the room. What was revealed was both jarring and exciting. All around the room were ancient maps and tapestries and drawings. Some were of battles and others of people looking like they were being tortured, some of them clearly bloody. On the walls between the pictures hung swords and shields and old Scottish tartans in their checkered patterns of red and black and green and blue. Lower on the walls, part-way around the room, rested bookshelves which were full of old books and manuscripts.

"Ian, come here, bring that light," Jacob whispered excitedly.

As Ian approached, he saw that Jacob was standing next to a large stone sarcophagus. Its white stone top was formed to look like a sleeping knight with shield and sword resting in his arms. Jacob brushed the dust from the top and struggled to get a good look.

"Look here, Ian," Jacob said, as his hand brushed down the shield. I have seen the symbol on his shield before . . . in a dream, I think, or maybe somewhere else, but I think in a dream." Jacob was pointing to the three rampant lions. The first wore a large ring on its right front paw. The second held a sword in its right hand and a bag in the left. The third stood with one foot on a large square stone and wore a crown. Across the shield was a banner with the word "Sporrai," in a very fancy and hard to read script. "I wonder what it means?" Jacob asked, without really directing the question to Ian.

Lying at the foot of the sarcophagus was a tattered old notebook. It was dark brown leather and in the dim light of the dark basement the boys could not make out the slight depression of a once proudly embossed seal on the cover. A paper was sticking from the book and marked a page of interest to whomever had been looking at it last. Jacob picked up the book and asked Ian to shine his light on the open pages.

The light brought to their attention a hand drawing of a sarcophagus. Both of the boys looked at each other in silence as they realized the drawing was probably of the stone case they were standing near. Ian removed his hand that was resting on the box, likely containing the remains of some long-dead man or woman and wiped it clean on his pants.

The title of the page next to the drawing of the sarcophagus was "Releasing the Protector of Andrew's Bones." Below it was a fragment of a poem;

Let this servant lie
Till one last deed
He is called
To save loves new seed.

There was room left to complete the poem and then what looked like three pine trees were drawn to the side of the page. The phrase "Aristotle's Grove" was written beneath the trees, and a bird was perched atop the central tree. Jacob then paged through the notebook quickly and found it filled with notes referring to sporrans and long-dead men who seemed to be part of some mystery the note-taker was trying to unravel. The page devoted to the "Green Elf of Feddinch" particularly caught his attention, as he remembered both Mr. and Mrs. Wood mentioning such a creature.

The noises upstairs reminded the boys of the urgency of their situation and Jacob laid the book back down on the stone slab where he had found it a moment before. Then Jacob paused and picked it back up.

"What are you doing? We don't have time to worry about old books!"

"Just a minute, this reminds me of something," Jacob picked up the book and opened it again, pushing the marked page into the beam of the flashlight. He stared at the image for several long seconds.

"Come on, Jacob!" Ian tried to grab the book.

"No, wait," Jacob pushed Ian's hand away and then asked, "What do these trees look like?"

"They are trees, so what!"

"No, I think they are *not* trees. Look at them. They also look like the tassels on our sporrans, don't they?"

"Well, maybe, somewhat." Ian was not convinced that Jacob was on to anything and wasn't sure he really cared, either.

"Yes, if these are tassels on our sporrans, or one of the sporrans, anyway, and there is a bird on the middle one, that might signify something important about it. And, remember, Jenny told me she got the message that 'things are not as they might appear; find the mean and you will find the answer'. Quick, where is your sporran?"

"It's up in the room, of course, you know that," Ian responded.

"Oh, yes, well, let's look at mine," Jacob said as he laid his sporran on the lid of the sarcophagus. Jacob motioned for Ian to shine the light on his sporran and then began to feel carefully in the hairy middle tassel. His excitement grew as something hard caught his attention and he rolled it in his fingers. Holding onto his new find with the fingers of his right hand, he pulled the hair back with his left and unveiled a small white claw.

"You see," Jacob said excitedly, "it must be the claw of the bird on the middle tree! Now, so what?"

"Yes, so what, let's get out of here!" Ian urged his friend.

Jacob ignored him and picked up the book again and began skimming through the pages. "Yes . . . yes. . . three trees, three lions. Middle tree contains the claw, so, middle lion must have some connection, right?"

Ian did not respond, but searched the room nervously for a way to escape.

"Shine that light over here on this shield," Jacob barked, and Ian responded. The middle lion on the shield of the sarcophagus held the sword in one hand and a pouch in the other. "This could be a sporran," Jacob offered. He then took the claw and awkwardly worked it around the outside of the lion. Then he put the claw on the sword. Nothing happened. He moved the claw over to the pouch and it caught. He pushed. The pouch suddenly gave way beneath the claw which surprised and shocked him.

"Its like a key! It fit, Ian!"

Ian reached over and stopped Jacob's hand. "Now, let's think about this, chap. We are in mortal danger. There is at least one guy and maybe two upstairs who want to hurt us and you are about to open a dead guy's coffin? Are you batty?"

"Alright, you are right. If we get through this, I can come back in the daylight, maybe." Jacob pulled his sporran and its hidden claw away from the sarcophagus lid but it would not budge. He pulled and pulled harder until it finally released and he took a stumble backward. "Darn it!" Jacob exclaimed as he noticed the claw had broken away from his sporran and stayed in the lid. He tried to remove it with his fingers but it held tight.

The sounds of shouting men and of a skirmish continued to come through the floor above the boys. "Come on, Jacob, you can get that later. We need to get out of here," Ian said as he gave a tug on Jacob's shoulder.

"Maybe, but, where are we going to go? Do you want to go back up there with that guy up there and probably angrier than ever?"

"Well, I suppose not, but. . ." A look of fear and confusion came over Ian's face. "Jacob, did you feel that?" he said.

"Umm, well, I felt something, but. . ."

Jacob jumped back as he felt a tremor emanate from the sarcophagus. "Probably an aftershock from that last crack of thunder, I bet!" Jacob offered the explanation but he didn't even convince himself.

The sounds of battle and argument grew louder upstairs just as they felt something tremble around them again, maybe from within the sarcophagus, but they were not sure. Something then scampered across the floor and Ian and Jacob both jumped.

"Just a mouse! Praise be!" Ian breathed a sigh of relief.

"Yeah, that must have been it," Jacob replied.

"Jacob, come on, let's get up these stairs and run for our lives!"

"No, Ian, it's too dangerous. If that guy is occupied fighting some other creature that was up there hiding, all the better for us! That other creature might be after us too, you know! I'm not going back up there into the house anywhere near that kitchen!"

"All the same, this place and that box," Ian was pointing to the sarcophagus, "are creeping me out and I want out of here."

"Okay, look, maybe there is some other way out," Jacob offered as he took a few steps into the center of the cluttered basement.

A bright flash of lightning followed by a crash of thunder called their attention to the small window near the ceiling.

"Maybe we can get out through the window, Jacob!"

Without answering, Jacob walked toward the window and examined the situation as best he could, considering the dim light. The window was at least nine feet off the ground and could be locked. Still, it was their best shot. A moment later, the boys began pulling a table across the room and then carefully stacking boxes and books on top of the table and under the window.

The climb up the stack was treacherous and Ian tried twice before giving way for Jacob to try. Jacob slowly teetered his way up the stack, occasionally feeling a foot fall through the top of one cardboard box or another. Stretching to reach the top of the window, Jacob was able to feel and unlatch the lock. The window swung in and up easily as Jacob hurriedly used the rough stone walls to scratch the cobwebs from his hands and tried not to think of the spider they might belong to. If there is one thing Jacob cannot stand, it is the thought of a spider crawling on him in the dark.

Rain started to pour in through the open window as Jacob reached up for something to grab hold of. His hand found a wet tree root exposed in the hole around the window and he pulled himself up and through the small opening. His knees were scraped and his hands sore by the time he emerged in the wet grass, but he was free.

Ian was calling Jacob's name and loudly whispering "Don't leave me down here! Where are you?"

Jacob popped his head back down into the window hole and extended a hand down for Ian. Ian hesitated, afraid of the possible fall.

"Ian, I suggest you come now, or be alone in the dead of the night with your very own *dead knight!*"

"Stop it, Jacob, just help me!"

Jacob struggled to help Ian's climb up to the window. In the dim light of the basement behind Ian, Jacob thought he saw something move again where they stood by the sarcophagus moments before.

"Come on, Iiaannnn, you can do it. . . ." The boys struggled until finally Ian emerged into the wet grass, his knees scraped and bloodied. Jacob leaned back in to pull the window shut and keep Mr. Woods' basement from flooding. This time he was almost sure he saw the shadows changing as if the lid of the sarcophagus was slowly sliding off.

Oh boy, maybe it's just the shadows playing tricks on me. Yes, that is it, get hold of yourself, Jacob! Jacob tried to convince himself as the boys turned to escape from the danger of being in the light cast from the flood light on the shed.

The rain was coming down hard and the boys instantly became soaked, the rain running down their faces and blurring their vision. Jacob led Ian around the back of the house where they could peer into the kitchen.

"What are we doing? Jacob, we need to get away from here!" Ian was grabbing at Jacob's back and urging him to stop. "To the trees! We should hide in the trees!"

"Shhhhh, wait, we also need to get to my dad!" Jacob pulled away from Ian's grasping fingers. "I can't leave him in there!"

Jacob slowly and cautiously snuck around the corner and peered through the edge of the glass window. He could see shadows but nothing more. "I need a better angle, I am going over under the window."

"You are nuts! You're on your own, pal!" Ian replied, as he hugged the wall tightly with his back and spit rain from his mouth.

Jacob crawled around the corner and under the kitchen window. He slowly raised up to peek in.

There he saw the dark stranger swing a fist at another man whose face was turned away from the window. The blow caught the second man hard, causing his head to jerk back violently before his body dropped hard to the floor. As his head hit the brick floor and turned, Jacob recognized the fallen man as Mr. Woods.

MISTY KNIGHT

J acob's heart raced and a salty tear slipped down his cheek and mixed with the rain as it did. The dark stranger picked up a sword that had been lost in the battle and raised it over Mr. Woods as if preparing to cleave him in two.

"Noooooooooooo!" Jacob yelled, and started for the kitchen door. He knew he had to save Mr. Woods even if it meant giving up the sporran or worse. As he screamed, the dark stranger looked up and smiled out the window.

Jacob had tied the sporran around his waist before the climb from the basement and now he felt something grab its belt and pull him backward. Then a hand smacked hard around his mouth. "Quiet, you fool!" Jacob could feel wet hair all around his neck and ears, as if he were being held by a bear. He kicked back wildly with his feet and struggled to get free.

"Quiet, and look!" the whisper came again. Something was happening in the kitchen. The dark stranger suddenly lost confidence, seeming startled and disoriented. He looked all around and hacked at the air as if fighting some invisible foe. Seconds later, Jacob could see a misty presence slowly encircling the stranger. Round and round it slowly turned. With each wispy step, the form took more substance until finally Jacob could make it out as a man in armor—a knight.

It's the knight of the Sarcophagus! The realization made Jacob completely forget he was being held by some hairy being in the middle of a terrible storm. Through the streaming rain, he watched in hypnotic awe as the stranger hacked wildly at the ghostly knight. His blows went right through his foe, finding nothing but misty air. Then, finally, one blow was stopped in mid-swing by the knight's sword. The knight's blade was now fully in our world and the stranger's blade shattered onto the kitchen floor.

What happened next surprised Jacob. He expected a terribly bloody blow to fell the stranger and he was rooting for it, too. Instead, the ghostly knight sheathed his sword and stepped toward the frightened and confused stranger. The knight's smoky arms wrapped around the evil presence and the man screamed as if being burned by a white-hot flame. The knight pulled him closer and closer until the tendrils of his misty body completely enveloped the leathery man.

Slowly the misty knight and the struggling stranger moved as if in a dance. Round and round they went, the man's screams growing silent, and then both began to disappear as if melting into the kitchen floor of Feddinch House.

The disappearance of the final parts of their bodies brought Jacob back to reality and he flew out of the arms that held him, as they had loosened during the final seconds of the battle in the kitchen. He ran around the corner where Ian stood wiping the rain from his face and shivering in the cold of the wet wind. Jacob grabbed Ian's arm and yelled "Ruuunnn!" as the two fled toward the woods.

Behind them they could hear Jacob's captor yelling. Then the man pointed his walking staff at the boys and both went down hard on the muddy yard.

"Now, you fools, stop your running before you get hurt! The danger has passed, Jacob and Ian."

Both boys looked at one another as they were sprawled on the cold, wet ground. This was no time for fun, but Ian couldn't help but snicker as he looked at Jacob who had mud dripping from all over his face. "Look at yourself, hotshot," Jacob responded, just as he felt a strong hand reach down for his arm and lift him to his feet. Ian was being lifted simultaneously.

A bolt of lightning cast light on a dark and very bearded face. Rain water splattered off the man's lips as he spoke. "I got your note, Jacob.

Seems you found help in some other places, though. Ian, we haven't met before, but I am Professor Hammish MacGregor and I would shake both your hands, but you are muddy messes. Now, shall we get out of this infernal rain and check on the Innkeeper?"

GIFTS OF DESTINY

Mr. *Woods! What am I doing?* Jacob led the other two on a run back toward Feddinch House. In the kitchen they found Mr. Woods had collected himself and was sitting at the kitchen table, dabbing blood from the corners of his mouth.

Jacob ran to the older man at the table and put his arm around his shoulder. "Thank you, Mr. Woods! You saved our lives! Thank you!"

Mr. Woods was still catching his breath and mending his wounds and could say nothing. The fight had clearly taken much out of him.

"Thank you, Mr. Woods," Ian added.

"Yes, Jack, you did well, old friend," MacGregor walked across the floor and gently touched the battle-scarred man on the back.

"You boys go over to the sink and wash that mud off you while I go check on your father and Mrs. Woods and make sure they are alright," MacGregor said as he headed through the door and down the hall outside the kitchen.

Before the boys were completely clean and dry, MacGregor had returned. "Sleeping like little lambs, they are, sleeping like little lambs!"

MacGregor began to boil a special herbal tea he created from the contents of jars he took from Mrs. Woods' cabinets. When it was ready, he poured a cup for Mr. Woods and then poured the extra through a towel that he would use to dab at Mr. Woods' cuts and bruises. Meanwhile, the boys took to cleaning the muddied and bloodied floor and straightening the battle-scarred kitchen.

When Mr. Woods' strength began to return, MacGregor prepared some regular tea and the four sat around the table to talk of what had happened to them that night.

MacGregor started the conversation. "Laddies, its time you learned a few things about those sporrans you have and about what happened here tonight. We can tell you some, but only some of what you will need to know. You must just trust that you will learn what you need to know when you need to know it. Now, Mr. Woods here is a very special man. He is not of 'the Remnant,' but he believes in the magic and was willing to take you two in when we got word that Jacob was being hunted and his sporran was in danger."

"Being hunted?" Jacob interjected, "But why me?"

"Jacob, you and Ian have been called to be sporran Bearers and there are people in this world who have tasted the power of the sporran and would do anything to get hold of one. One thing to remember is that a sporran only has power if it is freely given, it cannot be taken by force or stolen. I bet that is why our visitor tonight let you live as long as he did. He needed you to give it freely to him."

"Is he gone now?" Ian asked.

"We can only guess at his fate, but I am pretty sure your visitor has been taken from this world and will not trouble you further but that does not mean there will not be others. While the sporrans remain with you, you will need to be on guard always. I am afraid your lives as carefree young boys are at an end for awhile. It's the price we pay for the magic of the world."

"You know, Mr. Boyd and Mr. Nelson, you both performed your offices admirably tonight and I am proud of you," Mr. Woods was beginning to feel better and spoke for the first time.

The four talked for a short time more and then MacGregor suggested the boys needed to get some sleep.

"Jacob, have you opened the package you found inside the door yet?" MacGregor asked.

In all that had transpired through the night, he had forgotten the package that had begun the adventure earlier that evening. He reached into his back pocket and pulled out the small pouch of burgundy leather and placed it on the table in front of them.

"Well, go on Jacob, open it," MacGregor offered.

Jacob undid the leather strap that tied the pouch and pulled from it a golden ring. The ring was large, too large to fit him for sure, and very ornate. On one side were three lions on a shield, just like the one on the sarcophagus in the basement and the word "Sporrai" was written across it on a diagonal band. On the other side was a unicorn rearing back on its hind legs and holding a St. Andrews flag in one front hoof and bearing a shield with a red rampant lion in the other. Around the unicorn's neck was a crown.

Right in the middle of the ring was nothing. There was a hole, that is, where a jewel must have once been set, but no more. *Even without the jewel,* Jacob thought, *the ring must be worth a fortune.* Jacob stuck his finger in the ring and swooshed it around on his finger letting it drop and hang loosely on his right pointer.

"Jacob," MacGregor began to speak as he reached over and closed Jacob's fist around the ring. "This is yours and you were meant to have it. We can't say why but someday you *will* know. Don't tell anyone about it but keep it with you always, along with the sporran. You never know when it will be needed. Now, Ian, you reach into the pouch."

Jacob passed the pouch to Ian who took it with a long face. "It's empty, there is nothing for me."

"What seems empty can often hold the most valuable of gifts," Mr. Woods interjected, and motioned for him to go ahead.

Ian opened the top of the pouch and stuck his fingers inside. They went into the pouch empty but came out gripping a two-toned piece of horn. Ian turned the modest treasure in his hands. It was the tip of a deer antler about two inches long. On the fat end was a half-moon-shaped hole and on top was a wedge cut out of the horn and exposing an air chamber within the core of the antler. Ian recognized it as a whistle and raised it to his lips.

MacGregor reached over and stopped Ian's hand before it reached his mouth. "No . . . Ian, you are right that this is a whistle, but it has come from a place and time we do not fully understand and has power we do not yet know. You will know when it is time to blow it, and at that time trust the thought that you recognize in your belly before you find it in your head. Until then, put that in your pocket and keep it with you always."

Ian stared at the piece of horn in his hand and then slipped it into his front pocket.

"Laddies, you see, the force behind the sporran has chosen you to find these gifts." MacGregor was speaking while he removed a pipe from his coat and puffed it to life with an ember from the fire he caught on the edge of one of Mrs. Woods' butter knives. "I knew you both were special, but was not sure what it all would mean. You both will need to go on about your lives now, but know that someday you will be called to serve the cause that has brought us all here together tonight. Now, why don't you two head up to your room and get a bit of sleep before morning. It won't be long until the sun has risen."

Jacob hesitated. He wanted to know more and blurted out, "But, you can't just leave us like this? We need to know more. What is going on?"

MacGregor took a pull from his pipe and then set it down on the table in front of him. His exhale of smoke formed a ring that hovered in the air between the two boys and then separated into two smaller rings. Each ring of smoke drifted over to the two boys, slipped around their heads and then dissipated.

"There are things in this world none of us understand, Mr. Boyd," MacGregor spoke calmly and deliberately. "The challenge is to believe in the magic, even when it cannot be understood or even seen, and to accept what you are given. You must now wait until the time comes for you to learn more of the secret. Now, to bed with you both and I will take my leave and hope fate has scheduled another meeting for us someday."

Reluctantly, the boys pushed their chairs away from the table and turned toward the door into the hallway. Jacob turned at the door and looked at Mr. Woods, "Thank you again, Mr. Woods, for saving our lives."

"No, Jacob, thanks to both of you for saving mine!"

"Saving yours?" Jacob countered in confusion.

"I did only what I had to do." Mr. Woods stood and walked toward the boys near the door. "It was only a matter of time before that man would have cut me in two as payment for fulfilling my station. But you two found a way to release the knight from his tomb, something I have been trying to figure out for years. You saved my life and maybe much more. If the stranger had gotten hold of a sporran, our world would have been changed in ways only our nightmares could predict."

Mr. Woods bent down and put his arms around the boys, a slight hint of a tear at in his misty eyes. "Now, off with you!"

The boys climbed the stairs to Jacob's room. Jacob paused as he passed the window on the stair. The storm had cleared and the black clouds were being drawn up into one ever shrinking point of deep darkness in the sky. The moon was out again and now falling behind the trees on the west side of the house and to the east a faint hint of an orange sun crept through the lowest branches of the trees between the window and St. Andrews Bay. As he turned to his room, Jacob wondered if his life would ever be the same and what he could possibly tell Will and Jenny when he got back from the rest of his spring break trip through Scotland.

TO EDINBURGH. . .

THE STONE
OF DESTINY

BOOK TWO OF
THE REMNANT CHRONICLES

"NIBLICK"

"**J**acob," his father said with a chuckle already growing in his voice, "take a look behind us!" Mr. Boyd was looking in the rear view mirror of the car as he spoke. Jacob turned around to see what looked like a biker Santa Claus approaching fast.

It was an older man on a motorcycle and not just any motorcycle but a very old bike painted black with a green stripe that looked like a dragon's tail running down the sides. On the left side of the bike was a green sidecar. As it approached and began to pass, Jacob got a good look at the rider. The wind was splitting his beard in two and sending half up on each side of his head where they stuck out like two Nike swooshes behind his helmet. He wore golden goggles and long leather gloves up to his elbows, with feathery strips of leather waving off them in the wind.

In the sidecar was an even more bizarre site. A pug dog was standing with its little black face defiantly staring into the wind as if it were surfing down the road. One of its front legs was even tucked up under itself as if the dog was showing off by balancing on one foot. On its smushed pug face, it wore a tiny set of goggles and on its back was a leather vest with two green dragons locked in battle. As the man and his dog passed, the pug turned and looked at the Boyds, its tongue hanging out of the side of its mouth.

Jacob was laughing so hard at the sight that he bent over holding his stomach. Mr. Boyd was similarly laughing, but was trying to keep his eyes on the road. When Jacob looked up again the motorcycle had cut in front of them and there on the license plate of the bike was the word "NIBLICK". *Niblick!* Jacob almost called out the name. *Oh, I hope THAT is not Professor*

Chadwick von Niblick, he thought to himself. Still laughing, his dad slapped Jacob on the leg and said "If there are more like him in Edinburgh, we might not stay long!" and laughed.

Jacob and his father had been in Scotland for several days during this spring break and now they were heading south from St. Andrews to Scotland's capital city of Edinburgh. There they would spend the last couple of days before flying home. Jacob had been through a lot since the magical sporran entered his life, now nearly two weeks before. Flashes of the wizardly man MacGregor, the dangerous encounter with the leathery stranger that nearly cost him his life, and thoughts of his new friend Ian who had a sporran of his own, kept creeping into his mind.

Watching the strange man on the motorcycle now, however, all he could think of was the note he had received from MacGregor when he checked his sporran earlier that morning. He kept his leathery pouch in his backpack but checked it often ever since he discovered its power. "Make contact with my friend Professor Chadwick von Niblick in Edinburgh. Give him my regards. Stay strong, lad." The note was signed with "Hammish," the first name of Professor Hammish MacGregor.

"Dad," Jacob said, without taking his eyes off that fluttering white beard in front of them. "Dad, is there something called a 'Niblick' or is that, maybe, just that guy's name?" Jacob was directing his father's attention to the back of the motorcycle.

"Well, my guess is that 'Niblick' is his name or nickname or something," his dad answered. *Just what I feared*, Jacob thought to himself.

"But," Mr. Boyd added, "I seem to remember a 'Niblick' is also some kind of old golf club. . . actually, I think it might be the name of a seven wood. They are rare and I remember only seeing one in my life. I think your Uncle Doug bought one at a flea market once and was showing it off."

"Oh. . ." Jacob responded. Then his dad offered, "But if we catch up with this guy, I dare you to ask him!" He laughed. Jacob didn't.

GHOST TOUR

As the Boyds continued their drive toward Edinburgh, the white bearded man on the motorcycle and his dog eventually got farther and farther ahead and then disappeared. Jacob wondered if he could possibly be the man he was to contact in Edinburgh. If it was him, he wouldn't be surprised, the way things had been going.

It was an unusually warm day for Scotland in springtime and the Boyds took a break from driving, not far before they would cross over the Firth of Forth into Edinburgh. The Boyd men pulled alongside the road, took out a pair of baseball gloves and headed off for a walk and a game of catch in the field.

Back in the car, Mr. Boyd started calling bed and breakfasts to see if any had a room for the night. Most had no vacancies or were not answering their phones, but he eventually talked to a Mrs. Pitkin who had one room available for one night at her home. He took down the directions and they headed down the road and over the bridge to Edinburgh.

Mrs. Pitkin was a sharp-faced woman and answered the door in an apron. She immediately announced "I am cooking dinner for myself and will not be cooking for you. I do not make coffee, and breakfast will be two danishes and tea served in the parlor. I will put them there by eight o'clock. You can eat when you want. Any questions?"

Both Boyds stood for a moment in silence. "Well," Mr. Boyd asked, "how about our room?" "Aye," the cranky woman said, "first room on your right, just down the hall. You can leave payment on the dresser in the morning." Mrs. Pitkin walked back to her kitchen, leaving Jacob and his father to walk into the house and find their own room.

"I am glad this is only for one night!" Mr. Boyd whispered to Jacob as they headed down the hall. Jacob nodded in agreement.

It wouldn't be long until Mrs. Pitkin's Siamese cat would appear who, interestingly enough, was also called Mrs. Pitkin. She came to check out the new visitors and seemed to want them to know they would find no friend in her, either. Jacob tried to pet the cat, but Mrs. Pitkin just hissed and waltzed her way out of the room and back down the hall.

Jacob plopped down onto the bed and began to think about the sporran and the new ring he had gotten out of the leather bag he and Ian discovered behind the tiny door in Feddinch House. And, of course, that vision of the strange man and his dog on the motorcycle kept creeping into his mind. Mr. Boyd lay down on the double bed next to Jacob and the two looked over their guidebook for a place to eat and something to do for the evening. They eventually settled upon a restaurant off High Street and a candlelight ghost walk through some of Edinburgh's most haunted alleys and homes.

The Boyds caught a cab into town. Dinner was relatively uneventful, but as they approached Tron Kirk (Jacob learned that Kirk means church in Scotland), where they were to meet with the group for the ghost tour, Jacob began to feel apprehensive. "You aren't getting scared, are you?" Mr. Boyd asked.

"Me? Of course not!" Jacob replied. If truth be told, Jacob was a little scared, but he also felt something different than fright. He had that feeling running up and down his arms and neck that he'd experienced when he first got close to Ian who was bound up in the magic with him. Jacob wondered if this meant that another sporran or someone who was connected to the magic might be nearby.

Tron Kirk is on what is called the "Royal Mile" in Edinburgh which runs from Holyrood Palace, where the Queen of England stays when she visits Scotland, to the great Edinburgh Castle at the other. Along the Royal Mile are many buildings that are hundreds of years old and alleyways down which mysterious basement shops can be found.

As the group assembled on the darkening street, a tension hung in the misty air. In the shadows of the ancient city, Jacob thought he could see things moving. A man with a hood hanging low over his face walked by, brushing up against Jacob's backpack. He kept going and disappeared into the church. Then a scream from somewhere behind the ancient church seemed to startle everyone. Jacob's dad put his arm around his son. Movement in the shadows and the alleys continued as if a gathering were taking place.

To Jacob's right, a flash of light caught his eye. He turned to see a man with a torch coming up the street. Walking at first, he started coming faster and faster toward them until he was in a dead run. Then, a shot rang out and the man collapsed on the street just a few feet away from Jacob and his father. The burning torch bounced and rolled away from his body.

Everyone jumped back and many of the women on the street screamed. Jacob was startled and gasped loudly. The terrible memory of his confrontation with the tall leathery stranger in the kitchen of Feddinch House came rushing over him like a smothering damp blanket.

Two men ran over to aid the fallen man. Then another man's laughter was heard on the stairs of the church behind them. "Ha. . . Ha. . . Ha. . .Ha. . . Welcome to the Edinburgh Ghost Tour!" the man announced. "Please, give a hand to our actors . . ." People emerged from the shadows and the fallen man hopped to his feet, as the crowd applauded.

Jacob's dad laughed and made a fake swipe across Jacob's forehead as if he were wiping the sweat from his brow. Jacob was less amused. After what he had been through, there was no question left in his mind that mysterious forces walked the Earth and here in Scotland they seemed a bit too close for comfort and too brutal as well.

The tour led the group through a graveyard, through back alleys and tiny basement haunts, and through ancient vaults beneath the city. They saw where witches had been burned at the stake and every now and again someone would jump out of the shadows in old clothes and white make-up to try to scare them. Most of the time, they succeeded quite nicely!

When it was all over and the Boyds were back in their room, Jacob was very pleased there was only one bed and he and his dad would be sharing it. He had no interest in being alone after that tour! With Mrs. Pitkin the cat pacing back and forth like a sentry outside their door, the Boyd men drifted off to sleep.

Cowgate Street

Jacob woke the next morning to the sounds of his father already up and in the shower. Jacob lay in bed thinking about Professor von Niblick and how he would have to find a way to locate him and make contact, as Professor MacGregor's note insisted he do. Because MacGregor had come to his rescue at Feddinch House, Jacob figured he was a friend and should be trusted. Now he wondered about what would come next. Part of him hoped he would be asked to give back the sporran and it would be done. Another part of him, though, hoped this would be but the beginning of a more grand adventure still. Jacob lay and puzzled for a time on what to do. Finally it hit him. . . *of course! I'll look Niblick up in a phone book!*

Jacob pulled a pair of pants on over his pajama bottoms and headed out in Mrs. Pitkin's house in search of a phone book. Opening the door, he saw that Mrs. Pitkin the cat was still at her post watching their door. "Hello, cat," Jacob said as he bent over to give Mrs. Pitkin a pat on her head. The hair on Mrs. Pitkin's back rose as she hissed at him and then walked off.

In the parlor, where the promised danishes were waiting, he found a phone book on the bottom shelf of a very small wooden table that had a phone resting on its top. Picking up the book, Jacob made himself at home on a couch by the window and opened to the N's. There it was, on page 324: Professor Chadwick von Niblick, 333 Cowgate Street, Edinburgh. Jacob scribbled the address down on a notepad sitting by the phone and took a danish for his father and himself.

Jacob arrived in their room to find his dad out of the shower and almost dressed. "Good morning, son," his dad said as he peeked out of the bathroom.

"Morning Dad, got a danish for you."

"Thanks, Jake. I am glad you went out there. I didn't want to run into that old Mrs. Pitkin this morning!"

"Like I was on a covert mission, Dad, I snuck in and snuck out and she didn't even know I was there!" Jacob insisted.

Mr. Boyd laughed in reply and added, "Well, you get a shower now and get dressed and I will go see if I can find us a room for the next few nights."

As Jacob grabbed his clothes and headed into the bathroom, he called back, "Dad, the phone book is in the parlor just to the left of the door as you go in."

"Thanks," Mr. Boyd replied, and then paused for a moment heading out the door of the room and wondered how Jacob knew where the phone book was or that he was looking for one right then. "You are reminding me more of Mr. Woods with his psychic powers everyday, boy!"

By the time Jacob emerged dried and dressed, Mr. Boyd had finished his second cup of tea and had a room lined up for the night. The two packed and talked about what they would do once they dropped off their bags at their new place of lodging, then prepared to leave.

The air outside was clean and clear but a bit colder than it had been the last few days. Mr. Boyd went first down the few steps onto the sidewalk in front of Mrs. Pitkin's house. Jacob followed.

"Dad, where did you find a place to stay?" Jacob asked as he stepped onto the first step down toward the sidewalk.

"Oh, someplace I found in the phone book. I think it's called Niblick House and is on Cowgate Street."

Recognizing the name and address, a startled Jacob dropped his bags and sent them bouncing down the steps and into the back of his father's legs.

"What are you doing, Jake?" Mr. Boyd was a bit annoyed.

"Sorry Dad, nothing, just lost my grip, I guess."

As Mr. Boyd helped Jacob pick up his bags and they walked to the car, Jacob said, "You know, Dad, maybe we could find a Holiday Inn or something cheap like that. You must be spending a lot of money on these fancy little bed and breakfasts, you know!"

"Nonsense. Don't worry. I am sure the next place will not have a crazy woman who names her crazy cat after herself!" Mr. Boyd replied.

No, Jacob thought to himself, *I am sure of that, and I am also equally sure that what it will have is a crazy old man with a crazy pug dog who wears leather vests and rides around on a motorcycle!* As he looked back at Mrs. Pitkin in the window, for the first time since getting to Scotland, he thought maybe it was time to go home!

NIBLICK HOUSE

As he traveled the few miles to Cowgate Street, Jacob chewed on his nails and fiddled nervously with his backpack straps.

"What's wrong, Jake?" his dad finally asked.

Jacob ignored the question at first, but by the time his dad repeated it and smacked him on the knee for emphasis, Jacob had decided he had to tell him something. They were, after all, heading right into the arms of another strange man tied up in some way with the sporran.

"Dad," Jacob began to stammer, "it's just that, well . . . it's just that you have picked a bed and breakfast for us that is named Niblick House."

"Yes, so?"

"Well, if you remember from our drive from St. Andrews, we passed that very strange man named Niblick on the motorcycle."

"Oh, yes, you're right." His dad seemed to know where he was going with this. "Won't it be a blast to get to know him and his road surfing dog?"

Jacob's mouth dropped open. His father was just not getting it at all!

Cowgate Street was nothing but a tiny alleyway just off the Royal Mile and Mr. Boyd had to park the car several blocks away. Jacob was amazed by this part of Edinburgh. It was in the middle of such a large city, but nothing seemed even remotely modern in the buildings or streets. As they turned onto Cowgate Street, Jacob could feel his anxiety growing again. Nothing but a small metal plaque beside the door identified 333 Cowgate Street as Niblick House. Beneath the name was the year 1607. Mr. Boyd pointed to the date and whispered "Pretty cool staying in a 300-year-old house, huh?"

In the middle of the green wooden door was a large door knocker. It was made in the shape of a dragon's head, grasping a brass ring in its teeth. Mr.

Boyd lifted the ring and let it fall hard against the striker plate three times.

Jacob stood nervously trying to peek through the window into the house. A moment later and the door to Niblick House slowly began to open. The first things the Boyds saw inside the house were two big brown eyes about a foot off the ground starring at them. As the door opened further, they noticed it was the little pug dog they had seen the day before on von Niblick's motorcycle.

The dog took two quick steps out the door and then leapt off the top steps, crashing into Jacob's chest and causing him to fall back into the alley. Before Jacob knew what happened, the little dog was on top of him and licking his face wildly. "Get off me! Get off me!" Jacob kept ordering the dog, as Mr. Boyd laughed and introduced himself to the amply plump woman who answered the door.

"Pleasure to meet ya," said the older woman who introduced herself as Gladys Lafoon, housekeeper for Niblick House. "And don't worry about him," she said pointing to the dog who had now retreated back into the house. "His name is Mr. Nibbles and he won't harm ya."

Mrs. Lafoon welcomed the Boyd men into the house and Jacob instantly began playing with Mr. Nibbles in the hallway just inside the door. "Well, they seem to have hit it off," Mr. Boyd said to Mrs. Lafoon before she began to go over the rules of the house.

After talking about not smoking, making your own bed, and leaving used towels on the floor to be picked up, she came to what she said was the most important rule of all. Jacob stopped playing with the dog as he heard the name slip from her mouth.

"The most important rule of all," Mrs. Lafoon said, "is that Professor von Niblick, who is a most important scholar of ancient manuscripts and things, must never be disturbed when he is at work in his study. That door," she said pointing to the door immediately behind Jacob and to the right of the stairs, "is strictly off limits. It is the Professor's study where he does most of his thinking and studying and such."

Jacob would spend time staring at that door later, but right now Mrs. Lafoon was leading a tour around the rest of the house. There was a parlor to the left as one entered the front door, a staircase right in front of that door, and bedrooms at the top of the stair.

Mrs. Lafoon showed Jacob and his dad to their room and they settled in. By this time it was mid-morning and they had not even been out to explore Edinburgh yet. "Jake, we better get out there and buy you a kilt, you know!" Jacob's dad teased him. "No way! I am not wearing one of those man-dresses!"

"Well, it would go well with that *purse* I bought you," his dad replied.

"It's a sporran, Dad. Remember? And it's very manly!"

"By the way, I haven't seen you with that thing in awhile. Where is it?" Before waiting for an answer to that question, he added, "You haven't lost it, have you?" For a moment, Jacob let himself wish he had lost it, but didn't offer that.

"It's in my backpack, Dad, as always," Jacob answered.

The Boyd men left Niblick House just before noon and headed up to the Royal Mile. They walked directly to the old church where they had met the ghost tour the previous evening. Again today, Jacob felt strange as they approached Tron Kirk. Ascending the few steps into the old church, Jacob was shocked by what he saw. The church was no longer really a church but felt more like walking into a cave. The place was surprisingly dark and, though there were pamphlets for tourists and things to buy, there was also a huge chunk of the floor that had been removed to show the ancient streets that once existed below the church, which was itself built in the 17th century.

After looking around, the two walked out of the old church and down the steps onto the street. There a young woman approached them and pushed a flier into Mr. Boyd's hands with a "The lad will love this," and off she went down the street, approaching others who looked likely to be tourists.

The handbill was for a brass rubbing shop. Mr. Boyd handed it to Jacob and asked him what he thought. Jacob looked at the pamphlet and read that the shop was a place where people could do rubbings of old tombstones, etchings of knights and swords, Celtic crosses, and all things very old. "Just what my room needs, Dad!"

The two went off to call and check in with Mrs. Boyd back home and to get some lunch before heading to the brass rubbing shop. They would then go shopping for gifts for Jacob's mom and other members of the family.

TOMB RUBBING

After calling Jacob's mother and having some lunch, the Boyd men set off again down the Royal Mile to find the brass rubbing shop where Jacob would make something to hang in his room. Every shop seemed filled with stuff Jacob loved: swords, shields, fancy pewter cups, suits of armor. He was even coming to love all the plaid Scottish things that hung in every window. He had never thought of himself as a "Scot" before, but that seemed to be creeping upon him as well. Secretly, he was even starting to want a kilt, but that was not something he was ready to admit to just yet.

In those shops along the Royal Mile, Jacob also noticed things connected to the sporran and the dreams he had been having for the last week. There was the name MacGregor on almost everything imaginable from stickers to coffee mugs. And, one particular plaque he noticed had the name MacGregor written on the collar of a lion's head he remembered from a dream. It was an angry lion with its mouth open and a tongue like a flame. A crown sat atop his head and words surrounded it in a language Jacob could not understand.

There were crests to buy with the three lions lying down that he remembered from another dream, and unicorns. . . but very manly unicorns, as if they were ready for a fight, just like the one on the side of the ring he had found in Feddinch House. Jacob loved it all and was even warming up to the sound of bagpipes, which filled the air, from men and women playing along the streets in exchange for tips.

Jacob bought his mother a coffee mug with the name Boyd on it. His dad bought his wife a bracelet with a sapphire in the middle surrounded by Celtic designs like snakes wrapped around the band. They also picked out a kilt for her in a checkered pattern called the "Royal Stewart" tartan, and bought lots of postcards.

Arriving at the brass rubbing shop, they were met at the door by the nice young lady who had given them a handbill that morning. "Welcome, I thought you'd be along," she said, as she waved them into the shop.

The shop was filled with plaques of all shapes and sizes. There were small ones the size of a piece of paper and ones more than six feet tall with the outlines of a knight or Scottish warrior on them. A few people were working at tables scattered around the shop.

"You just pick out one of these brass plates," the lady said, "and I will get you all set up to do a rubbing." Mr. Boyd quickly picked out a Celtic cross and thistle bush to rub as a gift for Mrs. Boyd. Jacob, however, was more particular. Everything seemed interesting to him, from the swords and Celtic symbols to the coats of arms and helmets. But one caught his attention more than any other.

This brass plate was huge. It must have been two feet taller than Jacob and was of a fierce looking knight with shield in front of him and a sword in one hand. Mr. Boyd noticed Jacob keep coming back to it and staring. "Is that the one you want," Jacob's dad finally asked him.

"Well, sort of, I guess, but, it's too big and too much money to rub," Jacob replied without turning his eyes away from the eyes of the knight.

"Look, you might never be back to Scotland again so you better do it now. And imagine how cool he will look hanging on your wall," his dad encouraged him.

"Well, if you insist!" Jacob said eagerly, and turned to tell the lady. The shop girl was way ahead of him, however, and had already asked a red-haired young man from the storeroom to come out and carry the huge slab over to a table where Jacob could work on it.

The lady taped black paper over the brass plates and demonstrated how to rub the wax sticks (which were like fat wrapper-less crayons) over the carvings in the plates. As she did so, the image from the plate began to emerge on the black paper. She gave each of them several colors to work with and then went back to help other customers.

They rubbed the forms slowly and carefully, so as not to rip the paper. Jacob was frustrated at first at how slow he had to rub, but once the face of the knight began to emerge, Jacob's enthusiasm picked up again and he worked methodically.

Mr. Boyd's thistle and cross didn't come out quite as nicely as he had hoped and the lady from behind the counter helped him improve it with some careful applications of color and an eraser to remove his mistakes. As she passed Jacob, she glanced at his rubbing. He was just starting to rub the shield when she said, "You know, that rubbing you are doing is from an old tomb that was unearthed beneath Tron Kirk. No one knows who it might have been or how long ago he died."

Jacob smiled over at his father and flashed a "thumbs up" sign. His friends from home, Jenny and Will, would love this—a mysterious dead guy's likeness hanging on his wall! "Very cool," his dad said to him, before turning back to continue cleaning up his own rubbing.

As Jacob worked his way rubbing out the man's body, odd things began to happen. First, a word appeared on the shield. It wasn't in English and so he couldn't read it. *Hmmmm*, he thought, *I hadn't noticed that on the brass plate.* Then a dragon appeared peering around the man's right leg. Then, as he continued to rub the wax stick over the plate, other things began to appear that he hadn't remembered being on the image.

Jacob lifted the black paper that was quickly becoming a picture of a knight and looked at the brass plate beneath. He was right. Those things weren't there at all. *Where are they coming from?* He retaped the black sheet to the plate and continued to rub.

More symbols that looked like they might be words appeared. Then a crown and scepter appeared on the man's shield and, lying next to him, a stag came into view. The stag was lying on a large square stone. Then, around the man's waist he noticed a sporran, one that looked eerily like his own. On the man's right hand which grasped his sword, he noticed what looked like a large ring with little rays seeming to emanate out of it.

His dad had finished his own much smaller rubbing long before Jacob would finish his, and he took a walk down the street.

By the time Jacob was done, the shop was filled with tourists and the lady was too busy to check his rubbing very carefully. She just rolled it up and put it into a tube for him. He hurried out of the store, grateful that she had not noticed all those mysterious images that had appeared on his sheet.

Mogul Sword

J acob and his father spent the rest of the day shopping and touring
around Edinburgh. Jacob particularly enjoyed getting wet during the
brief afternoon rain shower when the only seats on the bus were on the
roof of the red double-decker touring bus.

Finally, coming home that night after dark, they were very tired. They
carried their packages up the stairs to their room and Mr. Boyd went straight
to bed. He hadn't seemed to be himself all day and complained occasionally
about being very tired and needing a rest.

Though he was tired as well, Jacob was not about to go to bed, and asked
if he could spend some time reading in Niblick House's parlor.

Coming down the stairs toward the study with a book about Scottish
castles in his right hand, Jacob glanced to his left at the door to von Niblick's
study. Even before Mrs. Lafoon told him the room was strictly off-limits and
no one was to disturb the Professor, Jacob had wondered what was in that
room and wanted nothing more than to get a peek inside. Knowing it was a
forbidden place made him want to get in there even more.

A slight movement at the bottom of the door caught his eye. There were
small tendrils of smoke slipping out through the crack of the door, curling
in on themselves, and then disappearing. The aroma was of a pleasant,
nutty-vanilla that Jacob recognized as pipe tobacco. The smell sent his mind
immediately back to Feddinch House and the night MacGregor lit his pipe
after the encounter that nearly cost him his life.

For a moment he stopped and thought of going back to the safety of
his bedroom. *No. MacGregor wanted me to meet von Niblick. I suppose it's
inevitable and better now than later.*

He turned and walked into the parlor where he found a tray on the coffee table containing a small plate of cookies and a small pot of steaming hot chocolate with just one cup. It was as if Mrs. Lafoon was expecting him at just that moment to come down to the parlor alone. He poured himself a cup of the hot chocolate and sat back on the couch to look around the room.

The shelves were full of old books, some in languages he did not recognize. In various corners of the shelves were dragons of all sorts and in all poses. Some were lying sleeping, others looked menacingly down from their perch. Carved into the mantel of the fireplace were two lions looking inward with their tongues flickering out of their mouths like flames. They were standing on their back legs with their front paws up, as if ready to fight one another. Above the fireplace was a round shield and above it was a bronze helmet with chains hanging from around its edge. In four corners around the shield and helmet were two old flint-lock pistols and two daggers with curved blades. Below them all was an ivory-handled sword in a well-worn sheath that looked like it was coming apart at the seams.

The room sparked his imagination and he lost himself in the haze of a vision of the sword hacking at one dragon or another from the bookshelves when Mr. Nibbles bounded in and up on the couch next to his new friend. The boy shared a cookie with the fat little pug dog and Mr. Nibbles laid his head to rest on his lap. The tip of his tongue hanging from the corner of his mouth, soon the dog began drooling slightly on Jacob's leg.

Jacob had always wanted a dog of his own, but never got one. It was a moment like this that he had dreamt of so many times before. *Just a boy and his dog, that is how things were meant to be,* he thought. Jacob laid his head back on the top of the couch and stared out into the hallway at the faint curls of smoke slipping from behind von Niblick's door. His eyes soon grew heavy and shut as his imagination took over his sleep.

Presently, he dreamed of a man holding a dragon in his hand. Smoke billowed from the beast and curled around the giant's leg. He ran to the fireplace in his dream and reached for the sword. Its ivory handle fit his palm perfectly as the helmet and shield fell upon him; both in their proper place. He took a defensive stand against the enemy when the giant spoke.

Jacob's head shot forward and Mr. Nibbles jumped from his lap. His heart was racing and he was disoriented as he noticed the figure of a man standing in the doorway. Jacob jumped to his feet. In the doorway stood a man with a long white beard, small reading glasses hanging precariously on the tip of his nose, and in his right hand was a smoldering pipe that must have been a foot long. *Von Niblick!* Jacob realized it could be no one other.

"Sorry to startle you, laddie," said von Niblick in a thick Scottish brogue. "I was wondering when you might be coming in."

Still feeling disoriented from being shocked out of his dream, all Jacob could muster was, "Sir?"

"I was wondering if you were just going to sit there all night with my dog, wanting to come for a visit, but without the nerve to knock."

After having now spent time with people in Scotland, Jacob no longer wondered about others seeming to be able to read his mind. Instead, he said, "Well, sir, its just that, . . . well, sir, its just that Mrs. Lafoon said we were never to disturb you in your study, sir."

"Did she now? Well, then, sounds like she is doing her job, but I have a feeling I might like being disturbed by you tonight. Why don't you come tell me a story?"

With those words, von Niblick turned and went into his study with Mr. Nibbles following closely at his heels. Jacob paused and watched the two disappear into the room across the hall.

"Quite a sword, isn't it? It's from the Mogul Empire and has seen much business. "Now, come along," von Niblick called back through the open study door.

Jacob stood, exchanging glances from the sword to the study door and back.

"Well, what are you waiting for?" von Niblick called through the remnants of grey smoke dissolving into the air in the hallway.

Jacob took a deep breath and started out of the parlor when a figure behind the door caught his eye. He pulled the door back and there, on the wall, was a framed rubbing just like the one he had done earlier that day at the brass rubbing shop. It was of the same tomb he had done, only this one was basic, without the dragon and other symbols that mysteriously had appeared in his rubbing but were clearly not on the brass plate at all.

I am beginning to think there are no real coincidences in the world, Jacob said to himself. Jacob pushed the door back against the wall of the parlor and, after a few very slow steps through the hall, peeked cautiously into the Professor's study.

ORDER OF THE SPORRAI

V on Niblick's study was a cluttered mess. There were papers and trinkets and books scattered everywhere. Just inside the door was a tall desk of dark black wood. Shelves came up from the desk's surface and slots in the shelving contained rolled papers like scrolls. The desktop was covered with papers and books and various small items. Von Niblick sat in a chair in front of that desk and motioned Jacob in to sit on a tattered leather chair by the window on the opposite side of the room.

"Well, come on now, we don't have all night!" von Niblick said as he again motioned to the chair.

Once Jacob entered the room and sat down, Mr. Nibbles got up and shut the door, pushing it closed with his pudgy nose. The dog then climbed on Jacob's lap as if to help him relax and feel more at home. The truth be told, Jacob had seldom felt so uncomfortable in his life.

"If this old smoke is too much for you in here, just open the window behind you, son. I'll put out the pipe now," the Professor told the boy. Jacob nodded, but said nothing.

"Now, we don't have much time, Jacob. Let's get at it, shall we?"

Jacob again nodded his head, but said nothing.

"Since you are not ready to tell me a story, let me tell you one," said the Professor.

Von Niblick was resting his forearms on his knees and leaning toward Jacob when he began to speak. His powerful grey eyes, starting at the floor in front of Jacob, moved slowly up to meet the boy's with a powerful glare.

"This story is about a boy that loved his father very much, but who had become separated from him. A different kind of man entered this boy's life and odd things began to happen. Things appeared; other things disappeared. Eventually he was reunited with his father and part of the mystery was revealed to him."

Jacob began to squirm as he heard his own story being retold by this perfect stranger.

"Then the boy was tested. Would he act selfishly, as most little boys do, or would he be noble and brave? The boy was on the Isle of Skye . . ."

"No," Jacob felt himself interrupt von Niblick, "I was in St. Andrews."

"This story is not about you, Jacob, it is about me."

Jacob's cheeks grew warm as he became ashamed for presuming the story was his. He was more confused than ever. *But, that is my story,* he insisted to himself. He did not add any more words to his mistake but sat back and listened.

Von Niblick sat back in his squeaking chair, too, and ran one hand through his beard as if he were thinking what to say next.

"You see, Jacob, you are not the first to have the magic. The sporrans have existed long before our time and will continue long after we are gone. They are part of the permanent things of the world, or, at least they are as permanent as things get in this world of ours."

Jacob could feel his unease start to turn into excitement at the realization he was about to learn more about the sporran and what was going on in his life.

"I was once a Bearer of a sporran, just as you are now. I was once in need of its magic and it needed me."

Jacob nodded as a knock came at the door. It was Mrs. Lafoon bearing more cookies, hot chocolate for Jacob, and hot tea for the Professor. "I bet it will be a late night for you two, so I thought you would appreciate a little something to keep you awake," Mrs. Lafoon said. She placed the tray on an old box made of brown leather with metal adornments and a Celtic cross on its lid. The box made a fine, albeit low, table for the snack.

"Thank you, Mrs. Lafoon," von Niblick said, as the housekeeper turned toward the door.

"Yes, thank you, ma'am," Jacob barely managed to say before the door shut again.

Von Niblick poured them both a cup, gave Mr. Nibbles a cookie in the shape of a dragon's tooth, and then began to unwind a story that kept Jacob spellbound.

He told Jacob of how there are a number of sporrans in the world, not all of which look quite like the traditional Scottish purse, but all of which hold great powers. They have been around since we began to remember and can be traced into the ancient Celtic people of northern Europe, Britain, and Ireland.

The Professor told Jacob of some of the legends of the place the sporrans had played in history. He walked him through many battles, love stories, and the rise and fall of numerous empires.

He told Jacob of his life's great ambition. He had spent his lifetime piecing together bits and pieces of the story of the origin of the sporrans that he had found in manuscripts, scrolls, shards of pottery, and on tombs all over the lands once held by the Celts. Coming into contact with the sporran as a boy, he grew up to become the world's most renowned authority on Celtic history and mythology.

Pointing to a stack of papers behind him on his desk, he explained that he had spent decades putting the pieces of the puzzle together and was completing the first translation of *The Book of Logres*—the book that would for the first time in nearly a thousand years tell the complete story of how a young man named Isildane brought the magic hide of a sacred stag into our world and from that skin the sporrans were cut. He was only a few clues away from getting it done and completing his masterwork. When complete, he said he was not sure what he would do with it. He did offer that he was sure the world was not ready to believe in magic again, and that in any case, the sporrans must always be kept out of the hands of evil people and so the truth must not be published as such.

None of the stories von Niblick told that night were as important, however, as his explanation of what was happening to Jacob and of the role Jacob might be called to play.

Von Niblick told Jacob that the sporrans come and go in time as they are needed. Most of the people that inherit them are completely oblivious about their power or that they are even impacting them. Most, even when miraculous things happen in their lives, just chalk it up to fate or good luck. In reality, often a sporran came into their lives but went undetected. To some, however, who are needed and who are worthy of playing a bigger role, more is revealed. He told Jacob that he was one of those people called to play a bigger role.

The realization that his story was not yet complete thrilled Jacob, but also scared him quite profoundly.

Jacob learned that he was a "Bearer" and that von Niblick and Hammish MacGregor were "Keepers" in an order called "The Sporrai." Bearers, like Jacob, were called upon to carry a sporran for a time and then to give it up. They were called because they had a need for the magic of the sporran and then proved worthy of keeping it for awhile and giving something back.

The Keepers were former Bearers who now serve as a type of wizard class to protect the secrets of the Sporrai and watch over the sporrans and the Bearers.

"Why haven't I heard of all this before?" Jacob asked, clearly showing he didn't fully buy all this just yet.

"You have, my boy," von Niblick responded, with a knowing smile creeping across his face. "The stories have been told throughout human history. The details have just been changed a bit to help keep the secrets."

Jacob's expression didn't change. He wanted to hear more.

"Heard of King Arthur, Jacob?"

"Of course," Jacob answered with a slight nod of his head.

"Well, King Arthur was a Bearer of a sacred sporran and his wizard named Merlin was a Keeper. Together they battled great forces of evil in their time and encouraged the light of the world to shine a bit brighter, just as we are called today to fight the forces of evil in our own, and to light a candle of goodness in our corner of the world. From the wizards of old tales to the ancient Celtic priests called the druids, to heroes like Arthur and William Wallace, we are bound up in an ancient story, Jacob, that will continue until the forces of light or the forces of darkness finally prevail forever."

Jacob felt a shot of electricity pulse through the nerves of his chest and right arm, causing him to shiver.

"You have felt that power before, haven't you?" von Niblick asked, again leaning closer to Jacob and looking deeply into his eyes.

"Yes. A few times," Jacob answered.

Von Niblick leaned back in his chair and stroked his beard. "Some of us call that feeling 'the quickening.' You will feel it when in the presence of another member of the Sporrai or near something bound up with the magic of the sporrans."

In response to an unasked question hanging in Jacob's eyes, the Professor told him no one could be sure yet if he was meant to someday be a Keeper or what role he might be called to play.

"For now, my boy, let us let this tale lie and you tell me about what my friend MacGregor sent with you." Von Niblick poured them both another cup and sat back to listen.

ISILDANE'S RING

J acob pulled from his pocket the golden ring that he had received from the pouch found in the wall of Feddinch House's kitchen and told the Professor of his close encounter with the evil leathery stranger. The gold had become progressively more bright as Jacob had fiddled with it in his pocket over the past few days. He handed it to Professor von Niblick without saying a word, but watching the older man's expression intently.

A thin smile crept out from behind von Niblick's thick white beard as he examined the small treasure. He turned to his desk and lit a candle, the light of which he used to more closely examine the images on the ring itself. Jacob could hear murmuring sounds from the Professor hunched close over the flame but could not make out what he was saying. He worried that if the older man got any closer to the candle's flame, his beard would surely catch fire.

Von Niblick turned, his glasses even more ready to fall off the tip of his nose. Jacob marveled at what force must be in play to keep them there balancing right on the tip of an otherwise tipless nose.

"My boy," the Professor said, his tone growing in excitement, "my friend Hammish must trust you very much to let you leave alone with this treasure. You have been given a key to powers even I cannot predict."

Jacob had taken a cookie from the tray but felt it crumble through his fingers and onto the floor in small bits. Without knowing what he was doing, he had tensed up and squashed the cookie in reaction to the Professor's words. "Oh, sorry, sir," Jacob stammered as he took notice of the last falling crumbs. Before he could even get the apology out, however, Mr. Nibbles was on the floor cleaning it up as thoroughly as any vacuum.

"You see," von Niblick began again, ignoring the cookie and Jacob's apology, "there is a legend of the keyring that will unlock an important chamber, but we don't know where that chamber may be or what kind of jewel or stone may have been in the ring itself." Von Niblick was pointing to the hole in the ring where a stone once sat and completed it. "It is even said that the ring empowers the wearer to reach into other realms of being."

We think a Keeper must have dismantled it many centuries ago to keep it from falling into the wrong hands, but we must be coming to a time when it will again be needed since it has resurfaced, as have other clues as well."

Jacob's mind was wandering, as images of great battles and ancient riches snuck through his head.

"So, did Hammish send anything else with you?" von Niblick asked.

"No sir, just the sporran and the ring," Jacob answered.

"Well, then, I guess there is nothing further for us to do tonight. Lets call it a night, shall we?" The Professor was standing and heading to open the door when he added, "And please remember that your father cannot know about this. No one outside the Sporrai can know. Do you understand?"

"Aaahhhh, yes, sir," Jacob stammered, as he stepped over a sleeping Mr. Nibbles on his way to the door.

"Oh," Jacob turned back to the Professor as he stepped through the door, "and I should tell you that I like that brass rubbing of yours in the parlor. I did one just like it today, only weird things showed up on it."

Von Niblick turned instantly back toward Jacob and grabbed his arm a bit too forcefully to be comfortable for the boy. "What do you mean weird things showed up on it?"

"Well," Jacob answered as he backed out of von Niblick's grip, "a dragon, a ring, a stag, strange writing . . ."

The Professor cut him off and barked at him to go retrieve the rubbing without delay. The older man's demeanor had changed drastically. Jacob could see a mix of fire and excitement in von Niblick's eyes that startled him and caused his feet to take the stairs two at a time until he reached his room and, without waking his dad or pausing to think about running away, he retrieved the tube containing the rubbing and hurried down the stairs.

Revealed Secrets

Von Niblick was calmer now, and apologized to Jacob for his reaction. "It's just that I have been trying to crack the code of that tomb for five years and . . . ." Von Niblick grabbed the tube and retreated into his study where he dropped hard into his desk chair. Relighting the candle, he turned the dim electric lights off that had illuminated the room.

Von Niblick unrolled the long length of black rubbing paper he had been handed by Jacob. "Hold this end down, lad," he said with a growing excitement in his voice. While Jacob held the top down on his desk to keep it from curling back up, von Niblick put a book on the other to hold the bottom down and began slowly passing the candle over its surface.

Jacob stood and watched the Professor as he excitedly studied the rubbing. "Yes. . . yes. . . hmm. . . of course. . . I knew it . . . ." Von Niblick was talking to himself and became almost oblivious to the boy standing there until Jacob finally spoke.

"Professor, what is it?" Jacob asked.

"Laddie, you may well have just provided the key to unraveling one of the most important and dangerous mysteries on Earth," von Niblick said without even looking up from the paper. "How did you do it? I mean, how did you get those images to appear?"

"I just rubbed it, I don't know. . ."

"Well, never mind about that. If it's one thing you need to know as a member of the Sporrai, it's that unexplainable things happen and are meant to happen. It can be no accident that the tomb rubbing gave up its secrets to you or that you have now brought it to me."

Jacob just stood staring at him, watching the Professor pass the candle back and forth across the paper, pausing here or there for awhile, mumbling things Jacob couldn't understand, then moving on.

"Son," von Niblick finally broke the silence, "it is getting late. . . perhaps you might want to go to bed or at least go sit down over there while I work this out."

Jacob was getting very tired again and, though his head was still swimming with the gravity of what he had learned so far, he decided not to go to bed but to go sit for awhile and watch von Niblick work.

Jacob slid easily into the tattered leather chair by the window and Mr. Nibbles was soon on his lap. Professor von Niblick poured himself another cup of tea and re-lit his pipe. Jacob watched the tendrils of smoke dance hypnotically above the Professor's head as the nutty-vanilla smell of the tobacco reached his nose. His eyelids began to droop, his head slipped back onto the chair, and he soon joined Mr. Nibbles in the land of quiet dreams.

Jacob awoke the next morning to find Mr. Nibbles gone and a blanket lying across his lap. Sunlight had begun to creep in through the window behind him and, through cloudy morning eyes, he noticed he was alone in the study.

He got up and walked out into the hallway where he heard sounds coming from the kitchen behind the stair. Opening the door, Jacob saw two men sitting at the table. The sight made his heart sink. He wished he could sneak off, but there was nowhere to go. He pushed open the door and stepped into the room.

"Well, good morning, sleepy head!" Mr. Boyd greeted his son. "The good professor here has been telling me all about your night together."

Holy cow! What did he tell him? Jacob stood confused and worried. This is exactly what Jacob had been afraid of. He had already felt terribly guilty for not telling his dad what was happening and now it would be that much worse if von Niblick spilled the beans and Jacob's dad thought him a liar.

Jacob couldn't muster an answer. He stood inside the door, glancing quickly from von Niblick to his father and from his father to von Niblick.

"Yes," Jacob's dad started again, "and he told me all about your plans and I think they are just terrific!"

Terrific? It's terrific that your son is part of some vast international conspiracy spanning centuries and involving forces of good and evil? Terrific that this man's son seemed to have developed powers to channel invisible symbols from dead men's tombs? What kind of father was this? Jacob felt confused and slightly dizzy.

"Here, laddie, sit down and have some breakfast," Gladys Lafoon pulled a chair from the table and helped Jacob to it.

"Yes, my boy," von Niblick began with a slight wink in his left eye, "I told your father all about your growing interest in my work on ancient Scottish texts and your interest in fly fishing for salmon." Jacob's eyes continued to dart from his father's eyes to von Niblick's and back and he didn't even notice Mrs. Lafoon putting a blueberry scone on the plate in front of him. *What is he talking about?* Jacob wondered.

"Tell Mrs. Lafoon thank you, Jacob!" his dad said forcefully.

"Oh, yes, ahhhh. . . thank you . . ." Jacob mustered without even bothering to look down at his plate or taking note of why he was thanking her.

"And we were just making final details for that trip to the river that you and I discussed last night." Von Niblick was now looking more intently into Jacob's eyes with both fuzzy eyebrows seeming to hover inches higher above his eyes than nature intended them. Then, the left eye seemed to close slightly with a wink.

I think he is telling me to go along with him, but what on earth is he talking about? Jacob was trying to make sense of it all.

"I have the car loaded up with our gear and as soon as you finish your breakfast and Gladys makes us some lunches, we will be off to the river," said von Niblick as he put his fork down for the last time and wiped away a bit of jam that had caught itself in his beard.

Jacob's father had a big smile on his face now and was clearly getting anxious to get to the river. "Well, eat up Jake, the fish are awaitin'!" his dad urged him.

Confusion swirling in his head, Jacob looked down at his scone and began to slowly spread it with jam as he attempted to make sense of what was happening around him.

LIA FAIL

Soon after arriving at the river, and after some basic lessons in fly fishing from von Niblick, the three hiked upstream to find suitable fishing holes. Von Niblick first placed Mr. Boyd in a spot he called "sweeter than the mead of the gods!" Then von Niblick took Jacob around the bend in the river where he would teach his apprentice the intricacies of luring a salmon to his hook.

Jacob found himself wishing the sporran stuff would just disappear. He loved fishing but could barely enjoy it today with the weight of all he had learned hovering over him and constantly wondering if von Niblick had something more in mind for this trip than just fishing.

"So," Jacob finally said, "what did you make of my rubbing last night?"

"Patience, laddie, patience, fishing always comes first," von Niblick said as he tied a fly to his own line to match the one he already had attached to Jacob's. "You Americans are always in such a rush!"

It was not long, however, before von Niblick asked Jacob to sit with him on a large stone in the middle of the river.

"Jacob," the Professor began as he dipped his right hand into the cold rushing water around him, "I spent last night decoding the rubbing of yours and I am afraid I have both great *and* terrible news."

Jacob laid down his pole next to his left leg, assuming his fishing trip was now over. He turned and glanced toward where he knew his father was posted, just as he heard a hoot of joy from around the bend.

"Don't worry, your father is having the time of his life! Those fish will keep him busy for hours!"

Jacob removed his hat and wiped his forehead. He took a deep breath and with the resignation of a child accepting the inevitable punishment to come said "okay, go on . . ."

Von Niblick started by taking Jacob back in time again into the history of the Sporrai and something he called *Lia Fail* or "the Stone of Destiny."

The Stone's history goes back at least as far as Jacob of the *Bible*, the Professor explained to his young friend. Jacob wondered if his sharing the Biblical character's name was just another accident or, yet again, there was more to it. Much of what he would be told was known to historians and much of the public. But, some of it was a secret closely held by the Sporrai. As von Niblick retold the legend of *Lia Fail* he did not tell which was common knowledge and which were the secrets.

According to the book of Genesis, Jacob laid his head down to sleep on a large stone. That night Jacob dreamt of a stairway leading to Heaven and of God's angels going up and down on that stair. They were entering and exiting our world. "As you will come to discover, Jacob, this was a very important night in human history," von Niblick assured him.

The Stone holds the key to great powers and many have attempted to take its control for their own glory. In ancient times, the Stone was secretly taken to Egypt and then eventually out of the Middle East by early members of the Sporrai. They brought it to Ireland to be held safe. Ireland was then thought to be at the very end of the world. There it was kept by a group of Irish monks and was blessed by St. Patrick himself. For centuries, the Irish used it as a coronation stone—Irish Chieftains being crowned while sitting on it.

As the centuries passed, word of its whereabouts eventually found its way to the great enemies of the Sporrai, those who would turn the world upside down by making right wrong and wrong right. Forming an alliance with Viking marauders, the enemy invaded Ireland in the first years of the fifth century. In a cataclysmic battle on the shores of eastern Ireland, the Sporrai and other Irish monks faced the Vikings with an enemy of light at their head. *Lia Fail* helped keep the Vikings at bay for many days. Then, at midnight on the fifth day, the Dark One divided his forces and hit the monastery from two sides.

The defenders did not have the men to hold their walls in more than one place and the Vikings soon breached the outer defenses. Many of the defenders were losing hope when a few of the faithful fell to their knees in prayer around *Lia Fail*. Suddenly, the night sky lit up and a bolt pierced the air, striking the stone and rending it in two. Seeing it as a sign to divide their force and counterattack, a dozen monks picked up the two halves of the stone and marched out of the monastery at the two parts of the Viking army.

The light in the sky had blinded the Vikings and chaos had erupted in their ranks. The Dark One had burned all the Viking ships when they arrived on shore in order to keep them from retreating if the battle turned against his army. Before the two halves of *Lia Fail*, and without a means of escape, the enemy marched itself into the sea and all were drowned. Fittingly alone, the leader retreated on the one ship he had allowed to survive.

Sometime after this battle, the Keepers decided to separate the two halves of *Lia Fail* and St. Columba, the patron saint of Scotland, brought half to the Island of Iona, which is Scotland's most holy ground. From that moment, it became the stone upon which Scottish Kings were to be crowned. Three hundred years after its arrival in Scotland's western islands, the enemy tried again with another Viking army. Before their arrival, however, Kenneth McAlpin and a group of Sporrai smuggled the stone onto the mainland of Scotland and eventually to the castle at Scone where it continued to serve as the seat upon which Scottish kings would be crowned until a little over 700 years ago.

In the year 1292, the English King Edward I stole the stone, or so he believed, and took it to England where it sat for the next 700 years under the throne of all English monarchs. In 1996, the English gave it back to Scotland and it now sits in a glass case in Edinburgh Castle for all to see. Trouble is, that is not the real *Lia Fail*.

In the year 1292, the Sporrai decided to let Edward I *think* he stole the Stone of Destiny as a way of throwing off the forces of darkness who will forever attempt to gain its control and its power. In reality, leaders of the Sporrai had taken the stone by night to Edinburgh Castle, and placed it somewhere in the secret catacombs that are hidden below the streets of Edinburgh, but of which very few people know. Of those who hid the treasure, only one emerged that next day from the catacombs. What happened to the others, no one knows for sure. And the one that did emerge immediately sailed alone across the sea to unknown lands where he could die alone without the risk of ever divulging his secrets. According to legend, however, those who were left behind in the caverns labored for years beneath the city, digging ever more catacombs, tunnels and traps to hide the real *Lia Fail* and other related treasures forever.

The legend also says that if the *Lia Fail* is ever needed to vanquish evil again, she will make herself known to the chosen one.

"We believe this is true, Jacob," von Niblick stated, as he stood to stretch. "We believe it is true because in 1815, Sir Walter Scott . . . Jacob, do you know who Sir Walter Scott is?"

"Well, I ran across a book of his in St. Andrews called *Rob Roy*."

"Ah. . . very good. Yes, he was a great novelist and his books on Scottish heroes like Rob Roy helped us reclaim much of our grand history.

But, anyway, back to my story. In 1815, he got permission from the Prince of Wales to enter the cellars beneath Edinburgh Castle. Scott is one of our great national treasures, you know, and, was a sporran Bearer himself. When he emerged, he held in his hands the lost regalia of the Scottish monarchy: Sword, Scepter, and Crown. They, too, are on display today in the Castle."

Jacob was caught up in the wonderful and exciting tale that seemed way too good to be true until it suddenly hit him. *Wait a minute, the sporran has drug me into this story. What is he getting at? What about this great "enemy of light"? That was nearly a thousand years ago or something, surely he is long gone. Why is von Niblick telling me all this?*

Jacob could feel his stomach turn and a bit of acidic bile slide up into his throat which he quickly spat into the water. He then leaned back on his hands, his face feeling cold and clammy.

CALL OF DUTY

Von Niblick could read the questions and concern in Jacob's eyes and put an arm around his shoulder. "Lad, none of us asks to be part of this story and yet we all have our role to play." The Professor stood and Jacob rose to his feet following him.

The Professor took off his fat-rimmed, green hat and held it at his side as he bent down on the rock in front of Jacob. He picked up Jacob's chin with his other hand and looked him straight and strongly in the eye. "Don't look away from my eyes," he began.

Jacob found it awkward and uneasy to look into the strong, grey eyes of the Professor and found himself instead focusing on his thick grey eyebrows that reminded Jacob of two fuzzy and elderly caterpillars following each other across the man's face.

"Jacob, the sporran came to you and brought you to Scotland and to me. It has given you the great gift of a father's time and love. Now I believe you are being called to serve that cause of love yourself. You can turn your back and take the easy road, but I assure you that you will never forgive yourself. Many years from now, you will lie in bed and wonder if you had done any good for the world at all and who may have been hurt because you lacked courage."

For the first time in his life, Jacob really felt essential. The feeling had been creeping upon him for days, but now was in full bloom. He felt like he was not just a kid but that things, important things, relied on him. That feeling did not sit easily with him, however. His legs grew tingly and weak and he asked if they could go to shore, where he could sit again without fearing falling into the river.

Stone-by-stone, the two made their way to the edge and Jacob sat hard in the tall grass by the bank.

"Jacob, MacGregor believes in you, that is why he tested you with his little hunt through Feddinch House and then let you bear Isildane's ring alone. I believe in you or I would not have told you all I have so far."

Jacob stared silently at the rippling water. He was glad von Niblick did not force him to look directly in his eyes any longer.

"And, most of all, the power behind the Sporrai must trust you or you would not have been told such secrets."

"What do you want?" Jacob finally asked without looking at von Niblick.

"It's not what I want, Jacob," von Niblick answered as he bent down to look into Jacob's eyes once more, "it's what is needed of you."

The Professor put his hand into the muddy bank at his feet and pulled a clump of mud from its rest. He began pulling it apart as he spoke. "You see, Jacob, we all have a role to play. This mud is made up of many different parts. There are tiny microbes and bugs in here. There are tiny parts of rocks and decaying leaves and droppings of birds and fish scales long rotted. They have all been brought together by this water rushing past that continues to change it by bringing new life to old."

So, what am I, a rotten fish scale or something? Jacob testily thought. He could feel his nausea turn to anxious anger as he felt his old and comfortable life slipping away. *Why can't I just be left alone to play and grow up normally?*

"We are all part of a story much older and much greater than any of us individually. To that story we owe our ears. To the storyteller, we owe our duty to play our part and play it well. And then, our last act of fidelity is to remember and pass on."

"What about my dad?" Jacob lashed out at von Niblick with a kick of muddy sand by the Professor's feet.

"Your dad? Why, your father has played his part very well. He and your mother gave birth to you, didn't they? He has nurtured and educated and loved you. He prepared you for this moment, whether or not he fully understood what he was doing all the time. He sent for you to bring you to Scotland and now has brought you here where you are faced with the choice of service or safety. This is no longer about your father, but about you."

Without saying a word, Jacob got up and walked to the turn in the river where he could watch his father fishing. His father's pole was bent forward as he fought a heavy fish that was pulling hard with the current. Out of the corner of his eye, Mr. Boyd saw his son around the bend and flashed a big, proud smile. Jacob waved, whispered "I love you," under his breath, and returned to where von Niblick was still seated.

"What am I to do?"

MISSION

Professor von Niblick put his arm around Jacob and squeezed tightly. Without his saying a word, Jacob knew how proud the old man was of him and it momentarily boosted his own confidence. His anger left with his resignation and the old man's approval.

"For some time now, Jacob," von Niblick began, "what remains of the loyal Sporrai, what we refer to as 'the Remnant,' have been getting information that the enemy was reconstituting its power in a distant land, gathering its forces, sending out spies and minions, and would be coming after *Lia Fail* and the other parts of the Sporrai treasure."

There it was again, the "enemy." Jacob's confidence took another hit.

"The great problem is," the Professor continued, "we can't mount a defense if we don't know where we are defending. The Sporrai who hid the *Lia Fail* in the catacombs provided a great service for awhile, but now it seems the enemy, by whatever name it is going these days, has gotten information of its own and is coming."

"What complicates all this is that the Sporrai who hid the Stone of Destiny and built the catacombs understood evil would most likely return for the treasure in the guise of a wise Keeper. They fixed it so only Bearers could ever enter the secret realm beneath the sod. MacGregor and I have already crossed over to the Order of the Keepers and so cannot enter ourselves. You, being a Bearer, must enter the catacombs and try to find, or at least retrieve information about the location of, *Lia Fail;* the Stone of Destiny. Failing that, we are sure there is something waiting for you down there in the dark."

The bile in Jacob's belly was now boiling and he leaned forward hard, attempting to keep his breakfast in his stomach. A dribble of spittle seeped from his lips.

"Aren't there other Bearers who could do it," Jacob murmured under his breath.

"MacGregor and I have reason to believe there may be a spy among the Keepers and so cannot risk even discussing it with others. You have been given the clues; you have passed the test. This is your burden to carry for the world, Jacob."

The top of Jacob's body lunged forward until he found himself near the water's edge on all fours. Mrs. Lafoon's blueberry scone, or what remained of it anyway, was now floating down the river and a cold bead of sweat dripped off Jacob's nose and into the water. He sat back and von Niblick passed him a drink from his canteen.

"Tomorrow I will send you into the caverns. There you must search for the Stone of Destiny, or at least for clues to its whereabouts. I will work tonight to put together things that will help you on the mission, but I am afraid you will be utterly on your own once you cross the threshold."

Jacob had nothing left in his stomach to retch, so just laid back in the cool grass. His skin was cold and clammy and his mind went utterly blank.

EDINBURGH CASTLE

F rightened and nervous, Jacob did not get much sleep that night. Von Niblick had given him an early briefing on the mission and sent him to bed. He awoke the next morning to awful sounds echoing off the walls of Room 3, Niblick House. "Dad, are you okay?" Jacob asked as he slowly swung his feet to the side of the bed. Mr. Boyd didn't hear him ask, but he might as well have. The retching sound told Jacob everything he needed to know.

Mr. Boyd turned out too sick that morning to worry about much of anything, or to go anywhere. Mrs. Lafoon said she would take care of him through the day and Professor von Niblick volunteered to take Jacob on a tour of the city, including Edinburgh Castle. In no condition to argue, Mr. Boyd readily agreed to the plan and immediately went back to bed. Mrs. Lafoon gave him some pills and a wet wash cloth for his head.

Jacob wondered if this was all a coincidence or if the Professor had a hand in making his father sick so that he could be free to enter the catacombs without his dad knowing. Either way, Jacob thought it best not to mention his suspicions, but to go along with the Professor's developing plan.

As Jacob and the Professor marched up the street toward Edinburgh Castle, as if reading his young companion's mind, von Niblick leaned down and whispered "I think your dad will be fine in the morning. No worries, laddie. No worries." The two were followed by Mr. Nibbles, his tongue hanging to one side as he panted up the street. They had to wait at the end of every block for their companion's short little legs to catch up with them. He made a comical sight in his little leather vest embroidered with dragons. Jacob felt the blush of embarrassment cross his face as people looked queerly at the three of them.

When they arrived at the gates of Edinburgh Castle and purchased their ticket to enter, Professor von Niblick pulled Jacob away from the rest of the crowd waiting to enter the fortress. "Now, for the plan to work, I have to get Mr. Nibbles into the castle, which the guards won't like at all. Keep up with me, lad. . . ."

Out of his long leather coat that reached down below his knees, von Niblick produced a pair of sunglasses and put them on. Then he put Mr. Nibbles on a leash, which the little pug dog did not like at all. Turning toward the guards and tour guides at the gate, he stretched out his walking stick in front of him and walked forward.

"Sir," a guard said as he took a step toward the Professor, "no dogs allowed, sir."

"Oh," von Niblick responded, "you wouldn't want to deprive a blind man of the chance to see the beloved castle, would ya now?"

"Well no, sir, but. . ." the guard responded as von Niblick dropped Mr. Nibbles' leash and began to walk directly into the castle wall. Smacking hard into the brown stone wall, the old professor fell backwards into a garbage can, sending it rolling back down the street, spilling garbage as it went.

Oh, no! What is he doing? Pretending to be blind? It will never work, Jacob thought to himself as he watched the mayhem unfold.

"Now, lad, see what you have done, An old blind man nearly kills himself because you don't want his dog in your precious castle! Do you want to be responsible for an old countryman getting himself killed in there? Well . . . ." The Professor was very animated and was waving his staff around in all directions and looking all over as he talked, as if he really was blind.

"Well," the guard attempted an answer, but not before the Professor interrupted again, "Fine then, lets go Grandson, before this young man causes me to fall over something else," von Niblick said as he motioned for Jacob to help him up. Jacob, the Professor, and Mr. Nibbles then hurried through the gates and were successfully in the castle and amongst a group of tourists that had assembled to wait for a tour.

"I was an actor in college, you know! Best Macbeth the stage at the University of Sterling has ever seen, laddie" whispered the Professor.

Edinburgh Castle is a huge fortress that resembles a small city. There are many walkways, grassy areas, small buildings, a chapel and even a cemetery for guard dogs within the castle walls. Jacob had no idea it would be this big or would be this open with streets and everything. He imagined castles as being one big building inside some great walls. Edinburgh Castle was bigger and grander than anything he could have imagined.

Though the three companions had approached it this morning from the street (which is the only way to get there unless you have a helicopter or are a very accomplished rock climber), the castle actually sits on a rocky cliff with sheer drops on all sides except the approach from the street.

There are stores, museums, restaurants, and a chapel, all inside the walls of the great castle. There are all sorts of paintings and statues of great men and women from Scottish and English history. On each side of the gatehouse entrance where Jacob and Professor von Niblick entered the castle, there is a statue. On one side is a statue of the great Scottish hero William Wallace and on the other is the Scottish King Robert the Bruce. In 1314, Bruce had taken back the castle from the English with only 30 men who scaled the cliffs and took the English soldiers by surprise.

To Jacob, it was all quite exciting and fueled his old wish to live in the age of knights and ladies and to brandish a broadsword against some great enemy of the realm.

The three wound their way through the castle tour with Professor von Niblick pretending to be blind, even as he pointed out many features of the castle and its furnishings that he thought Jacob needed to see. Mr. Nibbles was perfectly behaved.

On and off throughout the tour, Jacob felt that strange sensation up his arms and into his neck that von Niblick told him was called "the quickening." The feeling got particularly strong in the "Great Hall." The Great Hall is a massive room with big brown timbers for its roof and along all the walls are hundreds, maybe thousands of swords, knives, spears and pikes of all shapes and sizes. Jacob wondered how many had actually been employed to hack at some invading soldiers or some nasty orc or goblin.

The room was packed with hundreds of tourists who were there to witness the sword fight employees of the castle put on several times each day. When the demonstration began, Jacob couldn't see a thing, but he could hear the clash of metal as the swashbucklers went at each other in the front of the room.

Professor von Niblick led Jacob through the crowd toward the front. People were crammed together and every two steps Jacob would follow von Niblick in saying "Pardon me. Thank you. Excuse me. Cheers." They emerged from the crowd in front of the two men clad in traditional Scottish clothing and hacking at each other something fierce.

Jacob looked down but could not see Mr. Nibbles. *He must have been lost in the crowd somewhere,* he feared. Jacob pulled on the Professor's long leather coat to tell him Mr. Nibbles was missing just as he spotted a small streak of brown fur fly out of the far corner of the room.

It was Mr. Nibbles and he was running fast toward the two men putting on the sword demonstration. *What is he doing?*

Closer and closer he came until Nibbles leapt at the first man. His teeth snapped down hard on the swordsman's kilt and, as the dog fell, the kilt came down with him.

The crowd roared with laughter at the sight of the man standing in his underwear. Mr. Nibbles ran through the other swordsman's legs, causing him to fall backwards and his legs to flail into the air. Jacob could see the delight on Mr. Nibbles face as he dove to knock down one of the blades along the wall. Like dominos, the swords began slowly to fall into one another, knocking them down all over the room. As metal clanked against metal and then crashed to the floor, the crowd turned to watch Mr. Nibbles run to the back of the room, followed closely by the two men he had humiliated.

"Quick, lad," the Professor was pulling Jacob toward the fireplace in the front of the room. "Do as I told you, and quick!"

Von Niblick fiddled with a carving built into the fireplace and a small door opened inside the hearth. Jacob paused, momentarily feeling safe that he couldn't possibly fit into such a small doorway! *Yes, let's go home!* He thought.

"Now go!" ordered the Professor, pushing Jacob hard toward the little door in the fireplace.

Mr. Nibbles made it around the circumference of the room, causing havoc as he went, and leapt up into Professor von Niblick's arms when he again emerged in the front where he started. "Thank you all," Professor von Niblick announced to the crowd as they roared in approval. As the Professor had planned, they took it all as just part of the show.

The Professor and Nibbles quickly headed through the middle of the crowd and toward the door.

The distraction had worked. Jacob was gone.

Stranger in the Dark

J acob's heart was racing. He was frightened and alone. The smell of damp, stagnant air pressed into his lungs and clung disgustingly in his mouth. It felt like the walls were closing in to crush him, as if he could feel the very weight of the tons of rock and dirt that hung above his head. He and Professor von Niblick had talked the night before about this plan and he knew he might have to enter the vaults and catacombs below Edinburgh Castle, but he half thought the secret door wouldn't open or would not end up being there at all. Now he was here in the complete dark behind a wall in Edinburgh Castle and was utterly alone.

For a few moments he ran his hands along the cold damp wall behind him in hopes of finding a lever to open the door so he could escape and run to his father and then get a plane out of Scotland, never to return! He found nothing and sat down hard when he heard something in the chamber with him.

It was a low scratching sound as if someone were shuffling his feet back and forth nervously on the floor. As quickly as he could manage, with his hands shaking and panic taking control of his breathing, he opened his backpack to find the flashlight he had packed there the night before.

Finding it, he flipped the switch and quickly waved it about the rock chamber around him. The light shone upon nothing but the cold stone walls. Jacob heard the shuffling again. This time he could tell it was coming from just outside the chamber he was in.

Then Jacob heard a mumbling sound and he turned the light off, fearing whatever it was would find him alone and helpless if he kept the light on. The next sound he heard sounded more human than the others. Straining to make out the words, if that is what they were, Jacob thought he heard a quaking voice say "Bearer, serve, Order, Sporrai." Then it repeated the same words but a bit more clearly this time, as if the speaker was gaining some composure. "*Sporrai*," he was sure that is what he heard.

Hearing the word made Jacob remember the phrase Professor von Niblick told him to use if he got into any trouble here in the catacombs. Slowly he started to speak the phrase; "I am a Bearer. I serve in the Order of the Sporrai."

His words came back to him as if an echo from just outside the chamber. They were even in a tone that matched his own; nervous fright.

Jacob switched the flashlight back on and tried to angle it out of the entryway but nothing seemed to stir. Then he heard it again. "I am a Bearer. I serve the Order of the Sporrai." And then he heard it again, even more hurried this time. Then again the same phrase rang out and then yet again the words came back to his ears. He could also hear that shuffling/scratching sound between the repetitions of the phrase.

Mustering his courage, which only came because the voice echoing back seemed now even more frightened than he was (and there are few things that embolden a man's courage more than to be around others who have less of it than he) Jacob began making his way toward the arched exit of the chamber. Approaching close enough to get a better angle down the hall, he caught a glimpse of the tip of a shoe that was moving back and forth nervously on the rock floor.

As the beam from Jacob's flashlight moved up from the shoe to a leg, a loud cry rang in Jacob's ears. "Stooooooopppppppp!!!!!! Who are you?" Jacob could barely make out the words amidst the screams echoing off the walls and the foot began kicking wildly at the beam of light as if it could have kicked it away.

There was something strangely familiar in the voice. Jacob backed into the room turning out the light as he paused to think. *Could it be? No. Of course it couldn't be, could it? We left him in St. Andrews heading to Glasgow. He wouldn't be in Edinburgh!* Still, he couldn't think of anything else to say.

"Ian . . . is that you?"

"Ahhhhhhhh. . ." the person in the shoe replied, incoherently.

"Ian, it's Jacob, is that you?"

"Jacob?" the voice responded. "The Jacob from America, who left Feddinch House a few days ago on his way to Edinburgh?"

Jacob turned on his flashlight, put the light under his chin as he used to do when trying to scare his friends back home on sleepover nights, and stepped out of the chamber.

Ian screamed, and then swung a fist at Jacob's ghostly image. His hand met the flashlight and sent it flying to the floor. The impact made the light go out and everything went dark, again.

Reunited

"**I**s that really you, Jacob?"

"Yes, its really me . . now help me find my flashlight and let's hope it still works."

"Mine went out a while back and I feel like I have been wandering around in the dark for days," Ian said to his friend, as he felt on the floor for the light.

In short order, Jacob's hand ran into his light and he fumbled for the switch. To their great relief, a beam shot out against the wall. The two friends shook hands and began to trade stories about why they were here in the catacombs beneath Edinburgh Castle.

Jacob told Ian of Professor von Niblick and the clues and the Stone of Destiny.

Ian recounted how he and his dad were traveling along the border region of Scotland and ended up in the industrial town of Glasgow. There he had met up with a man named Mr. Whipsnade. Whipsnade had befriended Ian and his father and showed them many great sites in Glasgow and around the area. He lived in a small castle just outside town and let Ian and his father stay with him the previous night.

That evening, as Ian sat by the fire in his room reading a book, Whipsnade came to visit. The man, about the same age as Ian's father, brought tea and cookies and was very nice. Whipsnade asked him all sorts of questions about their trip and time in St. Andrews.

"You didn't tell him about the sporrans or what we found, did you?" Jacob interrupted Ian's telling of the story.

"Well, I don't think so but . . ."

"What do you mean you don't think so?" Jacob asked in a tone of accusation.

"Well," Ian attempted a response, "it was just that, well, he was so nice and brought wonderful cookies and even some Turkish Delight for me. And, well, I was so comfortable and he was so nice that I am not sure what I said."

Ian continued recounting the story of the night in Whipsnade's castle. He told Jacob that sometime that evening he found himself following Whipsnade down a set of very steep and twisting stone stairs. The stairs led to a kitchen and there, in the kitchen, was a small door, much like the one he and Jacob had opened in the kitchen of Feddinch House.

The only thing he remembered after that was Whipsnade whispering in his ear things like "You are a very talented boy . . . You deserve to have power and riches . . . Through that door, which I cannot go, lies great wealth . . . Bring back the treasure and I will share it with you . . . Your father will never have to work again . . . You are the chosen one . . . Be sure to bring me back the lion's eye . . . I will pay you very well for the lion's eye—more than you have ever dreamed of having!"

Then the door opened and Whipsnade kicked Ian hard into the passage and threw a bag in behind him. The bag contained a flashlight, a basic map of the tunnels and some tools.

Ian had gotten himself lost, then the flashlight went out. He wandered around in the dark for hours, and that is where Jacob found him.

"But, Jacob, what are you doing in Glasgow? You said you and your dad were going to Edinburgh which must be hundreds of miles away!" Ian asked.

"Either ten steps took me from Edinburgh Castle to Glasgow or you wandered hundreds of miles in the dark tunnels in just a few hours and somehow found Edinburgh," Jacob offered and then added, "Neither of those sounds very likely so there must be some other explanation."

"Maybe," Ian interjected, "Maybe there is another explanation and that is neither of us is where we think we are but the doors that got us here put us somewhere else entirely."

"Like two bedrooms that have doors which seem to lead you to two separate places, but somehow end up connected to the same bathroom?" Jacob asked.

"I guess that is what I am saying. . ." Ian responded.

"Where is the map Whipsnade gave you?" Jacob asked Ian, and put out his hand to receive it.

"Well, I set it down at some point in the dark and don't know what I did with it. I have been trying to feel around for it for hours but nothing," Ian answered.

"Well, the bottom line is that we are here now and I have an important mission to accomplish for Professor von Niblick." Jacob reached over and put an arm around Ian. "The way I know to get out is to follow my map and get what Professor von Niblick asked me to find, and then I am sure he will help get you back to your father in Glasgow. Are you up for another mission, friend?" Jacob said.

"I guess I will have to be, you Yank!"

The two looked over von Niblick's map and headed down the dark passageway that seemed carved right from the bedrock beneath Scotland's marshy turf.

THREE-HORNED BEASTY

The beam from Jacob's flashlight provided just enough light to barely make their way down the narrow passage. The boys walked closely together, with Jacob a mere step ahead of Ian. Walking slowly, as Jacob shone the light all around the ceiling, walls, and floor that surrounded them, everything appeared to be the same undifferentiated rock. Nothing seemed special, nothing different from anything else.

The feeling of being trapped was terrible. Jacob kept thinking about the fact that tons of rock and dirt and buildings and people rested above his head and he feared they could collapse at any moment. The walls seemed so close to him that occasionally he even felt it hard to breathe after he let himself think *too* much about where he was or what could happen to him. He was sure Ian felt the same way, but both boys were too proud to say anything to one another.

As they approached a point where the tunnel branched out in three directions, all of which seemed to lead further down into the earth, the boys stopped and Jacob took out von Niblick's map.

"Anything look familiar to you, Ian?"

"No," responded Ian. "My light was already dark by the time I found my way here, I just followed the wall with my hands. I don't know which tunnel I may have come up."

"According to von Niblick's map, we must be in something he called 'The Three-Horned Beasty,' " Jacob said. "Here, see, he has written,
'Beware the horns for they are sharp,

the teeth to watch but not the dark.
The eye remove but do not see
A fire within will guide thee.' "

"Dang, we are back to that stuff again!" Ian remarked, remembering their time in St. Andrews trying to discover the meaning of the clues left for them by Hammish MacGregor.

"Look, this is the best we have," Jacob replied. "Von Niblick told me he didn't understand everything he had discovered about the catacombs either, but that I would have to do my best once I got in here."

Jacob began to pan the room with the beam of light from his flashlight.

"Stop!" Ian shouted.

"What is it?"

"There, on the floor, I saw a flash of something."

Jacob panned back slowly across the floor until, again, the beam of light hit something shiny on the floor. Both boys approached it cautiously. A blue piece of glass or shiny rock about the size of one of their fists was embedded in the floor.

Jacob brushed some dust off of the stone and both boys inspected it carefully.

"Jacob, I wonder if that could be the beasty's eye?"

Jacob grumbled a low groan of possibility.

"If so, then look. . . the three tunnels must be its horns and the mouth must be back heeeeerrrrrrreeeee . . ."

Ian had taken a few steps back to where he thought the mouth might be and the floor had given way. As his friend fell, Jacob turned to hear the screams and see Ian's head disappear into the floor.

"Iaaaannnnnn!" Jacob crawled carefully, but quickly, to the edge of the gaping hole in the floor, his flashlight secured by his teeth and his hands frantically searching the floor in front of him, lest another trap door open and swallow him as well.

"Iaannnnnnnnn!" Jacob yelled through the hole and leaned close to look for his lost friend. Suddenly, a glint of light caught his eye in the hole and something gripped his collar and began to strangle him. Then something else grabbed his arm.

Jacob struggled and fought against the tightening grips and he pulled back hard, away from the hole. A gurgling sound emanated from the chamber and then, as fear gripped him tighter than the monster, Jacob pulled back hard and pushed himself away from the hole. The hands held fast to him and he realized he was pulling the creature with him out of the hole.

"Nooooooo!" Jacob felt himself grow momentarily stronger and pull back clear of the creature's grip. Looking down, he saw the hands of the beast reaching out to get hold of his ankles. He lifted his right foot to come down hard with his heel on the outstretched hand when he heard:

"Jake, it's me, I'm stuck, help!"

This was no creature from the depths of the caverns. Jacob could now see better in the shadowy light of the beam from his flashlight which had gotten knocked to the side of the cavern. It was Ian.

"I'm stuck, Jake! Help me!"

Jacob reached down and hoisted up the part of Ian's body still remaining in the hole.

Ian slowly emerged, flailing his hips back and forth, working his way up and panting hard.

"My backpack, it got stuck and hung me just inside the hole," Ian explained as he gulped for air. "You saved my life!"

"It's a wonder I didn't kill you! I thought you were some beast trying to wrestle me into your lair!"

"Jake," Ian said as he gulped air to catch his breath, "I think I saw the 'inner fire' that the poem referred to. Its down in the hole."

Jacob crawled back over to the hole and peered in. Sure enough, deep in the hole he could see a dim orange glow on the walls.

"Yep, I see it too. Hand me the flashlight."

Ian crawled behind Jacob and handed him the flashlight which Jacob held down into the hole. "Holy Man!"

"What is it?"

"If that backpack had not kept you from falling, you would have been impaled like a piece of meat on those stakes down there!"

Ian looked over the edge and then quickly backed away and against the wall, again panting heavily with the realization of his brush with a very painful death.

"What do we do now?" Ian asked, between large gulps of air.

"Well, let's see, the map warns us to beware of the teeth, which you weren't! And it says beware of the horns, so we better not try to go down one of the three tunnels. The key has to be that eye we found."

Both boys crawled over to the blue stone and inspected it in the light of the flashlight.

Jacob pushed on it. Nothing happened. He attempted to lift it out of the ground. Nothing.

Jacob reached for the knife on his belt. Von Niblick had given it to him that morning. He attempted to dig under the eye. When the blade of the small black penknife hit the underside of the crystal eye, it sent a shock through his arm, causing him to drop the knife and fall back.

"Here, take this kerchief and try twisting it maybe," Ian said to Jacob as he passed him the handkerchief from his pocket.

"Better not be snot on it!"

Jacob covered the palm of his hand with the handkerchief and very deliberately began to twist the eye. Turning it counter-clockwise, nothing happened. He tried again the other direction and the eye began to rotate and lift. Slowly, the dull sound of rock grinding against rock echoed off the cavern walls around them.

"Jacob . . . we are moving," a startled and trembling Ian Nelson muttered.

The floor beneath them was rotating slowly clockwise. The boys held tight to the ground. When the floor stopped, both looked up to see they were now facing back up the tunnel they had first come down. Turning around, they noticed a dull light emanating from the floor between the beast's horns.

Crawling over, Jacob was first to notice that the hole Ian had fallen through was now at the other end of the chamber and was revealing a twisting stone staircase going down into a deeper set of catacombs below. A light was burning enough to show them the way down the stairs.

"Well, looks like the blinded eye has allowed us to see. After you," Jacob said to Ian, while motioning him down the stairs.

"Well, ummmmmm, okay I guess, old chap, let's go."

As they descended the stairs, Jacob told Ian that von Niblick had said he would arrive at another level, but he didn't know how he would do it or when.

"Looks like now, and we are just walking down the stairs to get there, I guess," Ian replied.

TOMB OF SIX KEEPERS

Arriving at the bottom of the stairs, the boys noticed they were in a room not unlike the one they had just left, although it was well lit. Around all the walls ran a trench filled with a gooey black liquid that burned slowly without much heat or smoke but gave off a fairly bright light. The trenches ran down several passages coming off the room and continued to burn as far as the boys could see. Jacob put his flashlight back into his pack as they looked around.

"Look, Jacob, writing. . . ." Ian was inspecting the walls and called Jacob over to see. Etched in the walls were drawings and markings and words that reminded them both of the nasty graffiti they had seen from time-to-time in cities and along highways.

"Must have it," said one. Another read, "It's mine, it's mine, it must be mine!" Near the drawing of two stick figures that looked as if one was choking the other was written, "Beware, my treasure will come at a hefty price. It's mine, no one can have it but me!" Still other writings appeared to be in other languages the boys could not read.

At the far end of the room were the tall spikes that would have killed Ian if he had fallen through the hole. Intermixed within the spikes were spots of ivory white. Ian walked over to get a better look, but stopped short and turned in his tracks. Amidst the spikes and scattered on the floor around them were the bones of the less fortunate. One skull remained impaled on a stake. Having rotted off, its bottom jaw was now lying around the bottom of the stake like a horseshoe around a peg.

Jacob had begun to poke his head down the passage at the bottom of the stair when Ian caught up to him. He was amazed at how much more at ease he felt with the warming glow of the trench light rather than just the flashlight showing him the way. As Ian stepped into the passage, the room they had just left started to revolve again. When the slow-grinding sound stopped, the stone stair was gone and the hole they had come through in the ceiling was again at the other end of the room waiting to plunge more unsuspecting treasure hunters to their deaths. There was now no way for them to go back. Both realized it, but neither said a word to the other.

The two started down the passage with Jacob looking on his map for a clue as to where they were or where they should go next. But with a number of passages on the map all looking the same and von Niblick not being able to predict how they would emerge into this inner realm, the map was nearly useless.

Twenty yards down the corridor, openings began to come into view off the main passage. The rooms were dark, except near the front entrance where the trench of black ooze burned. Jacob pointed his flashlight into the first room and it appeared to be empty. They continued to the next, when Ian noticed that small dams had been built to keep the burning ooze from entering the rooms until it was needed. Ian gave a solid kick to the ones on the right and left side of the second door and the flame slowly crawled in and around the corridor of the room.

"Jaacccccoob, you better come see this!"

The chamber contained slots cut out of the walls, three on each side. At the end of the room directly opposite the door was a bench cut from the stone and engraved with symbols, including a large Celtic cross right in the middle of two panels etched with two dragons twisting themselves into two circles and both looking outward from the cross. On top of the bench were a golden cup and plate.

As the boys stepped into the chamber and looked more closely, the scene gave them an almost sickening feeling. Inside each of the six slots was the remains of a human being, his white bones clad in traditional Scottish kilt and armor. The realization hit them both at the same moment. They were standing in a tomb! The two boys tripped over one another as they hurried out of the chamber and into the passageway. If they could have run home at that moment they would have, but where to run?

The two boys went down the passage, away from the tomb room, to gather their thoughts and strengthen their resolve.

Jacob finally broke the silence.

"They are dead, Ian, they won't hurt us . . . ."

"Yes, so it is said of the dead, but do you believe it?"

Jacob ignored Ian's question because he really wasn't sure what to believe anymore. He looked at Professor von Niblick's map and found the room noted as "The Tomb of Six Keepers." They again had a reference point on the map.

"Here, Ian, look. This is where we are." Jacob spread the map out on the rocky floor, allowing the trench light to illuminate it. "According to the map, we are here at the Tomb of Six Keepers." Jacob's finger traced the way down the passageway on the map.

"Jacob, look," Ian interrupted, "Whipsnade told me to get the Lion's eye and bring it back to him and this place on the map is marked 'The Lion's Head.' Lets go to that point."

"Sounds as good as any other direction. Let's go."

As they headed down the corridor, Ian heard something behind them and turned. There was nothing he could see but he did notice the trench light in the "Tomb of Six Keepers" had gone out. *Turned out?* Ian felt his knees grow weak. "Let's not waste time. Come on, mate."

The two picked up their pace to a slow jog until they came to the point where the passage split, one corridor ascending to the right and one descending to the left. According to the map, The Lion's Head was to be right precisely at this juncture but there was nothing. Not even a sign that something once might have been there. The boys looked around for a clue and Jacob opened the map again. It sure looked like they were in the right place.

"Ian, listen to this little poem von Niblick has copied by The Lion's Head on the map. What do you make of it?" Jacob called to Ian who was pushing and pulling on the stones of the wall in front of him, trying to find a secret door or some clue.

> The answer is found
> In the eye of the beast.
> The *Lia Fail*
> Will never cease.
> But to approach the Lion
> Leap in the dark
> Sing to the angels
> Land on the mark.

The Lion's Head

"**W**hy can't he just write English and tell us what to do!" Ian exploded at the helpless feeling he got from hearing the riddle and not understanding. "My dad may be in danger, we are lost here in these tunnels somewhere, we don't know what to do or how to get out! Jacob, what are we going to do?" Ian kicked hard at the wall in the center between the two branching tunnels.

"Ian, I believe in Professor von Niblick. He told me that we were parts of an old story that stretched through time and that the right things would happen if I kept the faith and believed. I feel your frustration, friend, but if we are going to get out of here and get to our families again we must keep our heads and finish the mission." Jacob stood up and put his arm around Ian, who was resting his forehead against the cold stones of the cavern wall.

Ian was hiding his face as a tear dripped down his left cheek. He was frustrated and scared and worried deeply about his father and what this Whipsnade character might do to his dad if he failed to get what he asked for.

"Come on, let's work on this together," Jacob said, as he knelt again by the trench fire with the map and began to read the poem aloud.

> The answer is found
> In the eye of the beast.
> The *Lia Fail*
> Will never cease.
> But to approach the Lion
> Leap in the dark

Sing to the angels
Land on the mark.

"Jacob, what was that?" Ian said, his ears perked and his eyes darting.

"What was what? I just was reading the poem so we could untangle its meaning."

"No, I felt something, like the wall was moving or something, and I heard a grinding sound." Ian had wiped the tear from his cheek and walked over closer to Jacob.

"I didn't hear or feel anything."

"Well, read it again, Jake. And listen."

Jacob began to read the poem again. As he did, they both heard the grinding sound now getting louder and the floor under them began to shake. Then it stopped.

"Jake, do it again," Ian said with an assurance that lasted with him for only a moment.

"The answer is found," Jacob began the poem and the noise started again and this time it was louder and clearer. This third reading had set something in motion that even Jacob, pausing his recitation, could not stop. The wall in the fork between the two branching tunnels was moving, as if it were revolving back into the ground from where it had once been cut.

As it turned, a chamber was slowly revealed. The chamber was very narrow, but tall. It was barely big enough for two people Ian's and Jacob's size to stand in together. On the back wall there hung a golden lion's head. A crown on top its head, the Lion's tongue flicked out of its mouth like a flame. Jacob and Ian both had seen such lions on crests around Scotland, and Jacob remembered it resembling the ones adorning von Niblick's fireplace in his parlor.

Overcome with the chance to retrieve the Lion's eye and thereby gain the freedom of his father from Whipsnade and maybe get some treasure as well, Ian ran toward the Lion, grabbing at it in an attempt to reach the eye which was just beyond his reach.

"No, Ian, wait! We have to be careful!" Jacob tried to restrain his friend and urge him to be calm.

His impatient friend did not heed Jacob's warning. He continued right up to the golden head and jumped up and down trying to reach the eye. "Mine! Mine! Dang it!" the English boy yelled, as he stretched and jumped toward the head. Visions of wealth clouded his mind as he jumped and shouted. On the third jump, he came down hard on the ground and suddenly the floor gave out beneath his weight. Amidst a rushing sound and spray of water, Ian was gone.

Jacob ran to the hole that had appeared just outside the chamber and noticed the ground cracking around it, falling into the hole that had consumed Ian. Jacob called his friend's name repeatedly as he backed away from the collapsing floor. When the floor finally stopped crumbling, it revealed a shallow but fast moving underground river. A few yards from where Jacob stood, the river became a waterfall, taking the water ever deeper into the ground and Ian with it.

"Iiiiaaaaannn," Jacob called repeatedly into the hole. There was no reply. His flashlight revealed nothing but the rushing water in the river. He called for Ian again and again. Finally, Jacob sat back on the floor. Shock took hold of him at first. He stared silently at the hole. Then he dropped his head into his hands and began to weep. "Ian, what have you done! Where are you?" he muttered between sobs.

Eventually, Jacob's mind started returning to his own predicament and the realization that he was now alone again in the catacombs. He shook his head in an attempt to focus his mind. Jacob's last tear dripped down onto the map. *Ian's dead, maybe. I am alone. I may never get out of here. One mistake like Ian made and it's over for me, too! Why would you put boys through this! Why? Curse you, sporran, and you, too, von Niblick, for putting me here!*

As he sat pitying himself and trying to regain focus on the map, he noticed that a tear had hit the poem on the map right on the word "leap." The teardrop magnified the word and called Jacob's attention to it. He reached down and wiped the bead off the map as the word implanted itself in his imagination. *That is it!* He read the poem aloud again.

> But to approach the Lion
> Leap in the dark
> Sing to the angels
> Land on the mark.

To approach the Lion, it takes a leap in the dark, a leap of faith! Poor Ian just ran up to it without thinking, just wanting the eye! But you can't just run up to it, you must leap and trust you will land safely on the other side. Jacob could feel the excitement growing as he figured out the puzzle. It was an excitement tinged with guilt, as he worried about his friend lost in the river below.

Putting his backpack over his shoulders, he stood and held the map in his left hand. He looked over the hole in the cavern floor and the danger it revealed. He searched the Lion's chamber carefully with his eyes and found a small patch of dark shadow on the floor to the left of the Lion's head. *Leap in the dark.*

Jacob turned and hesitated for a moment as he looked back down the tunnel. *There is no turning back, there was no way out but forward.* He worked to convince himself to believe as he got himself in place to take two good steps and then leap over the rushing underground river and into the chamber.

Okay, Jacob, sing to the angels and give it a try! Jacob began to sing a prayer he remembered from church, took two steps, and leapt over the river. Landing hard on the other side, his momentum carried his forehead into the wall beside and beneath the Lion's head. His head snapped back on his neck. "Ugh!" *That's going to leave a mark,* he thought as he got up, rubbed his head, and looked around.

Jacob inspected the Lion carefully. Its right eye was closed, as if it were half asleep or winking. Its left eye was a blue stone, cut and sparkling in the dim light cast from the trench fires in the tunnels. Jacob tried to reach it but could not. After seeing what had happened to Ian, he was not about to jump for it.

Some cuts in the wall on the right side of the Lion seemed to hold promise that he might be able to climb on them and reach around the Lion's head to the blue eye. Jacob ducked under the Lion and noticed markings on the wall beneath its bearded chin. He took out his flashlight to inspect them. He recognized them instantly! It was the unicorn with the crown around its neck that was on the side of the gold ring he had retrieved from the secret door in the kitchen of Feddinch House in St. Andrews.

Just another coincidence, I suppose! I suppose not!

Jacob opened his pack and took out the ring. Something was different about it. It seemed, at once, more impressive and yet smaller. It shone brightly, even in the dim light of the cavern, and yet seemed of a more manageable size. He compared the etchings on it with those on the wall and they were a match. He put the ring on the ring finger of his right hand and, to his surprise, it fit! Either he had grown in the last day or the ring had shrunk to fit his finger. Either way, it felt good.

Looking at the ring on his hand reminded him of his grandfather who wears a big gold class ring from Davis & Elkins College. Jacob always admired that ring. If he made it out, he wondered if he would be able to keep the ring and what his grandfather would think of it, even if it didn't have a rock in the center as it was supposed to. *Maybe I can save my money and buy one to fit in it.*

But this was no time to worry about that, he realized. He thought he should get the eye and get on finding *Lia Fail* and his way out.

Jacob inspected the cuts in the rocky wall of the chamber and began climbing up the first few that got him high enough to be above the Lion's head. He leaned on the head, resting his right hand on the right cheek of the Lion and reaching with his left over to the blue eye. He fiddled with the beautiful blue eye but nothing seemed to give. *More leverage, I need more leverage.*

Jacob climbed another step that allowed him to reach the blue eye with more strength. Still, it didn't budge.

Leaning harder on the Lion to get even more leverage, he unconsciously moved his right hand up closer to the beast's closed right eye. The gold of the ring brushed against the gold of the lion's closed eye and the lid of the eye reacted. Jacob felt the skin on his hand crawl as the eye opened beneath his touch. He pushed back as the lid came fully open to reveal a small blood red stone in the socket of its eye.

Jacob released his grip on the Lion and held fast to the wall, as he stared at the red eye staring back at him. His hand began to move but he was not moving it. Up closer to the eye it was drawn. Jacob struggled to keep his hand down but it was no use. His hand had closed into a fist and as the ring approached the red eye, it shot to it and pressed hard into the socket. He struggled but it would not let him loose.

Jacob screamed in pain as the sensation of fire burned through his finger. His right arm shook. The fire seemed to pass through his arm and into his neck, then down his back. It was a feeling like he had felt before, when in the presence of another member of the Sporrai, but this was much more intense and painful. Finally, he lost his grip and the Lion let go of him as well. He fell to the floor beneath the beast. For a moment, he lost himself in a haze of confusing visions and searing pain.

His hand was still shaking when he sat up and looked at the ring. In the center of the ring the Lion's eye was fused tight. It was a bit duller than it appeared in the Lion's head, but the red was just as deep. On his finger around the ring were scorch marks. A small line of his own blood dripped down his hand from under the ring.

KELPIE

W hen Ian had slipped into the underground river, the intense cold of the water made him instantly tense every fiber of his body and then soon go limp and lose consciousness. His nearly lifeless body was battered around from rock-to-rock as it passed through the channels of the underground river and was eventually spat out from a cavern in a hillside some miles away. The sounds of his own gagging for air woke him from his dreamy state of carelessness.

He spent some moments gagging and spitting water as he lay on his side before he fully realized what had happened or where he was. He found himself wedged between two large boulders at the edge of a shallow waterfall. He was just a few yards away from the opening in the hillside out of which flowed the underground river. Hitting the boulders with great force had pushed the water from his lungs and saved him from drowning.

Every muscle and bone in his body ached like he had never experienced before. Simply to turn to get on all fours was difficult and he shivered with cold. His lungs burned with each breath.

He crawled his way out of the water and over to the bank of the small river. His head was pounding. Ian opened his pack and took out a sandwich. Though the bread was soggy and too disgusting to eat, the cheese and meat gave him strength and warmed him slightly.

Ian wondered what may have become of Jacob and worried about his friend and his own father and how he would now ever get back to either of them. Except for those first few hours in the catacombs, he had never felt so alone and hopeless in his life. He remembered once being lost in a department store and wondering if his mother had left him. He felt now like he had felt then;

intensely alone, frightened, and helpless.

Ian pulled the sporran from his pack and looked at it. He had not touched it in days. Now very much alone and frightened, he cursed it for existing and blamed it for his plight. Still, he wondered if it might be able to help him find his way. He opened the flap and looked inside. There, at the bottom of the pouch lay a note.

"Ian, are you there? Are you okay? Please tell me you are okay! It's Jacob. I have the eye. I am fine. If you are alive and find this, find Professor Chadwick von Niblick at Niblick House on Cowgate Street."

Jacob had taken a moment to write the note, as he lay recovering under the Lion's Head in the chamber. He sent it with little hope his friend was still alive. But he sent it because he realized that little hope is not the same as no hope at all.

Ian turned the note over and with cold and stiff fingers scratched out "Jacob. Am okay. Will try to find von Niblick. Good luck."

Ian stretched out his right leg and reached his hand into his right front pocket. He pulled out a small brown and tan item about the size of his pinky finger. It was the stag's horn whistle that the pouch had given him when it gave Jacob the jewel-less ring in the kitchen of Feddinch House in St. Andrews. Professor MacGregor warned him not to blow it except in the most dire of circumstances. "You will know when it is time to blow it," he remembered the Professor saying, "and at that time trust the thought that you recognize in your belly before you find it in your head."

He turned it over in his hand and wondered if this were the moment. He had resisted blowing it when he was lost in the catacombs, but mostly because his fear of calling attention to himself there in the dark outweighed his hope that it might bring help. Now, out in the light of day, he felt less trapped and more willing to give it a try. *Well, I might die out here of starvation and hypothermia anyway, so why not give it a go.*

Slowly he pulled the whistle to his lips. As they closed around it, a small shock pulsated through his mouth. He recognized it as a static electric shock like he would give his mother and sister after rubbing his sock-covered feet on the floor of their home in Oxford. He pulled it from his lips for a second but then returned it and took a deep breath. As the air entered his burning lungs, a shock ran through his shoulder blades and down his arm. He was used to that sensation by now, as it had occurred occasionally since the day he got his sporran more than a week before.

He exhaled into the hole of the whistle and out came a high-pitched whine that sounded not terribly unlike any other whistle he had ever blown. *Hmmmm. . . doesn't seem so special to me!* He blew it again. Ian was looking down his nose at the end of the whistle and didn't notice what was happening around him.

A silvery shimmer crawled across the water, the bark of nearby trees crawled around their trunks, branches and leaves blew back and bent hard away from him, loose rocks moved, birds abandoned their roosts and flew away. Ian didn't notice it all happening, but the whistle had caused a type of stirring in the world.

Just a dumb whistle, Ian thought, and then tossed it carelessly into the stream bed behind him where the water parted to meet the treasure and then closed gently in again upon it. Ian was oblivious to it all. He picked up his battered and bruised body and started following the river down through the field, hoping it would lead him eventually to a town or at least to someone who could help him. He walked several miles on his bruised and very tired legs. His shoes were full of water and were squishing with every step. The back of his heels began to blister as they rubbed against his wet shoes.

When he arrived at the location where the river opened into a small lake, or "loch," as they are known in Scotland, he saw a horse standing in the distance by the water's edge. *My way out of here!*

Ian approached the horse and, with each step, the beast's appearance became more beautiful. It had a new saddle upon its back made of grey leather with silver buckles and black stirrups. Its face was gentle, but strong, and it turned to look Ian in the eye, as if waiting to take him to safety.

Ian approached the horse slowly, but confidently. Within just a few feet of the horse, he turned as a shout rang out from the hillside above him.

"Get away from that horse! Get back, now!" Ian couldn't quite make out the features of the man scrambling down the hill toward him. A small animal ran beside him. *Darn. It's the owner, and he is mad! But, I haven't done anything wrong. Maybe he will get me to town. . . maybe!*

The stranger got closer and the feeling of being in trouble again overtook Ian. The boy made out a white beard flowing around the sides of the man's head. About 15 feet away, the man abruptly stopped. "Get away from that beast, now!"

Ian felt something wet drop on his head and start to slide down over his ears and onto his forehead. Slowly he reached up to find his head covered in a gooey, clear slime. *Oh. . . a flock of birds pooped on me . . . what a day!* he thought.

He craned his neck slowly up and backward until the true source of the slime came into view. He was now looking up at the underside of the chin of a huge, green head. Slowly he turned to face a wall of greenish white. It was the underside of a giant dragon-like creature of smooth skin.

Smlopp! Another glob of drool fell onto his head as the creature let out a loud bark. Ian's knees grew weak and he fell to the shore. The last thing he remembered was staring at a large, clawed toe resting beside his face. Then all went dark.

"Go back to your depths, beasty, and leave this one alone! He is not yours! In the name of the sacred power served by the Sporrai, I order you to your watery lair!" The older man was pointing his walking stick at the beast as he spoke. The little dog began to grow in size and change in looks, from a cute pup to something much more frightening and powerful. The man repeated the phrase and the beast snorted and turned to walk into the loch and disappear beneath its waters.

When Ian came to his senses the little dog was licking his face. "Laddie, are you alive?" Ian could hear the man saying as he stood over him.

"Yes, sir," Ian mustered as he sat up and pushed the dog away from him.

"I am Professor Chadwick von Niblick and this is Mr. Nibbles. He means you no harm and neither do I, though that kelpie there surely did!" Von Niblick helped Ian to his feet and continued, "You are Ian, aren't you? Well, Jacob sent a message to me that you had been lost in an underwater river and needed help. I figured this might be where that little river ended up, but wasn't sure. Good thing for you I heard your whistle and got here when I did!"

"Sir. . ." Ian's legs were still unsteady and he leaned against von Niblick as he spoke, "what was that thing?"

"Why, it was a kelpie of course. Have you not heard of the kelpies?" Ian shook his head no as they began to walk up the hill toward the road.

"Well, my boy, no wonder you were nearly eaten! We have kelpies here in our lochs in Scotland. What kind of books have you been reading, anyway? They have been here since before time as we know it. They are water creatures that can come ashore and turn themselves into a beautiful horse. When a boy or girl comes up to pet them or to steal a ride, the child's hands are stuck to the animal's hide. The kelpie then just walks back into the loch to drown and eat the poor victim."

Ian felt ill at the thought of almost being eaten and spit the sour taste from his mouth.

"Heard of Nessie, haven't you, lad? Well, she is a kelpie, though a pretty safe one as kelpies go. She is more ornery than beastly and prefers the taste of fish to boys."

Professor von Niblick had his motorcycle and sidecar waiting beside the road. Ian got in the sidecar and von Niblick covered him with several blankets before Mr. Nibbles jumped into his lap.

"We will have you home to my house, that kelpie slime gone from your hair, and warmed by the fire in no time, lad. Hang on!"

CASTLE WHIPSNADE

J acob slipped the ring from his finger and brushed the blood from his hand onto his pants. He examined the ring with its new jewel and noticed a small dark spot in the middle of the red stone, as if suspended right in the middle. As he held it close to his eye to try to make out what the small speck was, he was hit by a blindingly bright red light that dazed him momentarily. He turned the ring in his hand and looked through the finger hole at the back side of the stone. Now he noticed what was happening. The stone was gathering all the light from the trenches nearby and refracting it intensely through the back of the stone and out the top. The intense red glow was illuminating all the shadowy places and revealing new details about the chamber.

Above the Lion's head and to its right, the glowing light of the ring revealed a staircase through the ceiling of the chamber. He examined it and considered his choices of progress; two tunnels on either side of the Lion Head chamber which seemed to lead further down into the catacombs and this new staircase that led up. *Well, I could either jump the river and risk it all, or head up the staircase and try my luck up there on that level. Grandad always says 'go up, my boy, always go up!' So . . . here we go!*

Jacob had to climb the steep and narrow stairs on all fours. It was a difficult climb that left him very tired at the top. He emerged from the final step in a small chamber with a tunnel running through it from north to south. Across the way was a small door. As he approached it, Jacob wondered if he might now be back at the same level from where he and Ian started.

The door also made Jacob think about the Innkeepers of Feddinch House where he first saw such a small door. At least until that last night when he and Ian were nearly killed, he had had a delightful time. *What I wouldn't give for one of Mrs. Woods' waffles right now!* Jacob couldn't resist the possibility of emerging safely in Mrs. Woods' kitchen and approached the small door.

Jacob knelt down at the door and slowly pushed against it. It opened into an old-looking kitchen. He stepped into the inviting warmth and was surrounded by the pleasant smell of food being prepared. It wasn't Feddinch House, but it seemed friendly enough. The room was a mix of old and new. A large fireplace was burning on the opposite wall where a black kettle hung and was boiling. The stove and refrigerator and sink areas looked thoroughly modern. Three places were set at the table in front of three high-backed chairs.

"Well, its about time you got back!" The voice was coming from the high-backed chair at the table end closest to Jacob. The chair slipped back and the owner of the voice stood and turned. Jacob felt his heart race and he took a step back toward the door.

"Who are you?" The voice appeared angrier this time and the expression on the man's face seemed even more so.

"Aaahhhhhhhhhhh . . ." Jacob stammered as he back-peddled toward the little door and what he saw now as the relative safety of the catacombs. He turned for a mad dash through the door when it suddenly slammed shut.

"I asked you a question, boy!" The man had stopped and was staring hard at Jacob. "Who are you and where is that boy, Ian?"

Whipsnade! This is Whipsnade! The realization hit Jacob like a punch in the gut. He had just come through the door through which Ian entered the catacombs hours earlier.

Jacob would not get a chance to answer, even if he had wanted to. Whipsnade's eyes were drawn to the sporran that Jacob had tied around his waist when he sent the notes to Ian and Professor von Niblick. The man's manners immediately changed and a smile slowly opened onto his face.

"Well, now, where are my manners? You are surely a friend of Ian's. A fine boy, that Ian, and any friend of his is a friend of mine, that is certain! How about some tea and cakes? Or, maybe some creamy hot chocolate?"

Jacob was hungry and a cup of hot chocolate would certainly warm him up. He started to say "yes" and accept the man's hospitality but then remembered himself and how Ian and his father had gotten sucked in by this man's kindness and sugary treats.

"No, sir, thank you anyway," Jacob answered. "I really must be on my way."

"You'll go nowhere!" the man's voice and face had changed again. Jacob thought he seemed to grow larger with his rage. "Ian is your friend, isn't he? You must be Jacob, aren't you, boy?"

Jacob tried hard not to react.

"Well, since you won't talk, let me talk to you." Whipsnade turned his chair around to face Jacob and the door and sat down.

"Listen to me, boy! I don't know where Ian is or why you are here, but I have little Ian's father in my dungeon where he will rot until he is dead and then rot some more, unless you and Ian return with the eye of the Lion for me and then you give me that little sporran there. Do you understand me, boy?"

Again, Jacob tried to remain silently defiant.

"And to make sure you don't forget, I am going to give you a little something to remember our bargain!" The man walked to the fireplace and placed an iron bar in the fire. He turned it slowly as he kept an eye on Jacob. A few minutes passed as Jacob attempted to pull the small door back open. Then Whipsnade pulled the hot poker out of the flame. It glowed red hot. As he crossed the floor he spit on the red metal which sizzled and steamed ominously.

"Ohhh, don't be afraid, it will only hurt for a short while!" the man gave a wicked laugh as he stepped across the floor.

Jacob searched the room for a way to escape but found none. Whipsnade was between him and the doorway that led out of the kitchen and into the wider house. Suddenly, as Whipsnade came closer, Jacob felt the sporran slung around his waist grow heavier and sag. He reached in with his right hand, which bore the ring, but without taking his eyes off Whipsnade. His hand clenched around something and he pulled it from the pouch.

Jacob glanced down to see he was pulling a silver sword from the sporran. It felt light, but empowering. On the pommel was a lion's head and two intertwined dragons formed the rest of the handle and emerged on each end of the cross-guard.

Whipsnade thrust the red-hot iron at Jacob before the sword fully emerged. Jacob moved just in time to avoid most of the blow, but the hot iron caught his shirt and burned a small, but powerfully stinging slit in his left arm.

Whipsnade's next blow was met by Jacob's sword and broke the hot iron in two. Whipsnade dropped the part left in his hand and retreated momentarily to the table. There, he picked up a tall walking staff and Jacob felt himself fly back hard against the wall, pushed by an invisible force that seemed to suck the air from his lungs before hurling him backwards.

He got up with difficulty and readied himself for another blow. Whipsnade approached and Jacob leapt at him with his sword slashing the air in front of his enemy. The blade caught the man's garment and sliced into his leg.

Whipsnade uttered an obscenity and sent a crushing blow from his staff down across Jacob's back. Jacob's breath was sucked from his body as he hit the ground. The pain seared through his body and clouded his mind.

Whipsnade raised his staff again and was preparing to drop a deadly blow across Jacob's head when a sudden rush of wind from the catacombs threw the small door open and distracted him. Items in the kitchen flew across the room from the intensity of the rushing wind. Just before Jacob lost consciousness, he saw six white figures rushing on the wind through the door and brandishing long broadswords over their heads. Their bones clanged together like wind chimes and the faint sound of bagpipes floated on the air.

Jacob awoke some time later to find Whipsnade's cloak lying next to him, damp with blood. The sword he had pulled from the sporran was stained red, its blade resting on Whipsnade's cloak.

For years, Jacob would wake in the night with glimpses of the battle with

Whipsnade creeping into his mind. He never would fully understand what transpired in that kitchen, but he was sure he acted heroically and correctly. The memories he did have served to embolden him in difficult times.

Jacob heard a car and jumped to look out the window. It was Ian's father's car and it was speeding down the hill and away from the castle. He hoped Mr. Nelson had escaped unharmed and would go and find Ian.

As Jacob turned, he saw the six ghostly white figures kneeling beside the small door. They were resting their hands on their broadswords and their heads were down as if asleep or in prayer.

The small door was opened again into the catacombs and Jacob knew the only way home was back through those tunnels and caverns. He hesitated as he approached the skeletal knights and then, as if to avoid one of them reaching out and touching him, quickly rushed through the white gauntlet and stepped through the door and into the caverns.

Jacob stepped aside as a rush of wind came behind him and he watched the six Keepers float into the cavern, down the stair, and back to their tomb. The small door to Whipsnade's castle then slammed shut and disappeared amid the rocky walls.

The Professor's Study

As he lay in bed, still aching from the flu and his head throbbing with pain, Mr. Boyd could hear the sounds of people downstairs in Niblick House. *Jacob and von Niblick must be home,* he thought. Mr. Boyd had shown little improvement through the day and had taken only a bit of broth and tea from the tray Mrs. Lafoon brought him for lunch.

In his condition, there was little chance of Mr. Boyd coming downstairs to accidentally find Ian. Still, Professor von Niblick cautioned the boy to be very quiet and try not to leave the study unless it was absolutely necessary. "How would I explain you being here and Jacob not?" the Professor said as he ushered Ian into his study.

Ian was still wet and because of the ride in the sidecar of von Niblick's motorcycle, he was colder than ever. During the drive, he tried to duck down behind Mr. Nibbles as much as possible. But a little pug dog weighing less than 20 pounds doesn't provide much protection against the rushing winds of the road.

A moment later, the Professor entered the study again with a long black cloak hanging over his arm. "Lad, I am sorry to say we don't have any boy's clothes in the house but you must get out of those wet things before you catch your death! Here," von Niblick laid the cloak over a chair and turned to leave the room, "take those things off and I will have Mrs. Lafoon dry them. This will at least cover you for awhile!"

Ian stood alone in the study not wanting to take his clothes off and be naked but for some old wizardly coat. Still, he knew he should obey von Niblick as Jacob trusted him, too. And, he was eager to be dry and warm again.

A moment later and Ian was seated in the tattered leather chair by the window, trying to look comfortable and pretending to be brave. The bottom of his legs and feet were protruding in all their white pastiness from beneath the black cloak. Mrs. Lafoon soon entered with a tray of hot chocolate and scones. "Adventurous day, I take it?" she asked with a wink and then disappeared through the door with his wet clothes.

A scone and half cup of hot chocolate later and Mr. Nibbles entered the room and sat by Ian's feet. Professor von Niblick was not far behind. "Well, now, laddie, belly feeling a bit better now and your blood a bit warmer, I trust?" Without seeming to need an answer, the Professor pulled his chair closer to Ian and sat down across the tray from him. Taking his long brownish-red pipe from the table beside him, he prepared it to light, while asking Ian to tell him all about what had happened.

As Ian began telling his story, starting from the trip to Glasgow and the meeting of Whipsnade, Ian grew frantic at the memory of his father still alone in Whipsnade's castle. "Professor, you must help me, you must, my father is still there, still with that awful man who pushed me through the door! You must help him, you must!" Ian was standing now and pleading with the Professor.

"I will help your father as best I can, but to do that you must be calm and help me by telling me everything that happened. Come on, now, sit down and let's start at the point where you were pushed through the door. Here, another drink of chocolate and relax."

Von Niblick listened intently but silently to Ian's story and then stood, walked to the window behind Ian and stared out into the sunlit street. He turned a few seconds later with a large smile on his face and said, "So, he found the Lion's head and my map works! I knew it!"

Just then an odd look came over him and he rushed over to his desk, pulled something out of a side drawer that Ian could not see, and turned with a small piece of paper in his hand.

"A note from your friend Jacob! It reads:

'Whipsnade, I think, is dead. Terrible battle. Ian's dad has escaped, I think. Have you found Ian yet? Is he okay? My ring is complete. I am okay. No *Lia Fail* yet.' "

"Well, mighty good news, that! But, troubling, too. How does he know your dad has escaped and that this Whipsnade is dead?"

"And what about a terrible battle?" Ian interjected.

Without a word, the Professor turned to his desk and sat down. He turned the note over, took a quill from atop some papers on his desk, dipped it in black ink, and began to write.

"Have found Ian. Wet, but will live. Sounds like you are in trouble. Will send help. Make your way to Holyrood Palace to get out. You will know you are there. Be careful and please don't open any doors, I did tell you that, didn't I?"

Von Niblick put the note into something that Ian still could not get a glimpse of from where he sat and then both items went into the drawer.

"Ian, my boy, you wait here. Don't leave the study and certainly don't get into anything! Read a book or something until I get back. Come on Mr. Nibbles."

The dog followed von Niblick out of the room as Ian sat back with renewed thoughts and worries about his father.

A few minutes later and Mrs. Lafoon entered the study to find Ian in tears, which he quickly wiped away with the sleeve of the cloak as she entered.

"Ian, did your dad have a cell phone in his car?"

"Yes, yes, yes he did, can we call?" The hope of being able to contact his father made him forget for a split second that he was naked except for an old man's cloak. He jumped out of the chair and the cloak flew open. Mrs. Lafoon blushed at his nakedness and turned away.

"Come on into the kitchen, then, but be very quiet so as not to disturb Mr. Boyd. And, you might want to tie that thing shut!" Mrs. Lafoon waved her hand behind her as she left the room.

They reached Ian's father as he drove around Glasgow looking desperately for his son, and just before he went to the police for help.

"Dad, please don't ask questions just yet, but I am in Edinburgh and I am fine."

"Edinburgh!" Mr. Nelson yelled into the phone as his car slammed to a complete stop.

"Well, yes, Dad, I am at 333 Cowgate Street. I am fine, come get me and I will explain everything then."

Ian's father tried to get more information, but Mrs. Lafoon took the phone and convinced Mr. Nelson that Ian was alright and being taken care of and that he should just drive the several hours it takes from Glasgow to Edinburgh and come pick him up.

"He is never going to believe this!" Ian said, as he plopped his body into a kitchen chair and pulled the hood of the large black cloak over his head.

The Quaich Fountain

Jacob received von Niblick's note as he sat on a bench carved out of the stone walls of the passages. He had a snack and took a large drink from the bottle of water Mrs. Lafoon had packed into his backpack. "Don't open any doors! Don't open any doors! No, you didn't tell me! Thanks for nothing!" Jacob muttered under his breath as he read the note. Still, he was very glad to get the news that Ian had made it out alive. *Well, if I don't make it at least someone might tell my story.* He always wanted to be thought of as brave, and maybe even a hero.

Jacob continued his journey down the passage heading south toward · Holyrood Palace and away from Edinburgh Castle where he had begun. A small compass on his watch confirmed he was heading in the right direction, as did the continuing slope downward of the floor. Every few yards on both sides of the passage were small wooden doors. Obeying von Niblick's note and his experiences, he did not attempt to open any of them.

A few hundred yards down the passage, it abruptly stopped in a dead end. *What? I am sure I was heading in the right direction.* Jacob shined his flashlight against the bare stone walls but saw nothing. *What do I do now?* For a moment he thought about trying one of the small doors. *Maybe I will get lucky and it will lead me back to Feddinch House's kitchen where Mrs. Woods is probably making tea right now.* Oh, how he would like some tea and cakes. But trying a door had nearly gotten him captured or killed before, and he was in no mood to ignore von Niblick's belated warning now.

Jacob stood thinking about what to do and found himself playing nervously with the ring, spinning it round and round on his finger. When he realized what he was doing, he looked down at his hand and slipped the ring from his finger. The stone of the ring had helped him find the staircase in the chamber of the Lion's Head, now maybe it would help him find a clue or a way out, he thought.

Jacob took the ring in his left hand and cast the light from his flashlight through the inside of it. Looking up, he saw it had refracted in a bright red glow on the walls. Slowly he turned. Nothing could be seen but dull rock. Then, just to the left of where he stood, the light of the ring revealed an opening behind the rock and a lever to its right. Slowly he approached the wall, trying not to move the light and risk losing sight of the chamber and the lever. Slipping the flashlight under his left armpit and trying to keep its beam steadily flowing through the stone of the ring, he reached out with his right hand and touched the stone bump that the ring's glow had revealed to be a lever. He pulled it, and the stone wall began to slide away.

What was revealed when the wall had completely moved away was a narrow spiraling stair down into a lower level. Slowly, he started down and noticed the glow of the trench fires again lending their light to this lower level. He felt something comforting about the light and was glad to turn his flashlight off again and put it away. He also heard the relaxing sound of bubbling water.

Here the catacombs seemed more like a small, underground village, than simply a mine passage or tomb in the ground.

Along the walls were doorways, many small like the doors he had seen above, but this time they had no actual doors, only remnants of cloth that once hung to cover them. Other doorways were bigger. Not quite as tall as the ones he was used to back home, but close. Beyond the doorways, they were all dark.

In the center of the big open room at the bottom of the stair was a spring that bubbled up from the ground to form a fountain. One spout was made to look like a stag's head with water running through and out the tines of its antlers. A second was of a small boy, the water running through his arms and out his outstretched and open hands. The stream from his right hand emptied into a cup that overflowed into the base of the fountain.

The cup and the base of the fountain itself had similar flat handles on two sides and was shallow like a bowl. Jacob recognized them as traditional Scottish quaichs, a cup of fellowship. Jacob looked closely at the boy and thought he looked like he was presenting the water to someone through the cup.

Around the base of the fountain were words and symbols from languages and cultures he did not understand. He circled the base of the fountain looking at the symbols and imagined they represented about every civilization in history; Ancient Nordic runes, Latin, Greek, Egyptian hieroglyphics, cuneiform, Chinese characters, Celtic script.

Jacob reached a hand into the water. As his hand entered the liquid, his fingers took on a silvery sheen under the water. A barely perceptible tingling entered his fingers and crawled slowly up his arm. The sensation was surprisingly pleasant. Cupping it in his hands, he smelled it to see if it seemed foul or fair.

It seemed safe enough so he took his water bottle, which was nearly empty, and held it under the fingers of the boy statue until it was filled. He capped the bottle and returned it to his backpack in case he needed water before he got out of the catacombs.

He turned from the fountain and stepped away from the water. Jacob didn't notice that, as he walked away from the fountain, his reflection did not disappear with him but remained hovering silently in the waters. Eventually it would fade away as all reflections do, but much would happen before the waters would release the boy's imagination.

The trench fires around the edge of the fountain room did not cast enough light for Jacob to see far into the individual rooms. He turned on his flashlight again and pointed its rays into a few of the doorways. They appeared to be small sleeping rooms. Only a basic bit of furniture was found in any of them. A mat spread on the floor on one side, a wooden chair on the other and several shelves cut from the stone walls around the room. In each, a few basic personal items like cups and bowls could be seen, but not much more. Jacob wondered if this is where the Sporrai had lived when they brought *Lia Fail* to be hidden in the catacombs 800 or so years earlier. *If so, how long ago did they leave or die and what happened to them?* He wondered about their fate.

Anxious to get out to the light of day again, Jacob left the room and continued down the corridor that led south out of the fountain room. The walls of the passage were punctuated every hundred feet or so by smaller side passages and occasionally a bigger room. Jacob looked down each passage but never ventured from the main path south. The rooms here were enough to catch his attention and delay his progress.

First, he came to a room on the left with a large, round stone table. Like the benches and shelves he had seen, it seemed cut right from the very rock that formed the cavern. Remnants of tapestries hung on the walls but Jacob could barely make them out by shining his flashlight into the room. He kicked over one of the dams holding back the blazing black ooze at the base of the wall. The flame crawled slowly around the room and he followed it into a high-ceilinged space that felt much more open and comfortable than the close walls and ceilings of the passageways.

Walking closer to the table he noticed eight chairs sitting around it at eight spaces. The one furthest from the door was high-backed with carved designs of dragons. A faint outline of a design was at the center of the table that looked like it might once have been a heraldic shield. Great burgundy tapestries hung from the walls and contained pictures of battles and dragons and great knights. One of a boy about his age pulling a sword from a sporran caught his eye. He held his own sword up to the tapestry but they were not the same.

Jacob pulled the largest chair from under the table and examined the dragons and various rune symbols etched into its dark wood surface. Its arms ended in two clasped and long-fingered hands. Its legs ended with four-clawed feet. Jacob thought it was the coolest chair he had ever seen and wanted to sit in it, if only for a minute.

He moved closer and prepared to sit when he noticed a pile of dust on the seat. He reached down to wipe it clean before sitting. He bent closer and noticed the dust was actually gray and black ashes. He reached to sweep them to the floor but as his hand touched the particles, a shock pulsated in his neck and he pulled away. The hardness of the table began to melt and he rubbed his eyes, thinking they were playing some cruel joke on him.

He stared at the table which now had come to resemble a pool of water and, in the water, he saw his own reflection which presently vanished. Then another image emerged on the surface. It was of a man in fine silk garments. The man rubbed the tall chair, coveting it. He motioned for others in the room to stand back and then he slowly sat upon the chair by the table and smiled a proud and large grin. Suddenly, flames leapt up through his body, consuming his flesh, then charring the bones as they collapsed into ash on the chair. The scene horrified Jacob as he back-pedaled away from the table. *It could have been me! It could have been me!* His mind turned over the terrible possibilities in quick succession.

Suddenly a sound outside the room distracted him and the image vanished into the wood of the table. His heart raced as his eyes shot to the door. His breaths came in quick and shallow bursts. Since Ian was lost, the caverns had been completely silent except for the gentle gurgling of the fountain and his own steps. Jacob ran to the door and peeked into the hallway. Nothing. He could see or hear nothing. *Must have been my imagination, I hope! I have to get out of here!*

Libra Sporranus

J acob hurried down the passageway, looking behind him nervously
with every few steps. He slowed at each door and peeked down each
side passage that he passed as he went. Occasionally, he thought he
heard small footsteps but could never place them to a specific location. They
always seemed to be just around a bend he could not see. He also had a feeling
he was being followed, though nothing seemed obvious about it.

*Come on, come on, I can do this, I can make it, I can get out of here. It will be
alright. I will be alright.* He worked hard to convince himself to be confident
and calm but it was not easy. He kept his sword in his right hand and in front
of him ready to strike at anything that came near.

A hundred yards or so down the corridor and he thought he caught a
glimpse of a small shadow ducking around the corner. His breath raced again
in and out of his body, but his legs halted to a slow and silent tiptoeing sneak.
Maybe it won't see me. Maybe it won't see me.

As he snuck down the passage, under his breath Jacob began uttering the
phrase von Niblick had told him to say if he got into trouble. "I am a Bearer.
I serve in the Order of the Sporrai." Almost silently, he repeated the phrase
over and over as he stepped down the corridor. "I am a Bearer. I serve in the
Order of the Sporrai."

Jacob's right foot was about to hit the floor in front of one of the darkened
chambers when something suddenly grabbed his arm and yanked him hard
into the room. His body spun and he hit the ground hard on his left shoulder.
Before he could move, small hands were on him, holding him down to the
room's floor. He tried to scream but a hand grabbed him hard around the
mouth and held tight.

A whisper blew into his ear: "Shhh. . . We will not hurt you, Bearer. We serve the Sporrai, too, and you will die if you are not silent and still."

Jacob felt almost torn in two. . . he both wanted to rip away from these invisible creatures that had him pinned in the dark and he wanted to be silent in case they were keeping him from great danger. Within seconds, however, his dilemma dissolved as he saw a large shadow pass the door in the passageway and then heard a terrible guttural groaning from the same direction.

After the thing passed, the whisper again blew into his ear: "Be silent Sporran-Bearer, for a force has awakened that you know not how to control. We are friends and will help you. Will you sit still and silent if we release you?" The tone of the creature was very kindly and heavily accented with a deep Scottish brogue, thicker than any Jacob had heard since he arrived in Scotland.

Jacob nodded his head and the hands slowly and cautiously lifted from his body. His eyes had adjusted more to the dimmer light of the room and he could now make out two small men in simple black cloaks. They were no taller than barely above Jacob's waist, but were aged and obviously fully grown. Both were clean shaven and seemed well-groomed, at least in the dim light.

"I am Angus," said the one still whispering near his head, "and that is Fingus. We serve the Sporrai here in the caverns by protecting the secrets. We know why you are here but you are in great danger. You really must leave immediately. The recklessness and impatience of the other one that came with you awoke the beast that has long slept and it is seeking you."

Jacob's legs were pushing himself away from the two as he listened. "But how do I get out, and before I go I need to know of the fate of *Lia Fail*. . . ." He spoke haltingly and unsure of himself.

A small hand smacked hard around Jacob's mouth, stinging his lip and making him taste the saltiness of his own blood. "Do not utter that name while the beast is awake! You have found your 'stone of destiny,' young one. It is now upon your finger. Now, you must go and tell the one that sent you that this is not the time and you are not yet the one. That stone shall remain hidden until the world is again ready for its emergence. We must defeat the evil of the day with the other tools we have been given. You from the surface do your part and we down here shall do ours."

Jacob stiffened beneath the force of Angus' hand around his mouth and wriggled his head from side-to-side until he was again released.

"Now," Angus continued, "be silent or your tongue will not wag long once *she* gets hold of you!"

Jacob stared into Angus' eyes but did not speak. His anger at being struck so hard in the mouth had overcome his fright and his curiosity about these two strange beings.

"You will learn to thank him for that little smack someday Master Boyd!" Fingus said as he crawled on all fours up to Jacob's side.

"But, how do you know my name?" Jacob sputtered out, as he dabbed his mouth with his sleeve.

"Know your name? Why, you are a Sporran Bearer and one that wears the ring, no less. Of course we know your name." Angus was now standing and extending his hand to Jacob to help him from the ground.

"Come and let me show you something, Boyd," whispered Fingus as he walked across the room.

"I can't see to walk over there," Jacob said.

"Of course, Fingus and I can see well with little or no light but you Earth bats cannot."

"We can't risk a light in here. Boyd, take off that ring of yours and hold it up to your eye," Fingus added.

Jacob was wary of taking off the ring. He thought it had given him the power to pull the sword from the sporran and might help him now if these two turned out to be unfriendly. Still, he was in the dark alone with these two and some beast was prowling out in the passages waiting for him. He really didn't have much choice but to do what they said.

Jacob twisted the ring from his finger and held it up to his right eye. The red stone of the ring gathered what little bit of light was in the dark room and focused it intensely through its prism. In red shadows, Jacob could begin to make out features in the room as he followed Fingus to the far end of the chamber.

Through the inside of his ring, Jacob gazed all around the chamber. There were two great chairs directly in front of him with a long table between. On the table sat a pedestal with a large book lying open upon it. Beside the great book lay two other smaller and very tattered books that appeared very old.

"Come hence, boy, look here at the page of your age," said Fingus, motioning Jacob to the table. Jacob approached the book slowly and deliberately. When he looked down his knees began to lose their strength and his blood ran cold.

There, printed in letters both fancy and ominous, was his name "Jacob Thomas Boyd," followed by his birth date. As he stared at the page through his ring, however, his name began to fade and other names appeared in its place and other dates. Dates in the 1900s, 1800s, 1700s, 1600s and continuing back earlier and earlier still. As he stared he could see faces bubble out of the ink and then fade as if lives were passing before him.

"You are seeing back through time, Jacob. The sporran did not start with you and will not end with you. You are written in the *Libra Sporranus*, and have been since the book was given in the second age. If you would have the strength to turn the page, you would see your sporran passing on and you fading but you do not have the strength and we do not have the right." Angus now had his arm around Jacob's waist and was helping him maintain his posture as he spoke.

"Here," Fingus took the small book to the left of the great *Libra Sporranus* and unzipped Jacob's backpack. "Take this to the wizard who sent you."

"Now, Fingus, go take a look down the passage to see if *she* is still there while I help Boyd get himself together," Angus said as he turned Jacob from the table and the book.

"Here is the sword you dropped, Boyd. I suggest you put it back into the sporran where it will be safe until you may have need of it again. The sporran itself is of more use to you than any blade, human or elvish. You will do well to remember that."

Jacob took the sword by the hilt of twisted dragons and opened the flap of the sporran hanging from his waist. The blade slipped easily into the pouch and disappeared.

"Now, Boyd, listen carefully to me. You are nearly at your final exit from the catacombs. Holyrood Palace is just fifty yards away, but the exit is well concealed. You must go quickly down the passage to the left and then into the last room you see. There you must search with the ring to find the secret stair. It will lead you where you need to be."

"But, why can't you go with me?" Jacob said, in a voice that was almost pleading for help and companionship.

"Fingus and I will attempt to decoy the beasty while you escape. Whatever happens, don't turn back for you will not find shelter again here. Go forward."

Before Jacob could object or plead again, Angus was pushing him down the passage and then the two small men were running quickly away from him and north up the path from where Jacob had come. A low roar echoed off the halls and Fingus turned to see Jacob was standing frozen in the hallway. "Run, you fool!" he yelled.

DRAGONS

Jacob was running as quickly as he could, veering down the left fork of the passage, when he heard blood-curdling screams and a roar that shook the very rock walls of the catacombs. He paused as his mind conjured a frightful picture of what might be happening to poor little Angus and Fingus. Fear quickly shocked him into running hard again down the passage.

A second set of confused screeches stopped him again in his tracks. This time Jacob's fear quickened his instinct to fight and not to fly. He reached his right hand into the sporran and pulled the sword back into existence. The small dwarf-like men had risked their lives for him. He felt he owed them the same.

Tucking the sword under his arm again, he turned and ran back up the passage. As he ran he could hear the noises of battle getting closer until he sensed the necessity to turn down one of the narrow passages to his left. Shadows on the wall told the story of the battle raging around the corner.

Jacob raised the sword over his head and ran hard toward the angry shadows. As he turned the corner, his eyes caught clear sight of what was happening.

A giant beast was standing there, its breadth filling the tunnel and its back reaching close to the ceiling. Its head was pointed and its snout long. Its teeth were stained red with the blood of countless victims and its eyes were like molten gold, turning in on itself over and over again in two cauldrons. Its body almost looked orange with a blue tint, and darker spikes protruded from its back and arms. Angus was atop the beast's back repeatedly stabbing at its neck, but his blows seemed to have little impact. Fingus had fallen beneath its feet and the beast was lowering its teeth to tear the little man into chunks of meat.

Jacob did not pause to think but lunged at full stride at the beast's left leg. As he fell toward the floor, Jacob's sporran blade sliced through the flesh of the beast's thigh and it wailed back in an ear-shattering scream. The beast's sudden jerk caused Angus to lose his grip and slip from its back. His head smashed off the passage wall and he fell unconscious on the floor.

Fingus reached for Angus' loose blade and then stood defensively next to Jacob as the dragon gathered itself to renew its attack. The beast leaned back on its hind legs and then sprang forward, launching itself powerfully toward Fingus and Jacob. It glided through the air on outstretched wings of thin leathery skin just feet off the floor. Just before it crashed into them, Jacob managed to raise his sword again. The beast came crashing through, leaving Jacob and Fingus smashed hard onto the floor and covered in blood and mucousy ooze.

Bruised and battered, Jacob raised to his feet and helped Fingus to his. The beast gathered itself again and turned. Behind him, Jacob could hear the patter of small feet punctuated by a panting sound, racing up the passage to his rear. He dared not turn his back on the beast to see what was coming, but rather prepared himself for another blow.

Coming up the passage behind Jacob and Fingus, but without their knowledge, was Mr. Nibbles. The pug dog was running hard and panting as it went. As it rounded the corner, the small dog leapt. In mid-air, the dog stretched and grew and was compacted again only to be stretched again like taffy in a puller. When its feet again hit the passage floor, it was no longer anything anyone would recognize as the gentle "Mr. Nibbles." The dog had undergone an amazing transformation into a large and powerful dragon.

The newly-arrived dragon had a head that was large and round and dark. Its body was longer than the first dragon and laid out on four legs with two powerful wings and a short curling tail on its back. Its skin was brown underneath but was covered in an almost metallic-bluish hue.

Without seeing the new beast behind them, Jacob and Fingus fell to the ground as the first dragon leapt at them again. This time the creature did not crash through them but was met in mid-air by the newly-arrived dragon that was nearly as large as the first. Jacob looked up to see the two beasts locked in combat and hovering just over his head. He and Fingus crawled quickly over to Angus who was just regaining consciousness. They grabbed his arms and stood to drag him away from the fight. Angus stood unsteadily as the two helped him out of the smaller passage and into the main corridor.

"Run, you fool, run, and do not come back this time!" Fingus yelled at Jacob as he pushed him on his way.

"But. . ."

"Run and don't come back," Fingus cried even more forcefully this time.

Jacob pulled his backpack up on his shoulder, shoved the sword into his sporran, and started quickly down the passage as Fingus helped Angus into a small dark room down the hall where they could hide and tend to his wounds. As he ran, Jacob could hear the reverberating sounds of the two beasts locked in battle.

He tried to force himself to think positive thoughts about seeing his mom and dad again and being home in his room talking with Jenny and Will. Even school didn't seem so bad at that moment. Still, he sadly wondered if he would ever see Fingus or Angus again or any creatures like them. This was an adventure he knew he would never forget; *if I make it out alive*, he let his fear creep back in.

As he approached the final room where Angus told him he would find the hidden stair, Jacob paused to listen as the groans of battle changed. *What? Oh, no, its coming again!* Jacob hurriedly fumbled to remove the ring which slipped from his finger in the darkened room. *Darn! Where is it?* He searched the floor in panic until he felt the small jeweled circle in his fingers. He picked it up and peered through the stone.

There, I see it! There was nothing in the room except a very well-hidden stair that looked just like the undifferentiated rock from which it was cut.

Holding the ring in front of his eye he ran for the first rung of the stair. It was more like little ledges to climb upon than stairs, but Jacob started to climb as he heard the sounds of a fast-moving beast coming down the passage.

Jacob's legs and arms strained under the effort he had to make to climb quickly but safely. Some ledges were further than others and the strain on his arm muscles was immense. His muscles felt as if they were being torn from the bone. He pulled with his arms and pushed up with his legs as best he could. Looking up, he could see nothing but darkness. No opening. No light. Nothing to give hope.

Still, the sounds of the beast below moved him on. Those sounds were getting closer all the time and were punctuated on occasion by the sounds of combat. *Maybe they are still battling with one of them trying to get away* . . . his brain paused . . . *or fighting to get at me!* He climbed faster now at the renewed feeling of being hunted. Faster he climbed. His muscles strained. His heart raced. His breathing turned to panting.

Thud! His head hit the top of the shaft he was climbing. The crack to his head nearly made him fall but he struggled for balance and held on. "Nooooo!" he yelled, at the realization that there was no opening. Jacob looked down. The shadows had entered the room below. Now something was entering the shaft of stairs. "Noooo!" he yelled again, and punched his right fist up hard into the ceiling of the shaft. He heard feet above, as if he were under a floor. Then a voice. He turned to look down, as one of the beasts drew nearer to him and he felt hot air being pushed before it.

Suddenly a shaft of light hit his eye and he was stunned. He had not seen any light but the dim light of the trenches and his flashlight for many hours, and now the bright light of the open air hurt his eyes and caused him to be confused, disoriented, and blind. For a moment, he felt himself flying upwards into the light. *I am dead. That was painless. I am going up to Heaven. Farewell Mother!* His thoughts ran deep and calm.

Just as suddenly, he felt himself drop hard onto a cold floor. Then a rush of air blew him backward across the surface. As his eyes struggled to adjust to the light, many colored sparks flew down all around him. A slamming sound to his left followed by a thud and a deafening roar from beneath the floor shook Jacob's body to the bone.

As his eyes began to focus, he could see the dragon that had come to his rescue circling high in the room and then it burst through a window and off into the light. Shards of glass fell all around the room and Jacob tucked his face under his arm for cover.

Healing Waters

A bearded man approached Jacob who was lying on the cold floor. The boy's eyes were still not quite adjusted to the daylight and everything glowed in a hazy and painful light. "Is this Heaven? Are you St. Patrick, or God maybe?"

The man let out a bellowing laugh and said "St. von Niblick here, Chadwick von Niblick!" He laughed again and added, "No . . .this isn't Heaven, laddie, it's Scotland!"

"Professor!" Jacob exclaimed as he jumped painfully to his feet. "I made it! I made it out!"

"So I see, so I see . . . come, lets have a look at you," the older man said as he helped Jacob to his feet and brushed his clothing, looking over his arms and legs to check his well-being. After determining as best he could that Jacob was not suffering from any mortal wounds or broken bones, he grabbed the boy's arm and announced, "Come on, Master Boyd, we have to get out of here, that beast going through the window will have every bobby in Edinburgh here in a moment. And, I don't think we want to be trying to explain that it was a dragon and not you who broke that window, now do we?!"

"No, sir, but, who is Bobby?" Jacob asked, wondering what the man was talking about.

"Police, my boy, police . . . now come on. . ."

They were in Holyrood Palace. The two rushed out of the room and quickly found a group of tourists to blend into. "Now, appear as inconspicuous as possible, Jacob, we will get out of here at the first opportunity."

"Where is Mr. Nibbles?" Jacob whispered.

Von Niblick hesitated, considering how to stretch the truth a bit without breaking it. He was sure that Jacob was not ready to know of Mr. Nibble's truer self. "Well, I don't rightly know. I guess he is outside waiting, maybe . . . . Never mind that, let's break away and get out of here."

When von Niblick and Jacob exited Holyrood Palace, police cars were just starting to arrive and a scramble was taking place among the guards and tour guides in the area. In the confusion, they were able to walk out with the rest of the tourists, which were by then being ushered out of the area.

Just up the street, Jacob noticed a small brown spot behind a step. It moved slightly and kept Jacob's attention as he took a few more steps. With each step, the brown spot took on more of the form of a small dog.

"Mr. Nibbles, it's Mr. Nibbles and he is hurt!" Jacob announced as he ran over to the little dog who was licking the wounds on his back left leg and on his side. As Jacob picked him up, he noticed small little cuts around his head as well.

"Professor, what has happened to Mr. Nibbles?"

"Hmmmmmmmm. . . well, looks to me like old Mr. Nibbles might have gotten himself into a little scrap with another dog . . . is that right, Nibbles?" the Professor asked as he stroked the dog's head.

Jacob carried the wounded dog back to Cowgate Street and laid him down in the old tattered chair in von Niblick's study. Mrs. Lafoon was waiting on them when they arrived, and immediately got cloths and salves for Mr. Nibble's injuries. "I'll do that," Jacob offered as he took the rags and salve from Mrs. Lafoon. He knelt beside the panting and exhausted dog and stroked his head.

Jacob took the damp rags and began to gently clean Mr. Nibble's wounds. He cupped the dog's head in his left hand and whispered encouraging words as he cared for his wounds. The danger he had faced in the catacombs and the resulting wounds and painful limbs now seemed very distant as Jacob was absorbed in the care of his friend.

It was a touching scene that even the Professor's intense interest in knowing what happened in the catacombs could not bring him to interrupt. He and

Mrs. Lafoon backed out of the study and left Mr. Nibbles in Jacob's care.

An hour or so later, Jacob emerged from the study with bloody rags in hand. "Mr. Nibbles is sleeping now. I guess he will be alright," Jacob said without a reassuring tone.

"Thank you, Jacob, you do not know how much he means to me," said von Niblick as he invited Jacob to sit down next to him on the couch in the parlor.

"But, my father. . . how is he? I must see him!"

"Jacob, he isn't doing any better. Frankly, I have become worried about him," von Niblick answered, as he reached toward Jacob.

Jacob turned before the man's hand reached him, he grabbed his backpack and he bolted up the stairs taking two at a time where he could.

"Jacob, you don't . . ." von Niblick's voice trailed off as Jacob disappeared into his father's room. Mr. Boyd lay motionless on his back with a pillow being held down tight over his eyes by a thick book.

Jacob approached the bed with apprehension. Gently he lowered himself into a seated position on the bed. "Dad?" There was no answer. "Dad?"

"Jake, is that you?" Mr. Boyd's voice was gravelly and slow.

"Yes, father, how are you?"

"Oh, I will be alright," his father's answer was followed by a deep and raucous cough that exposed the lie in Mr. Boyd's words.

Jacob's heart sank. He had never seen his father in such a condition before. Seeing the man who had always taken care of him now so helpless, Jacob wondered about his own vulnerabilities here, still in a strange land.

"Jacob, could you get me some water?" His father barely managed to get out the words when a cough took control of his body and a small amount of mucous-filled blood dripped from the corner of his mouth.

"Sure Dad, whatever you need." Jacob stood and took the empty water glass from the nightstand and walked to the bathroom sink. He turned the faucet and watched the water stream into the basin. He put the cup under the water. As it began to fill, his mind began to cloud and he faded back into the catacombs. The sink became the fountain from beneath the streets of Edinburgh. The water began to pulsate through his fingers with a silvery shimmer. His reflection hung in the glass as the faucet took the form of a small boy smiling at him and presenting the flowing liquid through his hand. The runes and foreign words from the fountain's base spun in his head. His reflection began to dim in the glass and in its place appeared an image of his father lying on a golden couch borne by eight women clothed in white robes with golden ropes about their waists.

The glass slipped from his fingers and broke into shards in the basin. The crash also shattered the images conjured by his imagination. *The water! It's the water!*

Jacob's father was coughing again, as drops of blood fell undetected into the basin of the sink. Jacob ran to his father's side. The boy ripped open his backpack and removed the bottle he had filled with the water of the fountain from the catacombs.

"Here, Dad, take this," Jacob offered as he reached a hand under his father's head and lifted it slightly from the pillow. Mr. Boyd was so weak he had difficulty swallowing and most of the water fell out of his mouth and down his cheeks. Jacob reached up and wiped the water from his father's face when he noticed the bloody cut the broken glass had made across his index finger. Before his eyes, the water moved around and then into the cut and began to heal the wound upon contact. *The water! I was right!* he realized excitedly.

"Dad, Dad, you must take this water, you must swallow!" Jacob grabbed his father's head once more and lifted as he wedged his own body behind his father's in such a way that he could hold him upright. Reaching around, he poured the water into his father as the man gagged and then fell back into his son's arms.

Tears dripped down Jacob's cheeks as his head fell back and rested against the wall at the head of the bed. His eyes closed and he prayed for his father's life. More tears dripped into his ears and pooled.

"Jacob? Jacob? You can lay me down now, I am feeling suddenly much better. I guess I just needed a drink."

"Dad?" Jacob unwedged himself from behind his father and laid him back down on his pillow.

"Son, I don't know what just happened, but I am feeling much better now. There must have been something in my throat obstructing my breathing. Thanks for the water."

Mrs. Lafoon was now standing in the door with some warm towels. "Jacob, I think I can take it from here," she said, as she entered the room. "The Professor would like to see you when you are ready."

"Go ahead, Jake, I am feeling much better now. I think I might even be able to get up for dinner."

"Oh, no you don't," Mrs. Lafoon said as she pulled a chair to the bed and sat down.

"Okay, Dad, I will be back to check on you in a few minutes." Jacob squeezed his father's knee beneath the covers and mumbled some words as he turned to leave the room.

Mr. Nibbles! He suddenly felt like it was Christmas morning. *If the water could heal Dad, surely it can help Mr. Nibbles!* He grabbed the bottle with the remaining water from the fountain and ran down the stairs. He tore into von Niblick's study and slid on his knees the last few feet to the chair where the dog laid motionless.

Jacob whispered instructions intensely to the dog as he lifted the pug's head and poured the liquid into its mouth. "Just drink this, please. Please swallow, it is good for you, sir!" The dog sputtered and shook as the water slid into his mouth and down his throat. The boy took the remaining drops and dribbled them over the biggest wounds on Mr. Nibble's side, and then covered the dog again with a blanket and kissed him gently on his left ear. Mr. Nibbles did not move, but his eyes turned and looked at Jacob, who felt the dog was thanking him as well as he could for his efforts and care.

Jacob shut the door behind him and walked into the parlor where von

Niblick sat waiting for him on the couch.

After asking about Jacob's father's health and that of his dog, von Niblick got down to the business that had been pressing on his mind.

"Ian's father arrived a short time before you emerged from your little hole, Jacob, and all is fine with them. They decided to head back home to Oxford after all that had happened."

"Oh, too bad, I really was looking forward to telling him about what happened down there," Jacob said as he looked down at the carpet.

"Well, now, Jacob, about that . . ." von Niblick reached over and put his hand on Jacob's left knee as if to get his attention because he was going to say something very important.

"You see, Jacob, sometimes a sporran comes into someone's life only for a short time and for a specific purpose. Ian's sporran came to him for some purpose, maybe something to do with getting him into a closer relationship with his father, maybe to teach him patience, maybe to help you prove *yourself,* maybe as a test, we can't really say. But, his time has now come and gone. He and his father will have great stories to talk about on the way home, but by the time they cross the border into England, neither of them will really remember the magic that they encountered. He will probably remember you, and will retain deep in his mind the lessons he learned on his journey with you, but the magic is gone and his sporran will soon pass on."

Jacob turned to von Niblick with an expression of great sadness and loneliness crossing his face. "Don't feel sorry for him, Jacob. He is lucky to have encountered the magic at all and is now safe, for it has passed on. It is the ones who are called and prove worthy of bearing the magic longer that we must worry about." Jacob knew the Professor was talking about him and pointed to his own chest without saying a word.

"That is right, laddie, you have been called and I assume have proven yourself worthy of continuing to carry the burden. Now, tell me about what happened down there and don't leave out a single stitch!"

The excitement of being able to share the adventure started to well up in

Jacob as he turned to face von Niblick on the couch and began to recount what had happened. The Professor stroked his beard and nodded occasionally as he listened to the boy. "Aye! Aye!" is all he would occasionally say as he smiled in a way that made Jacob feel like he was confirming all the man's hopes and dreams.

All was enthusiastic retelling until Jacob came to the part about his battle with Whipsnade. Then the burn scar on his arm, which he had nearly forgotten about, started to burn intensely. It made him wince and he grabbed at it. Von Niblick pulled Jacob's sleeve up and looked at the scar.

For a moment, Jacob thought about retrieving his bottle of water from the catacombs, but then remembered it was gone. He had used it all on his father and Mr. Nibbles. He had given it all away. There was none left to heal his own wound.

"Gladys, the salve and a bandage, please!" the Professor yelled into the other room.

Mrs. Lafoon dressed the wound and Jacob assured her it felt better and it would be fine. As she left the room, a realization suddenly hit her, "Lad, you must be starved near to death!" Jacob was very hungry but had not realized it until she mentioned it. It was like her words suddenly opened up the pit of his stomach, which had been filled with cares about Mr. Nibbles, his father, Ian and the retelling of his story. "Yes ma'am," he answered enthusiastically.

Mrs. Lafoon turned and went into the kitchen. As she did, she silently raised her right hand as if to say "I'll be right back then!"

"That wound will never really heal, Jacob," von Niblick said as he touched the bandage on his arm. "You have been burned by a flame fed and wielded in the service of a bent and selfish love. I hope it will now forever serve to remind you of the danger that exists in this twisted world of ours."

"But, who was that Whipsnade and what happened to him?" Jacob's saying of the name caused the scar to burn again.

"Who he was doesn't really matter, Jacob. What you need to realize is that there are men in this world who have become twisted. They serve nothing higher than themselves and would do whatever they could to have their own will be done. Some of them know of the existence of the magic, though most, frankly, do not believe in anything at all and that is to our advantage. But those who quest to gain control of a sporran, and the other treasures that might lead them to the *Lia Fail,* will stop at nothing. That means that you, my young friend, will be in danger as long as you carry that pouch and wear that ring."

Jacob had stopped looking at von Niblick and was staring blankly into the fireplace.

"You must choose, Jacob. You have been through much and have proven yourself brave and patient and worthy. You have been called to join the myth, to become part of the Sporrai. But, our lives are not easy and our secrets are not kept without grave dangers. Even though you are a boy, you now have the fate of the world partially in your hands. You will have to choose if you can help us bear that burden or if you would rather go back to your own life of friends and school and fun, carefree living."

"How do I choose?"

"You will know when the time comes for your decision. It is not today, but the question will sit in your mind, needling your thoughts, until the day comes when you will make the decision of take up the yoke again or let it pass to someone else."

Mrs. Lafoon entered the room with tea, crackers and cheese. The conversation paused for a moment as she poured them both a cup and then went to check on Mr. Nibbles.

Von Niblick took Jacob's chin in his hand and turned the boy's face to his. "Now, continue your story, if you please."

The weight of a choice to be made and the thought of continuing danger drained Jacob's enthusiasm for the telling of the story, but he slowly continued to recount his adventure in the catacombs. As Jacob ended the story with the tale of how he furiously climbed the shaft of stairs where von Niblick found him in Holyrood Palace, he heard his father start down the stairs.

"Now," von Niblick hurriedly whispered to Jacob, "you have another choice to be made. You can tell your father of your adventures. After what you have been through, I would not ask you to keep them from him and I know you will want him to share your heroics. However, you should know that if you bring him into the knowledge of the magic, he will also have to share in the danger. One who knows of these things is not safe among so many of our world who do not believe. You should choose wisely."

Jacob desperately wanted to share his adventure with his father. For once he could show his dad that he was capable of great things and was brave and true. He knew his father would eventually understand and would be proud of him.

"What are you two doing!" Mr. Boyd burst into the room.

"Dad!" Jacob ran over to his father.

"My goodness, it hasn't been that long since I saw you, son!"

"Sure, Dad, but you have been sick, how are you feeling?"

"Much better, thank you," Mr. Boyd answered, "but, tell me of your day and your adventures."

Jacob looked at von Niblick and paused. He then turned back to his father and announced, "Oh, Dad, it was terrible, Mr. Nibbles got into some kind of fight and is badly hurt, I have been nursing him, come see the poor thing."

Professor von Niblick smiled at Jacob's quick and good thinking and all three men went into the study to check on the wounded dog.

STONE OF DESTINY

L ate that evening, Jacob remembered the book Angus and Fingus asked him to give Professor von Niblick. He snuck out of bed and then down to the Professor's study. He paused in the hallway, considering whether or not he should look inside the book. He opened its stiff and crackling pages but was disappointed to see it was written in a language he did not understand.

Von Niblick's door was slightly ajar and Jacob pushed it open. A candle burned on the Professor's desk and was the only light in the room. He set the tattered leather book on the desk next to the candle and turned to leave. As he did, a splotch of ghostly white in the other end of the room caught his eye. A bolt of fear surged through him and he backed clumsily into the desk. The candle rocked but luckily remained upright.

Jacob stared across the room until he recognized the specter. It was just von Niblick's white hair and beard moving up and down with his breath. He was asleep in the chair and Jacob took a deep breath of relief. Jacob blew out the candle and pulled the door shut before heading back to bed.

The next couple of days passed without great incident. Jacob and his father explored Edinburgh further, though his father could not understand why Jacob so steadfastly refused to visit Edinburgh Castle with him. They did pass by one evening when the flood lights were illuminating the inner walls of the ancient fortress. Jacob felt "the quickening" between his shoulder blades as his imagination crossed the castle walls into an older time of bonfires and trouble.

Jacob spent many hours nursing Mr. Nibbles back to health. He carried him from room-to-room and took to feeding him by hand so the little dog did not have to get down to reach his bowl.

Jacob and Professor von Niblick also found time to talk further about the order of the Sporrai and the ancient powers and secrets it protected.

When it finally hit Jacob to apologize for not getting a very satisfactory answer on the whereabouts of *Lia Fail*, von Niblick waved him off. "Lad, you went in to find the Stone of Destiny and, though you may not have found *Lia Fail* herself," he said as he pulled Jacob's hand up and looked at his ring with the blood red stone at its center, "I do think you found *your* stone of destiny!"

"Your destiny is wrapped up with Isildane's ring just as much as it is with the sporran itself. Centuries ago it was dismantled and separated to keep it out of the hands of evil forces. Now, it has found you and you have made it complete in the catacombs. It was the ring that allowed you to pull the sword from the sporran and defeat Whipsnade. It was the wearer of the ring of Isildane that called the six Keepers from their tomb to serve again. Keep it with you always, as no one can predict the next turn of the unexplored river of your life."

When the day came for Mr. Boyd and Jacob to head to the airport for their flight back home, Jacob was filled with very mixed emotions. He missed his mother and his friends, but something had happened to him in Scotland that he was not sure he yet understood and he would certainly miss the Professor and Mrs. Lafoon. Perhaps most of all, he dreaded leaving Mr. Nibbles behind. When he looked into his little friend's eyes, he saw the dog he never had but always wanted. He thought he even detected more.

That morning, Professor von Niblick pulled the pug dog aside and whispered in his ear. "Well, old friend," he said in hushed tones, "we have been together for a long time and I am going to miss you terribly, but I think your place is now with Jacob. He has already been hunted by two of the enemy and he may soon find himself again in dire trouble before he comes of age. Go with him and look after him, will you? But, don't show yourself for what you really are unless it is an absolute necessity. He has dealt with enough for now. I only wish we could have taken one last ride, old friend." The Professor hugged the dog and then retrieved a travel cage out of the cellar.

"Jacob," the Professor said as he walked toward the Boyd men who had carried their bags to the door, "you have shown such love of Mr. Nibbles that I would like you to have him."

"What? I couldn't!" Jacob said as Mr. Nibbles patted across the floor and sat at his feet. Jacob looked up at his father, but said nothing. His mind was torn between begging to be able to keep the dog and politely declining so the Professor and Mrs. Lafoon would not miss their long-time companion.

His father didn't need to be asked, however. "Sure, son, why not!"

Jacob bent down and picked up the dog, kissing his head.

"Mr. Nibbles is from China, you know," the Professor began as he started to recount how to take care of him and Mrs. Lafoon went to pack his favorite chew toys and blanket. "They bred pugs many centuries ago as lap dogs for the Emperor and his family. To this day, many Chinese think they have some special power or can bring good luck, so I hope Mr. Nibbles brings some to you."

Von Niblick helped the Boyd men carry their luggage and Mr. Nibbles' cage out to a waiting taxi at the curb. Mr. Boyd entered the car first as von Niblick held Jacob back.

"Lad," his powerful gray eyes captured Jacob's, "keep the sporran and Isildane's ring safely with you. But, above all, never forget that the magic is closer than you think and more powerful than the world will admit. Your faith may well save you in the days to come."

The Professor pressed something into Jacob's hand and gently nudged him into the car. Mr. Nibbles leaned his head out Jacob's window and licked the Professor's hand as the man quietly said "Farewell, old friend."

The car pulled away from the curb as Mr. Nibbles leapt into the back window for one more look at his old friend and his old home. The man's head was bowed and his gait slow as the dog watched the Professor walk down the street and disappear into Niblick House.

Mr. Boyd took one last look out the window as the buildings of Edinburgh passed. Jacob looked down and opened his hand. In his open palm there rested a small black leather book Professor von Niblick had pressed there a moment before. On its cover the word "Enchiridion" was stamped in gold. He slipped the book into his back pocket and turned to his father.

"Dad, I have a feeling I will be back someday."

~~THE END~~

Just the Beginning

DUNGAL'S CHARGE—A RECENTLY DISCOVERED LEAF FROM THE SPORRAI PAST[1]

The man with a tattered kilt wrapped around his waist and up over his shoulder stumbled down the hill of loose rocks, losing his footing several times and falling hard to the ground. Just across the stream was a series of crevices in the rocks where he could hide and get some much needed rest. He stumbled through the stream without caring to try to walk from rock-to-rock to avoid the ankle deep water.

He reached the cliff and worked himself up about ten feet to the closest and deepest crevice he could find. There he pulled his broadsword from its sheath on his back and laid it across his lap. Finally, he could rest. He leaned his head back and closed his eyes in relief from his run and in resignation that if they found him now, there was nothing more he could have done for the cause. Without rest soon, he surely would have collapsed before long and they would have him anyway.

Dungal had been hit by a sniper's musket ball the day before and the pain in his right arm was still excruciating, especially when he stopped to rest. He held his shoulder with his left hand as he listened to the hounds baying in the distance. The hunting dogs were leading a group of soldiers who had been tracking him for the last several days. They would stop at nothing to catch him and take the items he carried.

The Highlander was on a mission to deliver his package to St. Andrews where a ship was waiting to take it off the British Isles. Then it would be

1 Discovered, pieced together, and translated by Professor Chadwick von Niblick of Edinburgh, Scotland.

taken and hidden on foreign shores and he would find the kind of rest he had become unaccustomed to since the package found him. He did not ask for the mission but could not resist it either. Where he would spend his final days, he was not sure. It was a secret he had not been permitted to share. To some degree he did not care to know. On his final run, he could dream of a far away place where the power would be safe and where he would no longer be hunted but could rest satisfied that he had done all he could for his family and friends back home.

Three days ago, a group of soldiers in the service of Nidalas, had ambushed him as he came out from traveling stealthily through the moors at the edge of the Kingdom of Fife. He escaped that encounter unscathed, but two days later took a hit in the arm, when a sharp shooter caught him in the iron sights of his musket.

Now all he could do was hope that by crossing the stream, he would throw the dogs off his trail long enough to give him time to rest, gather his strength, and make it the last few miles to St. Andrew's Bay. His eyes closed tight, he listened as the dogs drew closer, then paused at the stream below, turned, and led their masters upstream.

Dungal slept long and deep that night, as he hadn't slept in days. In the dewy wet morning, he crawled down from his perch and spread his tartan blanket across the rocky ground by the stream and folded it into a kilt which he wrapped around his body as best he could with the one useful arm he had left.

He hadn't eaten in days and the emptiness of his stomach pained almost as badly as the lead slug in his right arm. He started walking east toward the sea and carefully looking over each ridge for any sign of Nidalas's men. No threats appeared anywhere, which both heartened Dungal and caused him to wonder. *Why am I having such an easy time this close to the goal?*

He discovered the answer to his puzzlement as he rose over the final hill before he would descend into St. Andrews. There, far below, he saw all entry points to the town were under guard and Nidalas's men patrolled the streets.

Worse still, the ship that was his destination was a floating ball of flame and smoke fifty yards out in the bay.

The exhausted and ill Highlander felt his arm throb around the lead ball as he gazed upon the terrible scene below. He sat in the tall yellow grass on the hill and wept at the failure of the mission that he knew was so important. Now his package was in danger of falling into the hands of evil. *Why couldn't I have traveled more quickly? Why couldn't I have seen that sniper and avoided his shot? Why have I failed!* He sat in the grass questioning his own failures and fearing the future of Scotland and his kin.

The sharp bark of dogs on the trail snapped him out of his self-pity and loathing about his life's failures. They were on to him again. He had to think quickly about an escape. Further up on the hill was a large home built around a central tower. It was obviously the home of some family of distinction. He crawled through the tall grass to avoid being seen and then sprinted from the field to the house. The horses were gone and no one seemed to be at home. He unlatched a door and walked into the house where he stashed his treasure and then immediately left.

The best I can do now is to lead them as far away from the prize as possible and hope my failure will not bear evil tidings for my children and theirs. The Highlander headed back the way he came, this time slowing his steps even more than he needed to in order to insure the dogs and men would stay on his trail—and away from the treasure he once guarded.

Nearing the stream and the cliffs above, the Highlander caught glimpse of movement to his right. A thick bush of brambles was waving violently back and forth. He moved toward the disturbance and found a white stag whose antlers were caught in the twisted thorn-covered branches. Momentarily forgetting about his own troubles, Dungal took a small knife from his boot and began quickly sawing at the branches to release the deer. Frightened, the deer whipped its head violently as Dungal used some of his last available strength to avoid the cuts and thrashes of its many-pointed rack. As the last branch was cut, the stag turned hard and drove two tines against the

Highlander's belly. The tines punctured his skin and ripped off a piece of his bloody shirt, which stuck between its tines as the animal ran off westward through the moors.

Making it back to the crevices in the cliff where he had spent the previous night, Dungal used the remainder of his strength to climb into his perch, pull his sword and lay its hilt upon his chest with the blade running down across his mid-section. He then covered himself with his tartan and closed his eyes. The last thing Dungal ever heard on this earth was the men calling after the dogs as they passed below and headed west through the moors in search of him.

More than three hundred winters have now passed since the Highlander freed the stag and then made his own tomb in Scotland's Kingdom of Fife.

About the Author

G.L. Gregg studies and teaches old documents and even older ideas at the University of Louisville in Louisville, Kentucky. He has traveled to Scotland several times to search for evidence of the existence of ancient Celtic magic and has not been disappointed. He often travels on such treks under the pseudonym "Doctor Kilt," and lives in LaGrange, Kentucky with his wife, four children, and golden retriever, Meg. Despite rumors to the contrary, he does not live with a dragon pug—yet!

For more information on *The Sporran, The Remnant Chronicles*, excerpts from upcoming books, and educational material related to the series and its real-life connections, visit

www.TheSporran.com

COMING SOON. . .

THE IONA CONSPIRACY

A New School—A Dragon Unveiled—
The Remnant Unmasked—Jacob Boyd's
New Call to Duty

BOOK THREE OF
THE REMNANT CHRONICLES